He Who Walks in Shadow

He Who Walks

in

Shadow

By
Brett J. Talley

JournalStone
San Francisco

JOURNALSTONE
YOUR LINK TO ARTISTIC TALENT

JournalStone books may be ordered through booksellers or by contacting:

JournalStone

www.journalstone.com

The views expressed in this work are solely those of the authors and do not necessarily reflect the views of the publisher, and the publisher hereby disclaims any responsibility for them.

ISBN:	978-1-942712-26-8	*(sc)*
ISBN:	978-1-942712-27-5	*(hc)*
ISBN:	978-1-942712-28-2	*(ebook)*

JournalStone rev. date: May 22, 2015

Library of Congress Control Number: 2015936226

Printed in the United States of America

Cover Art & Design: Becca Klein
Edited by: Michael R. Collings

For Annie

Prologue

Incendium Maleficarum, First Gate, First Key

In the beginning was the darkness, and the Earth was without form, and void.

In the abyss shone black suns of ancient days, Stygian orbs that ruled over ebon seas of endless infinity. The Great Old Ones were born of that emptiness, they who yet walk in foul and lonely places, who still call forth from the wilds of the world. From the maddened heights of the greatest mountains, to the roiling caverns of the deepest seas. In shadow-bound tombs, and empty passageways of lost antiquity. But they did not always haunt only the darkest watches of the night.

In the long ago they came to this world, spawn of shadow, when the stars wheeled round right. They seized it as their own, the realm on which they would build their glory. Upon its planes did rise great cities of titanic stone, cyclopean capitals of mind-breaking vastness. Carven by no hand of man, for humanity was but a whisper on cold winds that float back and forth upon the line of time. In unchallenged glory they ruled, for he who was lord upon them all needed but stretch forth his hand and whate'er he wished would be laid to waste.

The wisdom of the world—as it perceives itself now, at least— would call it mad, what they were and how they exercised dominion. But in an insane world, all shall dwell in madness.

So it might have been for all time. Forever might that shadow have fallen, a shade that covered the land and sea for all the sunless nights of black eternity.

But as with all nights, there came the dawn.

The darkness cannot comprehend the light, no more than it can abide it. It was but a single spark, a tiny, flickering flame. Yet it burst forth like the thunder that rides upon lightning. Then the Great Old Ones knew fear, as they had always known hatred, but it was upon a new enemy that their burning scorn was cast.

For there was one race whom the light favored. A slave race, a breed of mindless creatures which the darkness carved from the mud and gave form for its own amusement. As meaningless to it as an insect. As unimportant as the lowest beast.

And unto this forgotten creation—unto man—the light bestowed but a single gift. Knowledge of itself, and the spirit that comes with it.

Thus mankind came to know the light, though with that knowledge arose the memory of the darkness. And of that shadowed remembrance, mankind feared.

For as surely as the sun rises, it must also fall. As surely as one age ends, another must begin—an ever turning back to that which came before. To that which should not be. For in all truth is this—that is not dead which can eternal lie.

And the darkness does not forget.

Chapter 1

Journal of Carter Weston
February 19, 1932

There is a legend from the long ago, passed down through the ages on whispered words and shuddered sayings, written of in arcane and forbidden tomes, locked away in the dusty halls of abandoned libraries. It is history to some, myth to others, though the latter are never fulsome in their conviction. It speaks of the coming of a man from the east, if man he was, from behind the lake of Hali and the jeweled cities of Carcosa.

The wind rushed before his footsteps, while the sound of discordant piping floated in his wake. The vermin teemed around him, and the pestilence gathered at his feet. He wore the yellow robe of a king, but no king of this earth was he. For his raiment was tattered and stained with blood and mud and the tears of the damned. But his face was princely—the visage of command, the countenance of one to be followed, as a mystic might imagine the pharaohs of old. And with him always the book, the great crimson tome that bore the name of *Incendium Maleficarum*.

From the east he appeared, and like John of old, he preached the coming of another epoch of this earth. But no salvation was to be had through him. At least, not for mankind. He was a harbinger of the end of one age—and the beginning of another. The departure of mankind and the return of something more ancient. For on the wings of those he heralded rode death, and hell followed.

Onward he traveled, as the black tentacles of plague wrapped around his feet and spread from every town and city that his gaze fell upon, from every place in which he preached his sermon of the end times. The men and women and children died by the millions from that Black Death. They fell and they cursed the coming of the traveler, for to look upon him was to see the face of darkness, to taste madness and insanity.

Yet not all marked his coming with the evil eye. The most ancient cults, the nameless faiths whose adherents had howled the oldest rites into the wild winds on darkened mountain tops and in forgotten, ruined temples, they had long sought his coming. Their voices echoed across desolate plains and through unnamed valleys with one word, a name—*Nyarlathotep*!

For two years, that name was feared across Europe, and many died with the whisper of it on their last breath. Then, nothing. The ancient rites ceased. The vermin fled. The plague receded like a waning tide. As mysterious as his arrival, so too was the reason for his departure—so close to the end times, so close to opening the gate to worlds unseen and unimagined.

In legend and myth, much is false. But truth can be discerned, if the careful reader knows where to look. Within the tattered pages of a book that has no name, I discovered a story—to my knowledge singular in its telling—that holds a kernel of truth. It told of a simple farmer—of ancient stock of Greek or Roman or even Egyptian lineage—who came down from the mountains of shadowed Wallachia to face the child of Azathoth, the harbinger of that whence Cthulhu first came. But the farmer did not contend with Nyarlathotep alone. He brought with him a jewel, an object of unknown composition and origin, a crystalline tetrahedron, whose triangular facets seemed to shimmer with unnatural light. The writer of this tale held that it was the Oculus of legend, the Oracle of Truth, the Eye of God. The records are strangely silent as to what transpired on that blasted heath, all those centuries ago. All that can be said is that Nyarlathotep receded and the *Incendium Maleficarum* vanished once again beneath the shroud of history, while the fate of the farmer—and the Oculus—remains to this day a mystery.

An interesting side-show of history the story might have remained, were it not for the dark murmurings that swept across Europe on the eve of the Great War, the whispers of a preacher of the end times, wrapped in yellow garb, who spoke of the coming of a great darkness. That darkness fell upon us all with that conflict and the plague of influenza that erupted from it.

But I fear that this tribulation was but a prologue, the gloaming of a blacker night than we have seen since the Lord called forth for light in the first days. I will face this roiling chaos, as I have faced it before, but I fear that this challenge is greater than any I have yet seen.

And I do not know if I can defeat it alone.

Chapter 2

A forward for the interested reader, [Manuscript name TK]

A friend of mine—the oldest and finest of the men to whom I choose to give that title—once told me that when great or grave things happen, it is incumbent upon those of us who bore witness to their passing to record them for posterity so that other, future generations might learn from our mistakes and revel in our triumphs. Carter Weston was wise, but I do wonder if he knew that it would be his name that graced the pages of such recordings and that it would be his story that would inspire others to contend with the evil of this world—and the evil that lies beyond.

I remember well the moment I met Carter. It was a seemingly innocuous occasion, one of a hundred such introductions during our first few days at Miskatonic University, a place that would come to dominate both our lives as students and our adult undertakings. But I marked that incident, for some sense, something beyond the five commonly understood, told me that our meeting was auspicious. How right I was.

Life seldom continues along the path we intend, and one curve in the road leads invariably to another. So it was with Carter. He, the rare skeptic to grace the hallowed halls of Miskatonic, left, as they all do, a true believer. But his baptism into the faith of the cosmic and unutterable secrets of our world was truly by fire. For it was Carter who was chosen in the winter of our penultimate year of study to seek out a rare and powerful tome, a grimoire of horrible antiquity—*Incendium Maleficarum*, The Witches' Fire. It was Carter who was given this task by Dr. Atley Thayerson, a devotee of certain nameless cults, who masqueraded as a defender of the light.

Were it not for a chance encounter on a storm-wracked shore with four men who had faced the darkest of evils in their past, Thayerson might have accomplished his goal and opened the gate to the crawling chaos that waits in the vast emptiness of the cosmos. He might have seen it through even then, were brave men not ready to do all that was necessary as the future balanced on a knife's edge. For it was sacrifice that was required to send the dead city of R'lyeh back to the depths from whence it came. And it was only sacrifice that could silence what was awoken in the great citadel of that place, on that day when the stars came right and words were spoken that could have brought an end to all things.

Carter and I stood against the darkness that day. He recorded the history of our struggle many years later, on the very eve of his disappearance. The authorities called the words he wrote evidence of his madness. Perhaps there is no man alive but I who knows the bitter truth of those pages. The manuscript was to have been destroyed, but Carter was too wise to allow that to happen. I found it, just as he intended. And while much of the story was known to me, in its final pages I found a clue to the disappearance of Carter Weston.

From that clue I came to the strong conviction that Carter was alive. Weakened perhaps. In grave and deadly danger, certainly. But alive. For it was that accursed tome, *Incendium Maleficarum*, that his enemies sought, and no man knows better its workings than Carter. Now the book is seeking again, seeking a way to bring forth the Old Ones from their exile and their slumber. I would pursue it in any event, but I know that where I find the book, I will find Carter also.

I will keep a record of my efforts, as Carter would undoubtedly want. And when my journey is completed, no matter what the outcome, I will share that story with the world. But as a story is seldom told well when presented from only one perspective, I shall include whatever documents I deem relevant—edited, of course, to eliminate the redundant or the mundane—including my own commentary and the journal of Carter Weston himself, for his words were always strangely prescient and his foreknowledge uncanny. I hope that my readers will forgive an old man the clumsiness of his pen.

For now, perhaps it is best to begin at the beginning, on that horrible day when my greatest friend simply vanished.

--Henry Armitage

Chapter 3

Journal of Henry Armitage
December 15, 1932

For the first time in my life, words fail me. It has been a terrible day, one that will remain etched in my memory for as long as breath fills my lungs. Yet it is important to write it all down, lest time forget events that history witnessed. In any event, whatever is begun today, it will not end soon, and I fear it will not end well.

I visited Professor Carter Weston's office early this morning. Last week, we had planned to meet and discuss a class we are to teach together during the Spring term—a critical examination of Cotton Mather's *Wonders of the Invisible World.* I thought it strange that I had not seen Carter in the intervening time. It was rare that we went even a day without speaking to each other in some capacity. But I brushed it off, prepared to explain it away as work getting the better of him. I know more than most how terribly busy he has been.

It was rather early when I arrived at Dexter-Ward Hall, the sun having only just peeked over the trees that bordered Miskatonic Yard. It was a bitterly cold day; a week of unseasonably warm weather had given way to a howling blizzard the day and night before, and great mounds of snow made walking treacherous. But my preoccupation with my own difficulties was rather short-lived. They vanished when I realized Dexter-Ward sat quite empty.

The front doors were locked, and I opened them with my key, astonished that Carter had not preceded me. He had always been an early-riser, and I fully expected to find him waiting for me inside. And yet, as I entered, the only sound I heard in the darkened corridors of DW was the slamming of the door behind me.

I felt it then, as many who have stumbled upon a crime scene often claim. An energy in the air, a foreboding. A sense that something was off, that something was terribly wrong. I did not run to Carter's office. There seemed no reason to hurry, and I needed every ounce of resolve just to put one foot in front of the other.

Carter's office was at the end of the second-floor corridor. In the state I was in, it seemed like the longest hallway I had ever seen. Carter's door danced in front of me, swaying from side to side in my vision, but never really getting any closer. Yet long before I was ready, I found myself standing there, hand on the doorknob. All I had to do was turn. I did so. The lock was not engaged.

The door opened.

The office was empty.

I actually laughed out loud, standing there on the threshold, feeling foolish for my irrational concerns. Of course, Carter was just late. Nothing more than that. Nothing more sinister, nothing more unusual. And were it not for the envelope sitting on Carter's desk, the one that bore my name written in the angular pen of my good friend, perhaps I would have continued in my ignorance for hours more.

I picked it up, studied it, wondered why it would be waiting for me, here of all places. Everything in my being rebelled against opening it, even though I knew I had no choice. Inside was a letter, written in the same hand as my name on the envelope. I have recorded the contents below.

14 December 1932
My dearest Henry,

If you are reading this—and quite honestly, I have no reason to imagine you are not—then you have discovered that I am missing. My time is short. A week ago, I received a visitation from one who would have the book. The Incendium Maleficarum *seeks its owner, Henry. It seeks the one through which it can do the most harm, the one through which the gates can be opened and the Old Ones restored.*

And its true owner hears its song.

I have heard that song for the last forty years. I never knew the reason, and I tried not to question why the book chose me. But when that man, when Erich

Zann entered my office, the song of the book ceased. I must believe it sang for another. I must believe he heard it in his own ears.

That was seven days ago. Over the last week I have committed our story — and the story of the finding of the book — to the written page. You will find two copies in my wall safe, the combination which you know. Leave one. It is my hope that my executors will see fit to publish the truth to the world. If they should fail, I hope that you will do what they will not.

But whatever the case may be, you must follow this Zann and stop him from using the book. The fate of the world may depend on your efforts. I'm sorry I could not tell you sooner, but you know the price one pays for denying the book what it seeks. Zann will take possession of the Incendium Maleficarum. *He will likely kill me in the process, or the book and the dark forces it serves will punish me for my impudence. But whatever the case, Zann's plans will only have begun.*

I need not tell you about the signs we have witnessed these past few decades. I need not remind you of what we have faced, what we have lost. The portents are all come to pass. The harbinger will return. There's no one left but you to stand in his way. I only wish I could be there to stand with you.

Godspeed, my friend.
Carter Weston

The last few words I read with trembling hands. Could it be so? Could he be gone? And worst of all, could someone else have the *Incendium Maleficarum*? I opened the wall safe, and just as Carter had written, there were two manuscripts within. I took one, leaving the other behind. I put the letter in my pocket and called the police.

That was this morning. I left the police to their investigation, though I am certain that they will find nothing. No, I am the only one fit to undertake this task. I am no fool, however. I know that the difficulties I face will be arduous, and I fear that my age may prevent me from accomplishing that which must be done. This is a journey that I cannot make alone. Fortunately, there is one other in this world who cares for Carter as much as I—his daughter, Rachel. I only pray God that she can be made to forget and forgive the past.

For while Carter gave her life and love, it was also he who took them both away from her.

* * *

Arkham Advertiser, July 23, 1933, Page A-3

A ceremony conducted at Christchurch Cemetery on Saturday evening brought to a close a story that we at the *Arkham Advertiser* have been following with great interest these past six months. In a service conducted by the Rev. Alfred Pickman, the late Prof. Carter Weston of Miskatonic University was eulogized in a memorial that was among the more unusual we have witnessed here in Arkham. For while the family and friends of Prof. Weston were well in attendance, the Professor himself was notably absent.

As regular readers and Arkham familiars will well remember, Prof. Weston vanished mysteriously some six months ago. A search of his office and his home revealed no signs of break-in or other foul play, and police reports indicate that the Professor left no clue as to his whereabouts.

Intrepid reporting by this paper's crack staff revealed, however, that Prof. Weston did leave behind a rambling manuscript, written in haste and locked within the wall safe of his office. While the *Advertiser* has been stymied in our attempts to obtain a copy of that manuscript, our sources indicate that it included fantastic tales, stories that strained credulity, even by the standards of the hardened veterans of the Arkham police department. Despite our best efforts, the *Advertiser* has been unable to ascertain further the contents of this cryptic document, and it is our understanding that it was destroyed at the behest of the Weston estate.

With no evidence of Weston's whereabouts, certain distant family members and creditors of the professor moved for a declaration of death. As his only surviving daughter, Mrs. Rachel Jones (née Weston), did not object, a certificate of death was entered. This action was taken despite the protestations of Prof. Henry Armitage—also of Miskatonic—who has been adamant in his contention that Prof. Weston is, indeed, still alive.

While Saturday's memorial brings the matter to an official close, we at the *Arkham Advertiser* will be ever vigilant in discovering and reporting any new information to our faithful subscribers.

Chapter 4

Journal of Henry Armitage
July 21, 1933

This morning, after the service at Christchurch ended, I found Rachel where I expected her, at her high-gabled home on Lich Street, not a stone's throw from the Miskatonic campus. Knowing Rachel as I did, I prepared myself for a battle.

Six months had passed since Carter's disappearance, and despite my eagerness to begin the mission he had left behind for me, I'd been unable to discuss it with Rachel. There was always an excuse, always a reason not to talk to me. With her father's disappearance and the ongoing investigation into his whereabouts—and the court fight that followed—I couldn't rightly blame her, nor could I force her to hear me out. Now that the so-called "memorial service" was over I had to press the issue. Striking out on my own would be as foolhardy as it would be impotent. No, I had to have Rachel's help. Everything depended on it.

I had barely knocked before she answered the door with a smile, and somehow that worried me all the more. But even dressed in black with her chestnut brown hair pulled back in a bun, there was something enchanting about her, a gift from her mother's side of the family. I felt my guard slip. Perhaps she would be more willing to help than I had hoped.

"Henry. Somehow I knew I'd see you today. Come in." I followed her into the kitchen where she was making a late lunch, or perhaps an early dinner. "Care for a brandy?" she asked. "I know that was always your favorite…and my father's."

"That'll be all right, Rachel."

"Speaking of my father," she said, "we missed you at the funeral." As she spoke she removed a knife from a block and returned to slicing a pile of vegetables, a project that, given the pile of half-cut carrots, potatoes, and other sundries, I had apparently interrupted.

I smiled, without mirth. "I seriously doubt that anyone, present company excluded, missed me today."

"Well, Henry, you have been making quite a bit of trouble for my wretched family. And among the few of them who didn't just want their cut of his money, jealousy can be expected. After all, my father loved you more than most." She gathered up a handful of vegetables and dropped them in a simmering broth.

"But not more than you, of course."

Rachel looked at me and grinned. "You're up to something, Henry. I can tell. You were never good at flattery."

"And you are as perceptive as ever. Actually, Rachel, I was hoping that you could help me with something very important. I understand that you have some time, now that you've quit your job at the *Advertiser*."

Rachel coughed out a little laugh and wiped her hands on a dish towel. "Well, I always disliked the sensationalism, but when it was directed at my father I came to despise it. Besides, my editor didn't care for women in the newsroom."

I walked around the island to face her, taking her hand in mine. "Rachel, you know that I would have been there today if I believed your father were dead. If I didn't know he was alive."

Rachel closed her eyes tight, and I feared my words had given her great pain. "You've said that before," she said softly, "but I've seen no evidence to believe it's true."

"Only because you haven't given me the chance to show you. There are things you need to hear, proof you need to see. But you will have to have faith."

She cocked her head to the side, and I winced at the look she gave me. "Oh, Henry, you've always been like family to me, the uncle I never had," she said. "But you and my father... For you two, everything was always a mystery. There was always something deeper than the mundane. Something beyond the ordinary. You couldn't just take things at face value. Sometimes there's nothing more to the matter than what we see."

"Even if that's true, even if normally that were the case, can't you understand that this is different? Your father didn't just walk out and leave. You can't believe that."

"God, Henry," she said, and her voice was thick with frustration as she rubbed the bridge of her nose, "if I learned one thing from my father it is to never rule anything out. That there is nothing in this world that's so insane that it can't be believed. Can you honestly tell me that you know for sure he didn't just decide to leave? Take that book of his and just disappear? Maybe his mind finally snapped. Maybe he had a stroke and forgot who he was. Wandered into the woods and fell off of one of those blind cliffs just outside of town. Drowned in those god-awful swamps. Swept out to sea by the Miskatonic. How do you know he's still out there?"

"He didn't just disappear. He left a message. He left a clue for us."

"You mean the manuscript?"

"Yes! Did you read it?"

She shook her head. "I didn't. The executors had it. They told me it was all made up. And if my father did go mad and walk out and abandon us, I didn't want to see the evidence of it."

"Well, I did read it, and it is not insanity. It is an accurate record of the things we faced. The things we fought. I know that for a fact because I was there. And even more importantly, that manuscript tells about a meeting your father had mere days before his disappearance. A meeting with a man—a German—Erich Zann. He is the key. If we find this man, we find your father."

"We?"

"Yes, Rachel. I am going after Carter. I owe it to him, and I know he would do the same for me. But I'm old, and I'm weak. I can't find him alone. If I am going to see this through, I need your help."

"You want me to just to forget everything and go with you?"

"There's nothing tying you here."

She flinched, and I felt my heart drop as a wave of emotion passed over her face. What I had said was true, but that didn't make it any easier for her, and it didn't make the past any less painful. There was a reason she was alone in that house, with no family beyond Carter, and perhaps me, to consider. "I'm sorry, Rachel. I spoke hastily. I didn't mean any harm."

"No," she said, holding up a hand to stop me, as I had seen her father do a hundred times before, "no, you're right. You only told the truth. I think I'll take that drink now."

She turned and removed a decanter from a high shelf, pouring a draught of dark brown liquid. She looked at me and I nodded, so she poured a second.

"Rachel, I know the last few years have been difficult. I know that you never really forgave your father…"

Rachel spun on me in an instant. "That's not true," she said, pointing an accusing finger and cutting me off in mid-sentence. An awkward and uneasy silence followed. She picked up the second glass of brandy and handed it to me. "And you should know it's not true. Growing up with my father wasn't easy, but it taught me to be harder than most people. I never blamed him when you two went off for months at a time. I knew that it was part of his work, and I knew how important that work was. And I knew he loved me."

"But what happened to William, that was…"

"No different," she said, her voice quivering. "William was no man's fool. He knew the risks, and he accepted them freely. I accepted them, too. No, Henry. I never blamed my father for what happened. But he blamed himself. If there's been distance between us these past few years, it was his own guilt that made it, and it was his own guilt that kept it."

We stood in silence, the ghosts of the past thick around us. I downed my drink and opened my briefcase. I removed a ream of paper and placed it on the kitchen counter.

"So that's it, then?"

"That's it. Just read it, Rachel. That's all I ask. And if after you've read it you still think your father simply disappeared into the snows, then so be it. I just want you to give me this one chance. Will you do that at least, for an old friend?"

Rachel smiled again, and this time I sensed it was sincere. "For you," she said, taking my hand, "and for my father, anything."

And so we left it.

* * *

July 22, 1933

I had been awake barely a half hour this morning when there was a knock on my door. I opened it to find Rachel, the same wild look in her eyes that I had seen on occasion in her father's.

"All right," she said, thrusting the manuscript into my hands, "I can't believe I'm doing this. When do we leave? And where are we going?"

"Berlin," I answered. "Our search begins there."

Chapter 5

Diary of Rachel Jones
July 22, 1933

For the past six months, I've been coming to terms with the death of my father. It's an event every daughter—every child—dreads, but it is something that we all face. But I've been preparing for longer than most.

Some might call my father a fanatic, a crusader. To me he was always just a good man, doing the best he could to light the darkness so that his daughter might live in peace. Many times, he would wake me in the middle of the night to tell me that he and Henry had to leave. That he was needed somewhere in the world, that some wrong needed righting. He never said it, but I knew there was a chance he wouldn't come back, and I knew those late night visits were his way of saying goodbye.

Forever.

It was only later in life that I realized what exactly it was that he did. He was like Moses of old, standing at the edge of the Red Sea, holding back Pharaoh's armies with her waters, telling those who would do his people harm that they would come this far, but no farther.

But my father stood against something far worse than men and their ambitions. The tide he faced was one of swirling chaos. His tools—the ancient legends and texts that often contained as much folklore as fact. And yet he always came home from these adventures. He was always there for me. Until the day he wasn't.

I was sad, of course. Devastated, even. But I'm ashamed to say I felt some relief, too. The knock on the door I had always feared, the message of condolence I had always dreaded, it had finally came. At least now it was over. So I avoided Henry, even as I knew what he wanted to tell me, what he believed. That my father—somehow, some way—was alive. As absurd as that was. As impossible as it was to believe.

Then I read the manuscript.

I do not doubt for a moment that anyone else who read through those pages would have called them madness, the ravings of a man teetering on the edge, one who had finally gone over. Stories of demons, dark gods, and unnamed cults. Of sunken cities and the rising of great Cthulhu. Yes, madness. Unless you had lived my life. Unless you had seen what I had seen. Oh, there can be no question— my childhood prepared me well for today.

Is my father alive? I honestly don't know. It seems to me that it is more likely that he is dead, killed by this Zann for the book which evil men have always coveted, *Incendium Maleficarum*. But whatever the case may be, my father dedicated his life to a cause, to a war that has been raging for millennia. Another battle has begun in that war, and whether we fight for my father's freedom or in his memory, we will go on.

I am, after all, my father's daughter.

Chapter 6

Journal of Henry Armitage
July 23, 1933

Today we leave for Germany. I am excited, but apprehensive as well. Carter has been missing for six months, and even I must admit that the chances we will find him, and find him alive, are slim.

Of course, there is something else that weighs on my mind, something that I have tried not to think on, that I've tried to push away. I wish I could deny it, I wish I did not feel this way, but I am reminded of another trip overseas, some thirteen years ago, one I wrote about in a book that I never dared to publish and probably never will. Of all the star-crossed voyages Carter and I have made, none has ended in greater heartbreak than that one. For it changed the course of all our lives.

And if history repeats? If Rachel faces tragedy and death once again, perhaps her own?

How will I live with myself?

Excerpt from *Memoirs of a Crusader*, Dr. Henry Armitage, "The Tunguska Folly of 1919," (unpublished)

Rachel was born at the turn of the century, only a few years after Carter's marriage to Anna Stanton, a wonderful girl who was the daughter of Professor Thaddeus Stanton. Rachel's birth was cloaked in sadness, as her mother did not survive the ordeal. It was Carter's aunt, Mrs. Gertrude Partridge, who served in her stead and guided Rachel into womanhood. And Mrs. Partridge suffered for her kindness.

Although she had never known her, Rachel was the image of her mother in body and soul. She had the streak of rebellion that had marked Anna, and Carter encouraged her at every turn, much to the madam Partridge's eternal disapproval and dismay. But it served the girl well, and when she came of age she followed her father's footsteps to Miskatonic which, in keeping with its unorthodox ways, had recently begun to accept women.

It was there that she met William.

William Jones was one of the brightest men to come through the ancient gates of Miskatonic, and Carter and I battled over him for much of his tenure at the university. Carter could barely contain his delight when he seemed to have won him from me, though I had the last laugh when we learned that it was Carter's assets not as a professor but rather as a father that drew the young man to his side. Rachel and Will were married in the winter of 1918. She was 18 years old.

For a year, they were happy, and William worked at the side of Carter and myself, ostensibly as a graduate student. But on a particularly dark October night, Carter invited Will and me to his study for brandy and a cigar. It was there we informed William of our true purpose and the nature of our off-duty activities; the rumors that floated about Miskatonic were true. Forces moved in the earth, whose purpose was the end of mankind and the return of something older, something ancient, something primeval. And whether those forces were the embodiment of evil or simply so vast in their consciousness as to rate man no more than a pest to be exterminated, there could be little doubt that cohabitation on this planet was not an option. Thus, the war we fought was for the very existence of our species.

It is perhaps remarkable that William accepted this news so readily, but I suppose that years of study at our feet had prepared him for the strange and the uncanny. He joined us willingly. The die was cast, and it wasn't long before fate had its way.

The letter came in October of 1919. It was addressed to Carter from a Professor Anton Denikin of the University of Moscow, though at that time he bore the title of General. I have included it, in its entirety, below:

September 10, 1919
Brother Weston, my dear compatriot,

My how the years have flown, my friend. It seems only yesterday that we made plans to rendezvous at the University of Moscow and talk of our mutual interest in the forgotten corners of the world. I long for the days before the war. It has taken much from us; it will only take more.

I write to you from Kharkov on the southern front of our war against the Bolshevik. My men have fought valiantly, but I fear we have pushed as far towards Moscow as our limited supplies will allow. I am afraid that I will never again see that city, never again walk her streets or rest within her great cathedrals, not as a free man at least. It is upon that realization that I write you now.

As I am sure you remember, six years ago, in happier times, I spoke to you of strange tidings from the east. Long had I pondered the bizarre events on the Siberian frontier in 1908 when—as the peasants who lived to tell the tale reported—a great fire fell from the sky, night became as day, and the forest was laid waste for hundreds of miles. It piqued my curiosity, but it was another story that turned my blood cold and inspired me to extend an invitation to you then to visit me in Moscow and embark on an expedition to the area.

It was said that from the fires that burned the river Tunguska in those days emerged an object, extracted from the smoking crater that was dug out of the frozen swamps in that barren land. A jewel, one unlike any the men and women of the steppe had ever seen. Travelers through that region described a diamond pyramid, one whose pure, unbroken facets were carved with a perfection that bespoke techniques no earthly hand possesses. Within those facets seemed to burn a thin flame, a flickering red spark that glowed at the heart of the gem. You know of what I speak. The Eye of God has returned, in falling fire and consuming flame as was prophesied in certain ancient books that I will not mention here but that you know all too well. And those same books tell us that the Oculus will only appear when *his* return is imminent.

The darkest tomes speak of the coming of a man, one unlike any the people of this world have ever seen. At least, not for a very long time. A man tall and proud, with the face of a prince and the command of a king. The harbinger of a coming end, of an age beyond our own. Of the twilight of mankind and the return of something that ruled this world before. The one who wears the ring, the one who bears the mark, he of the Yellow Sign. I had reason to fear. For tell me, is there any other sigil that is a danger even to look upon? Is there any other mark of man that can bend the will and control the mind?

If the Oculus has returned, then the coming of the harbinger cannot be far behind. Alas, it seems the ancient writings regarding this man—if man he be—are correct, for turmoil and disorder have followed in the wake of the news from the east. The world has not been the same since the word came of the Oculus. Bloody conflict descended; famine and disease came with it. The Great War that interrupted our plans killed millions of my brothers and, indeed, my king.

I do not believe I shall ever have an opportunity to visit Siberia, and I am afraid that neither will you, if you delay. Even though it has been a decade since the event, I am certain that there is something to be learned from the wilderness of Tunguska, and it is even possible that the Eye remains there, waiting to be claimed by those forces of good who would banish the dark one again, holding shut whatever gate he seeks to open. One thing we can know for certain is this—we are not the only ones who seek the Oculus.

It is for this reason that I hope that your feet will walk where mine cannot, and your eyes will see what must remain forever hidden from mine. Perhaps one day, we can speak of what you discover there.

Finding your way will not be easy, but the White Army is strong in the east. Travel to Irkutsk, on the banks of the Angara River. The site of the event is far to the north, but there you will find a Colonel Rostov who has been told to assist you in any way you need. The pass I have included bears my signature, and it will provide you with safe travel through our territory, though, of course, I can guarantee you nothing if the Red Army is victorious.

I will understand if you see fit to forego this opportunity, but I fear for the future if you do. Until we meet again, my friend, I remain your brother in the light.

General Anton Denikin

It was grave news, indeed, and insanity to follow through on the General's request. In the weeks after he posted the message, the men under his command suffered disastrous defeats at the hands of the Red Army. And while the Republicans held firm in the East, no one could say how long that tenuous grip would remain. Yet as he read the letter, I saw a look of resolve spread across Carter's face.

It was a cold evening, and Carter had stoked quite a fire in the hearth. He sat down in a chair beside it, lighting one of the cigars that he seemed never to be without. I waited a good ten minutes before I interrupted his thoughts.

"So you mean to do it then?"

He arched an eyebrow. "I note a tone of disagreement. I am surprised. I understand that Siberia is rather charming in the winter."

"Putting that aside," I said with a grin, pouring a glass of brandy for each of us, "we'd be walking into a war zone. And I don't know if you followed the *Times* these last few weeks, but the Republican cause is all but lost in the west, and the Red Army is pressing hard in the east. They can't last long. We might arrive in Irkutsk to find this Colonel Rostov dead—or worse—and ourselves an enemy of the state."

"Your logic, as always, is impeccable," he said, taking the glass of brandy I offered. "Unfortunately, I don't know that we have a choice. There are things intimated in the General's letter that are grave indeed. I'll need time to consider them, and I hope that you will give me your trust on this matter until I come to some conclusions."

It was a request that Carter had made many times in the past. I had never refused him, and I would not do so now.

"But no matter what," he said, his tone changing from introspection to command, "I believe we must know the truth of the rumors from Siberia, regardless of the danger. Call William. We will be needing him."

Less than an hour later, William strode into Carter's office, wearing the same smile he always bore. William had the exuberance and hopefulness of youth, and these were qualities the two of us, jaded by many battles against the dark forces of the earth's forgotten lands, sorely needed.

I watched Carter's eyes light up as he entered. "William," he said, "thank you for coming on such short notice."

"Of course," he said, turning to me. "Dr. Armitage, how are you tonight?"

"Fine, as always, my boy. I believe your father-in-law has a proposal he wants to make to you."

"Yes," Carter said, rising from his chair to shake the boy's hand. "Have a seat, William, we have much to discuss."

"Is everything all right?" he asked, taking my seat next to the fire while I poured him a glass of brandy.

"It seems that things are rarely all right," Carter said. "It's an unfortunate consequence of the knowledge we possess, but the burden must fall to someone."

William nodded. "Of course." I handed him the drink and he thanked me.

"First, I must apologize for mocking your choice to spend so much time studying Russian. We will be in need of your skills after all."

"We're going to Russia?" William asked, sounding understandably confused.

"It appears so." Carter removed the letter from his pocket, handing it to the young man. Then we both waited as he read it. William let out a soft whistle and looked up at his father-in-law.

"I take it you think there's some truth to this note."

"I do."

"I also take it you've been following the news from the region. There's no guarantee we'll find a friendly welcome waiting for us. This pass from your friend might end up being our death warrant."

Weston nodded. "I wish I could say you were wrong. Dr. Armitage and I have discussed it, and we simply do not think we have a choice. If there is even the possibility of truth in Professor Denikin's assessment, we must investigate. Nevertheless, I will not hold it against you if you decide to stay. This is not an assignment; it is a request. In truth, I am sure my daughter would prefer you declined."

William grinned. "Rachel didn't have a choice when she became a part of this family. I did. I knew what I was getting myself into, and I wouldn't dream of letting you go alone. I'm sure Rachel will understand."

For the barest second, Carter hesitated, and I even wondered if perhaps he regretted asking the young man's assistance. He must have known as I did that William would never refuse him, no matter what the danger. But then Carter simply smiled and nodded. "Then it is settled," he declared. "We leave tomorrow."

Chapter 7

Le Temps, Paris (translated), 1 May 1933, Front Page

The denizens of Paris are living in fear today. A shocking crime of the most revolting and fiendish character that has ever taken place in France has been uncovered in the city's Latin Quarter. Early this morning, the gendarmes were called to the cellar of a house in La Cour du Dragon, between Rue de Rennes and Rue du Dragon. What they found inside is almost too horrible to describe within the pages of this publication.

In the center of an otherwise empty cellar was a crude wooden platform, and on that platform lay the body of a woman, though the state of that poor creature was so horrible as to make ready identification difficult. She lay on her back and was entirely naked, her arms and legs bound and pulled apart in a sickening mockery of Leonardo da Vinci's *Vitruvian Man*. Cause of death was impossible to ascertain, as any of the violations committed against her body may have been responsible for her final passing.

Her throat was slashed from ear to ear, and the cut was so deep that she was all but decapitated. But the fiend or fiends did not end their mischief there. Her ears and nose were missing, having been cut clean off. Moreover, the murderer's blade had gutted the woman from throat to gullet. Her organs were removed and spread about the room, apparently in some pattern which the authorities refused to reveal.

In fact, the police have been tight-lipped about many aspects of the crime—one that rivals the worst of London's White Chapel murders perpetrated by the infamous fiend known only as Jack the Ripper. But this paper has, through anonymous sources within the Prefecture of Police, uncovered details that should chill the blood of any Parisian.

According to our sources, the victim—whose identity may never be known—was a part of what can only be described as a religious ritual of the darkest and foulest character. Her organs were placed at the five points of a great, uneven star. Her heart was missing, having been burnt in a primitive altar placed at the head of the table on which she lay. And perhaps worst of all, the walls, floors, and even ceilings were covered in arcane and indecipherable symbols—all of which were written in the victim's own blood.

Such stunning news will shake this city to its core, and it raises many questions. Is this the beginnings of a new and terrible religious movement in the Parisian underground? Who perpetrated this horrendous crime? And perhaps most importantly, was this an isolated event, or can we expect more horrors?

Le Figaro, Paris (translated), 1 May 1933, Arts Page

Sad news today from the Latin Quarter as it seems that Henri Leroux, the renowned artist and perhaps the Quarter's most well-known denizen, has taken his own life. Famous the world over for his strikingly macabre and gothic style, Leroux produced such iconic paintings as *L'abîme* and *Les Dieux Aînés*. But lately he had spiraled into a deep depression culminating in his tragic death.

According to witnesses, at around 11 P.M. last night, there was a grand commotion in the Latin Quarter, consisting of the frantic cries and unintelligible shouting of a man, the very same M. Leroux. He was observed running down the Rue Barrée—completely in the nude—and flailing his arms in an erratic manner. Those who tried to stop him described M. Leroux as violently mad and quite dangerous. Despite the efforts of various passersby, M. Leroux ran all the way to the Pont des Arts, where he was seen to utter one last horrible cry before throwing himself into the waters of the Seine. His body was recovered this morning.

M. Leroux's death ends what had been a rather unusual chapter in the life of the famously eccentric Latin Quarter. In the last two weeks alone, five different young artists were admitted to various hospitals around the city, two in a completely catatonic state and three who reported suicidal depression brought on by particularly vivid and lucid dreams. The content of those dreams remains a mystery, though an anonymous citizen who is close to one of the persons in question reports that they centered on the end of the world.

Whatever wild and irresponsible imaginings were bred in the depths of the Latin Quarter, they seem to have affected M. Leroux more than most. His friends report that his already dark demeanor took on an even bleaker countenance in the weeks preceding his death and that he spoke endlessly and without bidding of his fear of sleep.

In any event, whatever the cause, the world of art has lost a true master. In this of all cities, he will be mourned and he will be remembered.

Personal Diary of Inspector François le Villard (translated)
2 May 1933

In the twenty-five years I have served as an inspector with La Sûreté Nationale, I have never seen the like of what I came upon in the Cour du Dragon last night. We were called to a small basement apartment in the Latin Quarter, within which we found a scene of such horror as any that heaven has ever bent above. A young girl— she couldn't have been older than eighteen—was ripped apart as if by some beast, though what animal could render such carnage I cannot say.

The press—scoundrels all—have revealed much of what the poor girl suffered and the indignities visited upon her by whatever devil even now walks the streets of Paris. These vultures pick at her bones. They have no respect for the living, and even less for the dead. My only comfort is that they have yet to draw a connection between the death of the artist Henri Leroux and that of the young woman whose identity remains a mystery. Are they somehow connected? Perhaps. I find it difficult to believe that such bizarre events could coincide both in date and location and have no common thread to bind them together. Was Leroux involved? Was he somehow complicit? What compelled him to throw himself from the Pont Des Arts? Could it have been guilt for such a heinous crime?

It is impossible to yet know, though I hope that our investigation will illuminate the facts. For now, I am focusing my efforts on determining the origin of a phrase found carved into the skin of the murder victim, a piece of the crime scene that the press—despite the leaks within my department—has not yet brought to light.

In the skin above her left breast, in the flesh that would have covered her heart—if it were still within her body—three words were inscribed. *Il est ressuscité*—he is risen! The words chilled me, this mockery of the true faith, this blasphemy. And the implication shook me to my core. Could it be that a Christian had done this thing? Or could it mean something else entirely, something darker, something far more sinister? Of what foul rising do these words speak? And what dark power did this poor girl die to resurrect, what black ritual did her sacrifice complete?

I will have answers to these questions. I will find this girl's murderer. That is my promise. That is my cause.

Chapter 8

Journal of Henry Armitage
July 23, 1933

It was early this morning when Rachel and I boarded a flight bound for Berlin. It wasn't long after we were in the air that she started to ask questions.

"So," she said, leaning forward, "this Erich Zann character, you think my father was right? You think he's responsible for his disappearance?"

I nodded. "He has to be. Other than to your father, the *Incendium Maleficarum* rarely calls to the innocent. Zann wanted what Carter had, and he was willing to do anything to get it. Like I said, where we find Zann, we find Carter. I'd bet my life on it."

Her eyes trailed to the window and the endless horizon. "That book. I always knew that it would come down to this. It's hard to believe, really. One of the first memories I have, one of the first things I remember from my childhood, is seeing it on my father's desk. The sun would hit it in the afternoon, and the gold lettering would shimmer. It was almost like a fire, the way it danced in the light. There was something about it, you know? Something that drew me even then. But I was afraid of it, too. It attracted me and repulsed me, all at once."

I couldn't help but smile. I understood exactly what she meant. "It is the book's nature. It's as much a living thing as you or I. It is a blessing and a curse, a man's ultimate desire and his greatest fear.

Within its pages is the power to save the world or to destroy it. But make no mistake, the book is wholly evil."

"Then why did my father keep it? Why not destroy it?"

"Were it that simple. The book has always been, as best anyone can tell. There is no burning it, no cutting it to shreds. It would survive, and besides, no one really knows what steps it might take to prevent its own end. It has a history of leaving death in its wake.

"No, destroying the book was never an option. Keeping it safe, protecting it from those who would use its power to do evil—that was the only choice open to your father. It was the mission of his life, and it is the reason for his disappearance."

Rachel took my hands in hers. "Tell me the truth, Henry. I don't want you to hide anything from me."

"Of course."

She hesitated, and I knew what she would ask. "Do you really think my father is alive?"

"I do. In fact, I'm sure of it. No one lives on this earth that understands the way the book works like your father. Maybe nobody ever has. Zann can't kill him. He is too valuable."

Rachel shuddered at the mention of Carter's possible murder. "What do we know about Zann?"

"Now *he* is an interesting character," I said, happy to turn to something I knew more about. "Zann's father was an incredibly talented, if largely unknown, musician. And he used that talent in a very special way. He was what we might call a 'closer'—a man who worked to keep the gates between our existence and those beyond tightly shut. I understand from those who should know that his music was his weapon, and he wielded it with a special ferocity. Unfortunately, as is too often the case it seems, others didn't recognize his importance. Instead, the wider world saw only a mad man who spoke of things unseen and unheard. He disappeared many years ago from his apartment on the Rue d'Auseil in Paris, a vanishing, if I might be so bold, that was as mysterious as your father's.

"They say the stars were different that night and that the signs in the heavens portended some uncertain doom. The last anyone saw or heard of Zann, he was locked in a garret apartment, sawing away at his violin, the song he played unlike any produced before or since.

"By the time of his disappearance, Zann's son had not seen his father in many years, the latter having abandoned the family back in Germany. Following the death of his mother, Zann went to live with relatives in Munich. After a sterling career at the University of Berlin, he became a prominent scholar, attaining the position of professor of ancient history at the University."

"With that sort of pedigree, I'm surprised he would be responsible," she said, as the rumble of turbulence shook the plane. She cast her gaze around the narrow metal tube. "I don't think I'll ever like flying."

"His reputation is spotless," I said, returning to the matter at hand. "And I can find nothing in the official records of his career to indicate he'd be involved in anything nefarious."

"And yet you're sure he's responsible?" she said as she gestured to the steward for a brandy to calm her nerves.

"Certainly. Carter always had an uncanny ability to judge character. Moreover, there is some evidence that Zann departed from the principles of his father. While his official records are spotless, there is often far more to a man than what he shows in the light of day. My research indicates that during his time at the University of Berlin, he fell in with a certain secret society, one that traces its roots back to the mythical sons of Aryas."

"The Thule Society?"

"You've heard of them?" I admit, I was both surprised and impressed.

"I did some research on the *völkische Bewegung* for a piece in the *Advertiser* on the new German government. Fascinating—if bizarre— stuff. It seemed that the Thule Society had been particularly influential in the halls of power at one point, but my understanding is that it was disbanded after falling out of favor with the authorities."

"And that is the official story. But in truth, Carter and I believed that the Thule Society merely went underground and that, indeed, its adherents were in high positions throughout Berlin. It's a frightening possibility, given that the Thule held the ancient ones in high esteem, worshiping them and seeking their return. But now, with Dr. Zann's promotion to Reich Minister of Cultural History, our theory seems to have been confirmed. And then, of course, there's the reaction of the *Incendium Maleficarum* to Dr. Zann's presence."

She took a long sip from her drink, and some of the color returned to her cheeks. "You mean the singing."

I nodded. "Your father confirmed the old legends. The book seeks its master, the one through whom it will accomplish its end. And only that person can hear its song. Your father heard that song for thirty years, right up until the moment Erich Zann walked through his door. From that point, Zann became its true owner."

Rachel sat silently in her seat, seeming to study a speck of dust on the floor. But I knew her mind was working. She reminded me then of Carter.

"Do you ever wonder why the book chose my father? If it's evil," she said, finally looking back up to me, "then does that say something about him? Does it expose some weakness?"

All I could do was shake my head. "I have wondered about it, and I know your father wondered, too. It was a terrible burden, one that might well drive a weaker-minded man mad. But in the end, Carter was only a means to an end. The book is patient, and it knew this day would come. Your father has been at the heart of a secret war raging just beyond the borders of civilization and the boundaries of our world. I fear that Dr. Zann seeks to deal a final blow to our side in the conflict. He needed the book to do it, and now he has it."

"And he has my father, and all that he knows."

"Correct, and that is why we must stop him."

"God," she murmured, slumping into her seat. She waved her empty glass at the steward, who came and refilled it. "This is all so unbelievable."

"And I wouldn't believe it myself, were I not a witness."

"How many times have you done this, Henry? How many times have you and my father set off for some godforsaken part of the world, doing godforsaken things most decent people would call insane? How many times?"

I grinned. "More than I can count, my darling. Many, many times."

"Like the time you and my father and William went?"

My smile faded and I looked away. I could not bear to meet her gaze. "Yes, that was one of the times."

"He didn't even tell me where he was going, you know?" she said, her eyes trailing off as she looked out the window to the sky beyond. "He told me he'd be gone for a month, maybe longer, and not to worry. He said, 'Carter knows what he's doing. He'll take care of everything.' But even then he offered to stay. I think he would have, too. But I told him that was silly. I told him to go. I insisted. So he kissed me on the cheek, told me he loved me, and was out the door. It happened so fast, like a train passing a station without a stop. I had barely registered that he was leaving before he was gone."

What to say to that? How to make up for a crime committed so many years before? I had no words, so I said the only thing that came to my mind. "I'm sorry, Rachel." It was pathetic and insignificant and clichéd, but it was not empty. Rachel looked at me and took my hands in hers.

"You don't have to apologize, Henry. I'm fine. I've been fine. And I know that William would want me to help you. We're going to find my father. I can't imagine a better way to honor Will."

As she looked in my eyes, I knew she meant it. She was putting her faith in me. It was a faith that had been betrayed before.

Chapter 9

Excerpt from *Memoirs of a Crusader*, Dr. Henry Armitage, "The Tunguska Folly of 1919," (unpublished)

With William's assent, Carter was anxious to depart. Our trip was urgent, and time was not in abundance. Unfortunately, the air routes of the modern age were still in their infancy in those days, and so it was by ship that we were to travel. In better times, we would have sailed for the continent and then traveled east by rail. But with the Red Army now in firm control from the Dnieper to the Ural Mountains and beyond, an eastern route was impossible. Thus, we set forth for San Francisco and a ship that would take us to Vladivostok.

Carter brought with him a veritable library of arcane and esoteric works. He studied them relentlessly on the trip to San Francisco, but he did not speak of his suspicions about what had happened in the Russian wilderness. I knew that William was as curious as I, but neither of us asked any questions.

When we arrived at the port of San Francisco, Carter had most of the books posted for return to his office at Miskatonic. All but one, the one he never was without—the *Incendium Maleficarum*.

We'd sailed for three days when Carter called us into his cabin. He stoked a fire in the hearth, and as he did, I had the feeling that this night would be unlike so many others before, when we had chatted on inconsequential things over brandy and cigars. Tonight, Carter had the look of a man who meant business.

Which is not to say that the cigars and brandy were not present. Carter had his vices, and one of them was his love of tobacco. He'd smoked a pipe for a while but had complained incessantly of the hassle it entailed. I'd bought him a box of cigars one Christmas, and he never looked back. The brandy was a habit of older vintage, but one that went well with his new obsession. He poured three glasses, and after we each lit a cigar, he began to speak.

"Tell me, Henry. Did you ever have the honor of meeting the good General during happier times?"

"General Denikin? I can't say that I did."

"And of course, young William here would have had no such opportunity. It's unfortunate, really. Anton Denikin is a great patriot and a lover of his country, and I am sure he has made a fine leader of men. But he was, before the war began, a brilliant professor. His work on the belief systems of the Ankara civilization is quite remarkable."

"The Ankara?" William asked. Carter had opened the door to an obscure—and one might even say shunned—epoch of ancient history. My curiosity was piqued.

"Well," Weston said, taking a long drag on his cigar and blowing the smoke toward the fireplace, "the Ankara were a truly ancient civilization, making their homes in present-day Turkey, Iran, and along the Mediterranean coast. Many mighty kingdoms rose from the remnants of their empire, and it is said that the knowledge of the Egyptians, the Babylonians, and the Mycenaeans was, in fact, nothing more than a decayed imitation of their own. They had no system of writing that we know of, but their legends survived in the oral traditions. It was the Sumerians—devotees of the Ankaran myths— who wrote them down, and it is their tablets and scrolls that have come down to us through the ages. The University of Moscow possessed the only extant copy of these works, and Professor Denikin is the world's foremost expert on their contents. I have never seen them in person, but the Professor was kind enough to provide me with copies and detailed descriptions."

The room seemed to grow darker as Carter spoke, and though I told myself it was merely the setting of the November sun and the vastness of the empty oceans, I could not help but feel that something more had descended. Words have power in this world, and at the mention of the Ankara, the air had changed around us. But Carter did not seem to notice. He sat there, smoking his cigar, staring into space as if he were looking into the past.

"The scroll is known," he continued, "as the Bel Xul. Within its pages are recorded the visions of an Ankaran holy man, who the Sumerians knew only as Nabu Sebet Babi, the Seer of the Seven Gates. It was said that he received secret knowledge of the time before time, when the moon had not yet found its place in the heavens, and no sun had ever dawned upon the earth. Within these visions Nabu Sebet Babi witnessed impossible visions across infinite vistas of time and space. And within those vistas he looked upon an age of earth's history before the coming of man, when, as the Bible records, 'the earth was without form and void, and darkness was over the face of the deep.' But that does not mean the world was empty."

I nodded as he spoke. The truth of his words I had seen with mine own eyes decades earlier when one of the older masters of this world had risen from the deep. Were it not for the sacrifice of a brave and honorable man, a sea captain named Jonathan Gray, the world might have ended then and there, all those years before.

"The Bel Xul is thus in keeping with much we have seen in our travels, and it reflects the legends of other long dead cultures that speak of the elder gods, those ancient forms that ruled primordial earth. The Old Ones, who built the titanic cities of Ib and R'lyeh and Tikalt and that nameless necropolis that lies beneath the sands of Arabia. In fact, the Bel Xul may well be the primogenitor of these legends, the seed by which a thousand different mythos came into being."

"But what," I said, leaning in close to Carter, "does this have to do with what happened in Siberia?"

Carter looked down at the letter he had received from Denikin, rereading its key passages. "The Bel Xul is voluminous," he said, still scanning the missive, "but the good professor has directed us to one passage. The Old Ones, of course, are unimaginable to us, and attempts to conceptualize them are as if one were to stare into the unreverberate blackness of the abyss—impenetrable. That is their nature.

"But there is one," he said, holding up a finger, "whose relationship to mankind is entirely different. When the Old Ones were overthrown, when light came to this world and they were cast into outer darkness, there was one who remained, who still walked the earth and sowed destruction and confusion in his midst.

"He is the harbinger, the messenger, he who stands in between. A god to the legendary Mi-Go, a demon to early man. He wears a thousand masks, or so they say, and thus is known by many names. He is the crawling chaos, the 'Black Man' of the ancient witch cults, the haunter of the dark. But one name, taken when he walked along the River Nile in the city of Shem in the Old Kingdom, he wears as his own. And that name," Carter said, the light of the fire reflected in his eyes, "the one that has come to us across the darkness of forty-seven centuries, is Nyarlathotep."

He leaned back in his chair, relighting the cigar that had gone dead in the telling of his story. The name of Nyarlathotep was well known to me, as were the tales of his wanderings across the earth. And black stories they were. It was said that he possessed power over the mind of man and that he could, merely with his words, sway the masses. He had the ability to possess and control the powerful—kings, emperors, popes—leading entire kingdoms to death and destruction. Disease followed in his wake, and there was no land that his feet fell upon that was spared an ill fate. Even William, who was but a neophyte in his knowledge of the true nature of the world around us, had heard that accursed name.

"And that is why we are on this voyage. I believe that Nyarlathotep will return. Now, the Oculus can banish the dark one from our world, but it has been lost for a millennium. It is said that it will only reappear when the stars come right and the rise of Nyarlathotep is imminent. If it is possible that the Oculus has returned, then we cannot ignore the threat. If others were to attain it first, all hope might well be lost. And given that the last few years have brought us death and destruction never before imagined, I must believe that Denikin's words are more than idle chatter. Then there is the matter of the ring he is said to wear."

"Yes," I said, "the one that bears the yellow sign."

Carter nodded. "It is that sign by which he is known, the sign that heralds the aligning of the stars and the opening of the gate. The same sign that Denikin mentions, the one that rumor tells has arisen again. Rumors seldom bear the whole truth, but they rarely bear none, either. The fact is," he said, folding the letter carefully and placing it in its envelope, "we are fortunate that Denikin wrote to us when he did, while time remains to us, even if it is short."

"What does the book say of Nyarlathotep?" William asked.

I watched as Carter's eyes trailed across the darkened chamber to the tome that sat upon the desk of his stateroom, the book that I rarely saw him without. The flickering light of the fireplace seemed to play along the crimson cover, and the gold-flaked inscription, *Incendium Maleficarum*, sparkled in the night. When I had first met Carter Weston, he was a skeptic, a naïve unbeliever who knew little of the world. But now he was the master to whom I looked for answers, and the book was one reason for his wisdom.

"Little more than we already know from other sources. Whereas the knowledge contained within the book is often secret and hidden from mankind, it is not so with the stories of Nyarlathotep. These are well known. He has walked among us for centuries. It is for this reason, perhaps, that the *Necronomicon* speaks so often of him. Some say that it was he who gave the mad Arab inspiration for that work."

"What do you think we will find in Russia?"

"Possibly nothing. But I don't think so. I think the signs are clear. I think the Oculus is there, and we will find it. And that's a good thing, because I fear we will need it in the days to come."

The conversation ended then. Carter leaned back and smoked his cigar, peering into the distance. William and I sat in silence, pondering what we faced, hoping for fair winds and clear skies. Alas, whatever god watches over us all did not hear our prayers.

Chapter 10

Excerpt from *Memoirs of a Crusader*, Dr. Henry Armitage, "The Tunguska Folly of 1919", (unpublished)

We arrived in Vladivostok early in the morning of November 21, 1919, to chaos and madness. Word had come late the night before of the fall of Omsk and the defeat of Admiral Kolchak's forces in Siberia. The eastern White Army was now in full retreat towards Baikal, with the western army and General Denikin bottled up in the Crimea. Kolchak was rumored dead, though the worst news was yet to come. The British and Americans, who had to that point provided support in the form of both men and materiel, were pulling out. The war was all but lost. The host of civilians gathered at the port confirmed that bitter truth in the starkest way possible.

We disembarked into a maelstrom. Men, women, and children of every possible background and distinction were everywhere, surrounding us. Some stood shivering in the cold, while the wealthiest were wrapped tight in their finest furs. They came at us, each with something to sell. Diamonds and jewels were thrust into my face, while the prices asked were but a pittance, no more than the cost of transit to anywhere but Vladivostok. Others offered the clothes on their back, and at least one woman tried to sell me her daughter. When it became clear that we weren't interested, the swarm moved on to their next victims.

"What the hell was that?" William spat.

"That," Weston said, "was desperation."

"And theft," William replied. "I had a woman try to convince me she'd sell a pair of diamond earrings for a few dollars. Fakes."

"Those weren't fakes. The same thing happened in Europe when Moscow fell. The cream of Russian civilization fled with nothing but the clothes on their backs and the diamonds around their necks. But even the market for rare jewels can be flooded. You just witnessed the wealthy of the old order, cut down by the very capitalism the Bolsheviks abhor."

William and I looked back at the crowds of desperate people, a thin sliver of paper between them and freedom, between life and the advancing Red Army. I've rarely seen such horror, but even worse awaited me as we made our way to the military train that would carry us to Irkutsk.

The streets were thick with carts carrying the dead and wounded from Vladivostok station. They had been streaming in for days, every arriving train bearing more casualties from western battles. So many shattered bodies. Men shorn of arms and legs. The stench of death, the sickly sweet smell of rotting flesh, both of the still-living and the long-dead, all thrown together in a horrid testament to the evils of war. The snow drifted down gently around them, reminding me in one macabre instant of Christmastime. And now, with the collapse of the Eastern resistance and the fall of Omsk, this stream of broken men would soon become a flood. As bad as things were in Russia's great eastern port, darker days were coming.

"Let's just get to the station," Carter said, perhaps sensing our growing discomfort. "The sooner we are away from here, the better."

"I know we've come a long way, but perhaps..." I was certain of our purpose, but the chaos surrounding us made me question whether we could accomplish it. Carter cut me off.

"I will understand," he said, turning to William and me, "if either of you wishes to abandon this errand, foolish as it may be. Certainly our time is even shorter than we thought. But I must continue, no matter what the cost. So, if you are with me, I need your word now. There's no turning back once we get on that train."

My doubts notwithstanding, I was unwilling to challenge Carter so directly. If he was determined to see this through, who was I to disagree? And William, he would never go against Carter. No, our answer was clear. He saw it in both our eyes, nodded to each of us, and we continued on our path.

The station was on the edge of town, a scene of even greater din and clamor. The dead and dying were being removed as quickly as the men who bore them could act. Each body was replaced with supplies—guns, bullets, food—all desperately needed on the front lines. Above the screams of the wounded could be heard the shouted orders of the officers, each tinged with the threat of severe punishment if the men did not move faster.

We entered the station to find it deserted but for a man in a booth at the far end. The floors were covered by old newspapers and discarded flyers from happier—and busier—times. The high dome of the station with its great windows must have been something to see in a different age. Now the place was but a tomb to the old regime, a monument to what had been and a warning of what was to come. The man, despite his lack of customers, sat at attention, as if at any moment he expected ticket buyers such as ourselves to appear.

"Excuse me, sir," Carter began, "we need to speak to someone about passage on your train."

The man stared at him in seeming bemusement, then said, "Ya ne govoryu po-Angliski."

William leaned over Carter's shoulder and began to speak to the man in his own tongue. Carter and I waited. Without William, we would have been lost.

"He says that there are no tickets for the trains. He says the army has taken them all for their own purposes."

"Tell him we understand that," Carter said. "Tell him we are on a mission for the army and need to find someone in authority to speak with."

William nodded and turned back to the man, relaying the message. He gestured to a door to our left. "He says a Captain Aleksandrov is in charge. Says we can find him on the loading dock."

We nodded our thanks to the man, while William added a *spasiba* for the three of us.

We walked back into the chill wind and gently falling snow. Before I could ask how we would know this Aleksandrov, we came upon a man standing on the platform, watching the loading and unloading. He had the obvious air of command, and if he was not the Captain, he would certainly know his whereabouts.

William led the way, excused himself in Russian, and began to explain our situation. A quizzical smile spread across the man's face before he held up a hand to stop him.

"Your Russian is very good, my friend, but perhaps not as good as my English."

"And much preferable," Carter said with a laugh, "as my friend and I here speak not a word of the former."

"Understandable. It is not an easy language, as I know well. My parents moved to England when I was young, so I struggle with its finer points even now. I returned on the eve of the Great War, to defend my homeland. I never thought," he said, gesturing to the tumult around him, "that I would be defending her from my own brothers. And I certainly did not expect to see three Americans here, in Vladivostok, seeking my assistance. What brings you to this godforsaken place?"

"We come at the behest of General Denikin," Carter said, handing him the pass. "We seek passage to Irkutsk, on an urgent errand for him, an old friend from well before the revolution."

"General Denikin? I'm sorry to say that I'm not even sure he still lives. And besides, I do not believe he would have called you to Irkutsk if he knew the situation there now. What you see here is but a fraction of the chaos there. We will hold her as long as we can, but Irkutsk will be overrun by the Red Army by the spring, if not sooner. It may not see Christmas. I must advise you to abandon this plan."

I watched as Aleksandrov handed Carter the pass, who shook his head.

"I'm sorry Captain, I can't do that. We have obligations, and we must see them through."

Aleksandrov's eyes narrowed, and something of the friendliness he had offered us melted away even in the freezing cold.

"I don't know what those obligations entail, and I won't bother to ask since, if I judge you rightly, you wouldn't tell me in any event. But I must ask you, are they worth your life? Are they worth the lives of your friends? If you travel to Irkutsk, you are putting all of them at risk. I'll tell you what I should not, but what every Bolshevik knows already. Transbaikal is lost, my friends. We intend to halt the retreat at Chita and establish a new line there. But even that plan is suspect, and Chita lies several hundred miles east of Irkutsk. Go if you must, but know well what you face if you do. There is no help for you beyond the Baikal."

"I thank you for your assistance, Captain. And I thank you for your warning."

Aleksandrov nodded, not bothering to argue further.

"This train departs within the half-hour. The accommodations leave something to be desired, but they are the best I can do. I have no doubt you will find Colonel Rostov in Irkutsk. It is his home, and he will never leave it. I only hope that the same will not be said of you."

Aleksandrov turned to his duties, and Carter glanced at William and me. We were committed, and he saw it in our eyes. We entered the train and made our way to the corner of a half-empty troop car. There we passed the next few nights as the train traveled inexorably west into the jaws of the advancing Red Army, a menace that now far outshone in our eyes anything we might find in Tunguska.

How naïve we were.

Chapter 11

Journal of Henry Armitage
July 24, 1933

Rachel and I arrived in Berlin's Tempelhof airport late on the night of July 23, 1933. A storm came with us. The howling wind cut through us, and torrential rain rode on it. By the time we hailed a cab, we were soaked to the bone. We had not much dried when we arrived at the Hotel Esplanade at the Pottsdamer Platz. I would have preferred to go straight to our room and straight to bed, but alas, fate was not to be so kind.

We entered the hotel and came upon an explosion of sound and light. The roar of a live band poured through the open double doors of what I could see—even with a mere glance—was an ornate ballroom.

"Looks like we came to the right place," Rachel said to me with a sly grin and playful eyes.

"Maybe for you, young lady. I think my dancing days are done."

"My dear Henry," she said, putting her hand on my shoulder, "I dare say there's more to you than you let on."

I wouldn't have expected an opportunity to test that hypothesis, but one came sooner than I imagined. Before I could even open my mouth to respond, a young man in a black military uniform appeared. He clicked his heels, bowed, and said, "Dr. Armitage, Mrs. Jones, welcome to Berlin. Please, forgive my intrusion."

"No," Rachel said with no small amount of hesitation, "not at all." She looked at me for direction, but I had none to offer. "I'm sorry, but I didn't catch your name."

"It is not important, ma'am," the young man said, his smile never wavering. "It is my privilege to invite you to a small gathering." We waved his hand towards the ballroom where raucous laughter did much to undercut his assertion about the size of the party.

"Well, we thank you for that," Rachel said, "but how did you know who we are?"

The smile remained, but the corners of the soldier's mouth seemed to tick up ever so slightly as he said, "Oh, Mrs. Jones, we in Germany are most interested in our visitors, particularly those with such a fine pedigree. Now, if you please, I know you must want to change out of these wet clothes. I'll be waiting."

"So much for a discreet entrance," Rachel said as we made our way to our room.

"Yes, it would seem as though we were expected."

"Nothing for it now, though."

"Should we go to this party?"

Rachel glanced over her shoulder at the man in a suit standing at the end of the hallway trying—a little too hard, it would seem—to appear inconspicuous.

"I don't think we have a choice."

"Right. I'll meet you downstairs."

"Maybe I'll get to see you in those dancing shoes after all," she said with a grin as she opened the door of her room, located next to mine.

I frowned, and she laughed.

* * *

Ten minutes later I emerged in a suit identical to the one I had been wearing, sans the soaking rain. I waited on Rachel in the lobby, and when she appeared, with her dress trailing down the grand staircase as she walked, the golden-globed necklace Carter had given her more than a decade before catching the light, I was struck speechless. It is a strange thing, one that so many a father or uncle has experienced—for I considered Rachel to be my own kin as strongly as if it were true—to watch a child grow into adulthood. Where had the little girl with skinned knees and pigtails gone? I suppose she had vanished many, many years before.

"Another thing my father taught me," she said upon seeing my expression, "was to always have at least one nice thing to wear. You never know when you'll be invited to a party."

"Quite," I mumbled. "And you still wear that necklace."

Her hand went to the globe that hung around her neck on a golden chain. Her fingers ran over the indentations of the Arabic script, as I knew they had done unnumbered times before.

"Always."

She glanced over my shoulder, and I didn't have to follow her eyes to know where she was looking. "I see our friend is waiting on us."

"He hasn't left. I suppose we shouldn't keep him in suspense."

"Certainly not. Lieutenant!" she called, sounding positively ecstatic to see him. "The party is waiting."

"Of course," he said, gesturing to the double doors.

We followed him into the grand ballroom. It was a stunningly beautiful chamber. Six chandeliers hung from the ceiling, their sparkling electric lights adding to the glow of a full moon that beamed down from the newly broken clouds through the glass dome that was the hall's ceiling. The light glittered off the gilded walls, imbuing the assembled revelers with a golden glow.

Nor was it an inconsequential gathering. It seemed as though all of Berlin society was present, and all were dressed to the nines. I felt a rare moment of self-doubt, embarrassed at my ill-fitting suit. But Rachel was radiant. She belonged in this place.

As I glanced around the ballroom, I noticed a man in expensive attire, a beautiful young woman in a gossamer dress hanging from his arm. He was surrounded by party-goers, many of them in military uniforms. But what made me notice him was the fact that he was looking intently at us. He mumbled something to the young lady—who also turned and glanced in our direction, with no shortage of disdain, I thought—and then started walking towards us. Before he'd gone five feet his face erupted in a brilliant smile.

"Dr. Henry Armitage," he cried, throwing his arms wide, "and you, madam, must be Mrs. Rachel Jones." He bent and kissed

Rachel's hand before turning to me and grasping mine. "We've been expecting you."

The lieutenant, who had not left our side, saluted the man before turning to us. "May I introduce to you Dr. Erich Zann, of the University of Berlin."

"Charmed," Rachel said, "though I must say I'm surprised to find a welcoming party for Dr. Armitage and me. We didn't exactly come announced."

"Well, the party was to happen regardless. But surely you must know, Frau Jones, that we in Germany are always honored by the presence of such a fine academic as Dr. Armitage. And your father," he said, pausing almost imperceptibly—but not quite—at the mention of Carter, "is known and respected around the world. I was most distressed to hear of his passing. I saw him, only weeks before he died."

"Yes," Rachel said, "I'm quite aware. Though we continue to hold out hope that he is merely missing. Perhaps detained somewhere."

Zann's smile, which had never really faded, seemed to grow even wider. "Perhaps," he said simply.

"And I must commend you, Doctor. It must be difficult to monitor the thousands of people who venture in and out of Germany every day, just so you can greet every scholar that comes across your borders."

"Well, Dr. Armitage is not just any academic. His reputation precedes him."

"As does yours, Dr. Zann," I said. "I read your work on Hindu mythology. Most intriguing, though I found your hypothesis linking the religion of ancient India to early German folklore somewhat... tenuous."

Zann laughed, perhaps too enthusiastically. "Ah yes, that old thing. I may have been too exotic in some of my conclusions. But I find that youth often suffers from over-exuberance. You can leave us now, lieutenant." The young man clicked his heels and bowed again before withdrawing.

"And," I continued, "I understand that you've recently been offered the position of Reich Minister of Cultural History. Quite an honor. They must think rather highly of you in the Reich Chancellery.

"Yes, well," Zann said, his smile fading, "we reward loyalty in Germany. Even more, we reward results."

"Quite."

If Zann had dropped his guard, it didn't last for long. He grinned at me again, slapping me on the shoulder, "Come, let us have a drink."

I glanced around for Rachel, but she was no longer at my side. I would only learn later where she'd gone.

Diary of Rachel Jones

I went with Henry to the ballroom of the Esplanade, though everything within me rebelled at the idea. I was fairly certain the young lieutenant was directed to arrest us if we resisted. I had traveled to Germany once before—as a girl with my father, sometime before the war—and had found Berlin to be one of the most beautiful cities in the world. I loved it then, but a pall had fallen over the country. I know little of these Nazis but their tactics are of force and intimidation. And if a man like Zann—whom I now believe knows something about the disappearance of my father—has found favor with them, then they will always be my enemies.

Zann was there, of course, as I suspected. His shark-tooth smile and fancy suit could not cover the evil in his heart. If I had doubted before, seeing him was enough. This man was corrupt, and he meant to do us harm. Still, he approached us exuding the thick aroma of false charm, and I was forced to endure this charade as Henry tried to poke holes in his story. That is, until I noticed another young man hovering about us.

If it had only been his face, or his hair, or even the way his suit hung awkwardly on his too-thin frame, perhaps I would have let it pass. Maybe, if it had only been a passing resemblance, I would have said nothing. But he had William's eyes. The same spark. The same kindness. And when he smiled... It wasn't that he looked just like William. God no. Nothing so clichéd, nothing so ridiculous. It was so much more than that.

I turned so quickly that I think it took him by surprise. "Do you always make a habit of eavesdropping on others' conversations, or is this a special occasion?" I watched with some pleasure as that grin faded.

"Oh...no... Sorry ma'am. I didn't mean any harm." I winced a bit when he called me "ma'am," and I had to remind myself that I was far too old for this young man, a college student who knew little of the world. "It's just I heard you mention Dr. Carter Weston."

"No, no offense," I said. I glanced at Henry, who was still engaged with the German. Then I took the boy by the shoulder and led him away. "What do you know of Dr. Weston?"

"Well, ma'am..."

"Please," I said, interrupting. I grabbed a pair of champagne glasses from a passing waiter and handed him one. "If we are to be friends then we mustn't be so formal. My name is Rachel. Rachel Jones."

His face lit up again as he took a sip of champagne. "And I am Sebastian Leblanc, but my friends call me Guillaume."

I smiled. "And what should I call you?"

"Why, Guillaume, of course."

"Then Guillaume it is. That's not a German name."

"No, no," he said, a thinly veiled look of disgust passing over his face. "I am from Paris. I came here to study ancient religion with Dr. Zann. He is one of the foremost experts in the area, you know? Almost as famous as Dr. Weston."

"Yes, you mentioned Dr. Weston," I said, looking over my shoulder. One of the party-goers seemed entirely too interested in what we were doing for it to be natural. In Germany, one is never alone, it seems. "May I ask why?"

"Oh, no particular reason. I just thought I heard you mention him when you were speaking with Dr. Zann, and as he has always been a personal hero of mine, I couldn't help but listen in."

"I see." I don't know why I thought he might help us. Was there any reason to believe that things would turn around now, when they had seemed so dark for so long? But then he said something that sent my heart into my throat.

"And also, I would have sworn that I saw Dr. Weston only yesterday."

Journal of Henry Armitage

I followed Zann to the bar, though not knowing where Rachel had gone troubled me deeply. Curse me for not thinking things through. We'd walked like lambs into a den of lions, and Zann was chief amongst them, the blood-soaked leader of the pride. But there was nothing for it. He had begun the game, and it was mine to play.

He said something in German to the man behind the bar, holding up two fingers as he spoke. The man gave him two glasses of white wine, one of which he passed to me.

"An excellent dry wine from Alsace. One of the best that Germany has to offer." I took a sip, and indeed, it was a fine vintage.

"Most excellent," I said. "Though I was under the impression that Alsace now belonged to France."

A tremor of rage flashed across Zann's face, and I wondered again if I had gone too far. He was a man of roiling emotions, just below the calm surface he portrayed to the world. I little doubted that he was given to bouts of unbridled passion, nor did I doubt he was the kind who had no compunction about killing someone who stood in his way. But control was there as well, and after only a moment, Zann had reasserted it.

"On the maps, perhaps. But I can assure you that Alsace is still very much part of the fatherland, as it was and as it always will be. Surely you would agree that culture and its influence know no borders? The German nation is strong, and we are one people, no matter what the politicians may say."

"As long as Germany remembers, this time, that borders do have meaning, then I can see nothing amiss with that view. Cheers."

Zann watched with cold eyes as I drank half of the wine left in my glass.

"Is that why you came here, Dr. Armitage, to debate German politics and German foreign policy? I must say, it's not my area of expertise, nor are they subjects which I enjoy discussing."

"No, politics has never interested me." I downed the rest of the glass, gesturing to the man behind the bar for more. His incredulous glance towards Zann was met with an irritated flick of the hand, and my glass was refilled.

"Then what then? A tour of our wineries, perhaps?"

"No," I said, downing the glass in one drink and calling for yet another, "I never cared all that much for wine, either."

Dr. Zann sighed. Deeply, and I relished the moment.

"Actually, Dr. Zann, I came here to discuss Dr. Weston with you."

Zann arched an eyebrow. "Carter Weston? I'm not sure I understand."

"Surely you know that you were one of the last people who saw him alive?"

"Well," Zann said, leaning on the bar, "I did go to see him. At the end of last year, if I recall correctly. I was sent there on business for the University. He had a book in his possession, one of rather ancient lineage. The University was interested in borrowing it. All and all, nothing extraordinary."

"But he didn't give it to you."

"No, actually, he did not. I was surprised. I had heard that he was a reasonable man. So I left empty-handed."

He was lying, and I knew it.

"I think you know more than you let on. I think you got exactly what you were looking for, and I think you know exactly where Carter Weston is."

The corners of Zann's mouth started to creep up, and his tremulous lips could not be kept from breaking into a smile.

"Do you now, Dr. Armitage? Ah yes, we come to your true purpose here. Tell me, if I was the sort of man who could make a person simply disappear, even thousands of miles from home, then what powers do you think I might possess here, in Germany?"

His eyes flashed from the left to the right, and it was only then that I noticed the men closing in on me.

Diary of Rachel Jones

"Saw him?" I almost screamed it, and when I grabbed Guillaume's arm, I thought he might jump out of his skin from shock. "Where?"

"At the University," he stuttered. "It was late. Very late as a matter of fact." He scrunched up his brow and rubbed his chin, trying to recall every detail. "I couldn't sleep. I rarely can these days, it seems. And I was walking about the grounds. There's a building on campus, an old army barracks. Built before the war, in the 1800s. And I could have sworn I saw Dr. Weston and two other men go inside. It was strange. I only noticed because I recognized him from his books…and because he seemed ill. The two men were helping him, carrying him even."

Guillaume rambled on, but I was barely listening. I reached down and found a chair to steady myself. If it hadn't been there, I might have fallen straight away. I'd come with Henry out of a sense of obligation, whether to him or my father I can't rightly say. I had expected to find little. Perhaps the man who was behind my father's disappearance, the man who had likely killed him, the man whom I was sure was now in this room. But to hear that my father might live? And in Berlin? That was too much to be hoped.

And in that moment, I felt a rage towards Erich Zann greater than I thought possible. My eyes searched the room, and then I saw him. He was standing next to Henry at the bar. Men in dark suits— the same suits in fact, subtlety not becoming them—were closing in on them. And they weren't the only ones. The man who'd been trailing me was moving in my direction.

Guillaume had stopped talking and was staring at me. If we were going to get out of this, I'd need his help.

"Okay," I said. "Okay. I'm going to need you to do something for me."

"Madam?"

"I'm going to need a distraction."

"What? What do you mean?"

"Something like this."

Poor Guillaume. He didn't know what he was getting into. I grabbed his arm, and in his shock it was easy to throw him into the approaching German. The party was in full swing, and with the blast of the band and the dancing couples around us, no one even really noticed as Guillaume and the suited thug went flipping over a table. Guillaume jumped up, apologies pouring out of his mouth.

"Come on!" I said as I yanked him back, "I don't have time for it and he doesn't care."

"What were you thinking? Do you know what you just did?"

"It doesn't matter! Let's go!" I grabbed his shoulder, veritably dragging him through the crowd to the bar. "Can you throw a punch?"

"What?"

"Do you know how to hit a man?"

"Um...yes, I suppose?" he stuttered, not grasping the point.

"Good, cause I'm going to need it."

Henry noticed us before the good doctor, and I saw real fear in his eyes.

I clasped Henry's hand and pulled him towards me. "Excuse me, Dr. Zann, but I think we've outstayed our welcome."

The smile was now a sneer. "Quite." The first of his goons came running up behind him.

"All right, Guillaume, time to shine." I spun him around, and by God if he didn't swing with all his might. By some miracle, his fist connected with the German and down he went. But then I heard a woman scream, and I knew our cover was blown. I grabbed the open wine bottle and turned. The other German had already wrapped his arms around Henry's shoulders. I brought the bottle down hard, connecting with the side of my target's head. The bottle smashed, and wine exploded along with shards of glass, one of which dug deep into my palm. Blood mingled with wine, and pain was the product. Now the whole room was in chaos. Women were crying and men were screaming, and the police were already at the door.

"Let's go!" Henry cried, pointing towards an exit in the back. We started to run. Zann raised his glass and grinned.

"Farewell, Frau Jones. Something tells me we will be meeting again very soon, indeed."

The three of us left him behind, bursting through the rear door and into the cold night.

Chapter 12

Diary of Rachel Jones
July 24, 1933

The rain had stopped, but the storm was just behind us. Henry grabbed a metal rod and jammed it between the handles on the doors. I wasn't interested in waiting around to see if it held. Guillaume was cursing in French, but not so loud that I didn't hear the sound of police whistles getting closer with every moment.

"We have to go, and go now," Henry said.

I turned to Guillaume, who was still muttering. "We need to get off the streets. Some place safe, just for a little while. Do you know somewhere?"

He thought for a moment and was about to speak when someone slammed into the doors behind us. The bar held, for the moment.

"Now, Guillaume!"

"Yes, yes," he said. "There is a woman. A friend of mine. Come."

I grabbed him by the arm. "Can she be trusted?"

He hesitated, but then nodded. "Yes. At least, as much as anyone."

"That'll have to do."

He led us down the alley before turning into an even smaller one that ran off to the right. I had no idea where he was going, but the faster we got away from the Esplanade, the better. We stayed in the shadows, avoiding the streets and the light. Though if anyone had seen us—three well-dressed foreigners dashing from alley to alley—no amount of talking would have allayed suspicions.

We emerged only when we were close, following Guillaume across the street to a nondescript walk-up. We made our way to a garret on the top floor. Guillaume knocked twice. There was a voice from behind the door, and he answered in German. It opened and, before the woman could say a word, we pushed our way inside.

Guillaume slammed the door behind us and locked it, while the woman—a beautiful girl of no more than twenty—screamed at him in words I did not know. Guillaume held up his hands and began to shout over her.

"Can we keep it down? The last thing we need is someone hearing us," I said to Guillaume. "Hi," I said, turning to the girl. She fell silent, assessing me with suspicious eyes. "I'm sorry to barge in. It's hard to explain, but we need your help."

"Guillaume says that the police are after you. Is it true?" Her English was nearly perfect, even with the accent.

"Yes," I answered. She was young, but something about her told me that she suffered neither fools nor liars. "But we didn't do anything wrong."

"I am sure they would beg to differ. Still, the police have never been friends of mine, so for now you can stay."

She turned to Guillaume and spat something in German. That she was opening her home didn't mean that she was happy about it.

"Thank you," I said, trying to spare Guillaume another tongue-lashing. "My name is Rachel Jones. This is Henry Armitage."

"And my name is Margot. You are American?"

"Yes, we are."

"Foreigners," she said, turning towards the kitchen before casting yet another angry glance at Guillaume, "always bringing trouble. I'll make some tea, and I'll get a bandage for that cut on your hand."

Guillaume collapsed into a chair next to us and buried his head in his hands. I couldn't help but notice they were shaking.

"Friend of yours?" I asked him.

He looked up at me over his splayed fingers, and he seemed totally exhausted.

"She was. Before you two showed up." He cursed again in French and stood up, pacing back and forth in front of the window, peeking nervously through the curtains every time we heard a sound from below. Margot returned with a tray on which sat four porcelain cups, all but one chipped badly. Not that I cared. I was just glad to have something to calm my nerves and, perhaps more importantly,

Guillaume's. She sat down beside me and took my hand in hers. She dabbed iodine on the cut with a cloth. I winced from the sting.

"Now that we are acquainted, why don't you tell me what happened?" Margot asked, as she wrapped a bandage around my hand.

"Yes, why don't you?" The color was only now beginning to return to Guillaume's face. "I hope you know the mess we're in. If anyone recognized me..." He trailed off. There was no need for him to finish.

"Carter Weston, Dr. Weston, you say you saw him?"

"Yes," Guillaume said, confused. "What of it?"

Henry leaned forward in his chair. "Carter Weston is dead." He let it hang in the air, watched the effect wash over Guillaume's face. "Or at least, that is what we have been led to believe. Seven months ago, Dr. Weston disappeared. When the police searched his office, they found nothing amiss. No evidence of a struggle. Nothing taken. Nothing, except a single book, one of a pedigree both ancient and profane."

"*Incendium Maleficarum*," Guillaume whispered. He saw the surprise in my eyes and chuckled. "Of course, I know of it. It is the work that made Dr. Weston famous. I would have killed to get my hands on it." The smile faded as he realized what he had said.

"Yes, and it seems as though someone may have done just that."

"But I saw him. I know it. I would have known him anywhere."

"And that is why we are here. The last person to meet with Carter was your very own Dr. Zann. We know from a message Carter left behind that the good doctor had but one request."

Guillaume leaned back, his chair creaking beneath him. "The book," he said, his tone one of resignation.

"Exactly. But if my theory is correct, Dr. Weston is too valuable to kill, his knowledge of the book too great. No, I believe that he is here, in Germany. Your eyewitness testimony merely confirms that."

"But why have you come? Why didn't the University send someone else?"

Henry and I caught each other's eyes across the room.

"I see," Guillaume said with a sigh that bordered on a moan. "So you are alone, then."

"Carter is my father," I said. I noticed Margot, who had been paying little attention to the conversation until that point, perk up. She leaned forward in her chair, suddenly interested. "I don't know if he is alive or dead, but if there is a chance that he is here in Berlin, I have to see it through. Henry and I can handle this on our own. All we need from you are more details about where you saw Carter. We can take it from there, and no one need ever know you were involved."

Guillaume nodded, but before he could answer, Margot spoke.

"You should not go alone. What two can do, four can do better. We will go with you." Guillaume looked as if she had slapped him in the face.

"Margot!" More words followed, in German, a language with which I am completely unfamiliar. But no understanding was necessary. An argument erupted immediately, and after only a few moments, it was clear that Margot had the better part of it. Or at least, enough to beat Guillaume into submission.

She turned to me, and there was purpose in her eyes. "My mother was, in her younger days, a beautiful woman," she said. Looking at Margot, I could believe it. "And the thing I remember the most about photographs from her youth was her smile. It was a big, brilliant, perfect smile, the kind that I am sure lit up a room. But that was only pictures. By the time I was old enough to remember, my mother didn't smile much anymore. These two teeth," she said, pointing to her mouth, "were missing. Perhaps my father wasn't always a bastard, but when he drank, he got angry. And when he was angry, he liked to hit us. He threw me out when I was fifteen, and it was the happiest day of my life. I pray God every night that he will die, and that my mother will have some peace. But to this day, he remains. We will save your father, because your father is worth saving. And when death loses its prize, perhaps it will take another."

I understood then why Guillaume had fallen silent. How does one answer something like that?

"We must move quickly," Henry said. "Zann knows we are on to him, and it is impossible to say how he might react."

"Then we go tonight." We all turned to Guillaume, who suddenly flashed a smile that I imagined was his trademark in happier times. "After all, if we go to our deaths, no reason to keep the Reaper in suspense, eh?"

"In that case," I said, "what are we waiting for?"

Chapter 13

Excerpt from *Memoirs of a Crusader*, Dr. Henry Armitage, "The Tunguska Folly of 1919", (unpublished)

We arrived in Irkutsk to the sound of distant thunder. But the booming was too regular to be natural.

"One of the big 305s," I said. "Probably a hundred miles out still."

If we were lucky, it was a hundred miles out. The 305s were not mobile weapons, and if the Red Army was using them, then they had arrived in force and with only one purpose—to sweep over the Republicans like a crimson tidal wave.

"Let's find Rostov," Carter said. "And quickly."

We stepped out of the train into a swirling chaos that made what we had seen at Vladivostok seem calm. The shouts of commanding officers, the cries of wounded soldiers. The evacuation was in full swing. I looked into the eyes of the men—boys, really—who poured off the train with us, set to replace the wounded being ferried back to Vladivostok, to plug the holes they left behind. In those eyes I saw a fear that was heartbreaking.

"The General said you would come, and come you did."

I turned to a bear of a man, a thick, fur-lined great coat hanging from his massive frame. He was the perfect image of a Russian aristocrat, ripped from a Victorian novel. In the chaos that surrounded us, he was the picture of calm, and when he clasped Carter's shoulders in his huge hands, I could not help a smile.

"I'm glad you found us," Carter said. "The General was vague about where you would be."

"In truth, if you had come a month later, you would have found me in the ground." His booming laugh carried over the tumult of the station, though no one else was paying him any attention. "And it was not hard to find you, my friends. We receive few visitors in Irkutsk these days, the tourist season having long passed. Though," he said, as cannon fire boomed in the distance, sounding closer than before, "it appears the Bolsheviks are eager to try our local fare." He chuckled, though now the mirth was gone. "Yes, my friends, it is good that you arrived when you did."

"General Denikin told you why we came, then?" I asked. Rostov nodded, putting his arm around my shoulder and leading us off the platform.

"Indeed he did."

He directed us around the station and down a side street. I was glad for that, as the main avenue was packed with the dead and wounded. The chaos of war had swallowed that place whole.

"When I received the General's directive," continued Rostov, "I admit to being stunned that he would think anything more important than defending the city. I have never refused an order, but I certainly questioned this one. But now..." he said. "Well, it's only a matter of time now. I know little of your mission, but whatever help I can give you on your quest, I will provide it."

We came to a boarding house, and Rostov shepherded us inside. There was a tavern on the first floor, and after exchanging some words in Russian with the owner and giving him our bags, we joined Rostov at a table in the back.

"You'll stay here tonight, and then we will leave first thing in the morning. Ah yes," he said, as an attractive young woman delivered four mugs of beer and four shots of a clear liquid that could only be vodka. "To safe travels," he said, raising one of the small glasses. "Dlya pobedy nad nashimi vragami!"

The clear liquor burned more intensely than I expected. William and I couldn't help coughing, and only Carter seemed unfazed. Rostov smiled so broadly I thought his face might split apart. "The nectar of the gods, my friends. The water of life!"

"I think I prefer the beer," I muttered.

"Oh well, I suppose it is not for everyone," Rostov said. "But the Russian people are of a strong stock, or so they say. And it is only vodka that can match our character."

"So what do you anticipate for this trip?" Carter asked, taking a deep drink from his stein.

Rostov let loose a whistle, long and low. "Well," he said, "it will not be easy. Anything but, I fear. The place you seek is located in a wide valley, far to the north, along the banks of the Tunguska River. It is eight-hundred miles at least to Vanavara, and another forty beyond that to the site of the explosion. The train line to Vanavara hasn't been used for a couple years, so we need not worry about any delays. The road will be ours and ours alone. I intend to make good time. The longer we take, the more likely we will find Irkutsk in the hands of the enemy upon our return."

"And hopefully," Carter said, "the whole journey will be a waste of our time. If all we found was a barren crater, I would be overjoyed."

Rostov rubbed his expansive beard. "This is my home, you know? And I remember stories of the event, from the traders who went north. They say something fell from the heavens, that it came with thunder and fire. That the early morning sun was blotted out by a flash of light not of this world, and that the earth shook with a brutal power. It is an event of great infamy in the lands to the north. Finding our way should not be difficult, though who can say what we will discover at the conclusion of our journey."

"And I cannot tell you how much I appreciate your help."

Rostov waved him off. "It is my pleasure. General Denikin is an old friend. It is the least I can do for him."

"Do you know if the General still lives?"

Rostov nodded as the girl brought him another glass of vodka. "He is alive. I received word from him only yesterday. He and what is left of his men are retreating toward the Crimea. He ordered me to do the same, taking our forces beyond the Baikal. As I said, I've never refused an order. This will be my first. That is, if we ever return here." Rostov threw the fiery liquid back, slamming the glass onto the table. "But for now, my friends, we rest. Our journey begins on the morrow. It will be long and hard. I only hope that you find what you seek."

Rostov stood, nodding once to each of us, and then we were alone again. We sat there, finishing our beers, saying little. Whatever destiny awaited us, we were ready to face it. Or so we thought.

* * *

Tunguska Field Journal of Dr. Carter Weston
December 5, 1919

Rostov's men readied the train for the northern wilds as the bitter wind carried the sounds of artillery fire from somewhere beyond the borders of Irkutsk.

"It's an advanced position," Rostov said. "They are trying to frighten us, make us leave the city freely. We can hold them here for a month, maybe more. Do not worry. We have time."

He slapped me on the back, and I hoped he was right. Henry came to me last night and expressed his well-founded fear that time had already run out for our expedition. Part of me wonders if I should send him and William back to Vladivostok. I am convinced that we must go to Tunguska, that if there is even a chance that the Oculus is there, we must seek it. But can I risk Henry's life on that conviction? Can I risk that of William, my son-in-law? Still, I need them, and I choose to put my trust in Rostov. If we return to find this city in the hands of the Red Army, I suppose that we will deal with that development accordingly. Presumably, they will simply expel us from their territory. And while Rostov will insist on a fight to the death, there is no reason to think we have to join him in that endeavor. Yes, the risk is minimal, and the potential for a discovery of untold importance too great. We must proceed.

* * *

We'd been on the train for a few hours when William came to see me. Our train consists of only an engine, a coal-car, and a passenger car. Not only are we making good time, but the accommodations are far better than the train we took from Vladivostok. In fact, we are afforded a level of comfort and privacy that one could scarcely hope for. I was enjoying that precious seclusion when I was interrupted by William's knock—an interruption I would ordinarily welcome any time. But when Will entered, I could see that something troubled him, troubled him deeply. I closed my journal—this very one—and bade him sit down.

"You've looked better," I said, drawing an uneasy smile from the young man.

"I have news," he said. "Good news, really."

One would never have been able to tell.

"Well," I said, "I'm certainly glad it's not bad news. I can't imagine how you'd look if it were."

William leaned back and sighed. "Rachel's pregnant."

"Pregnant!" I exclaimed, loud enough that even Henry must have heard me. "Good news, that's fantastic news!" And yet the look on William's face didn't show it. "What's the matter? Is it something with Rachel? Is everything okay between you two?"

"Yes, yes," he said. "Absolutely. Things are fine. Things are wonderful. But this will bring a change, one I had hoped to avoid as long as possible."

"A change?"

"You know how much I admire you. What you and Henry do. And I know you were looking for someone to follow in your footsteps. And I know that you had hoped that person would be me." He looked up at me with a mixture of sadness and resignation. "I can't do that. I'm sorry Carter, but my future is in a classroom, not in the field."

"I take it you've discussed this with Rachel."

He nodded. "To tell you the truth, I wasn't going to go on this expedition, but she insisted. She knew that I wanted this last chance. And she knew that you needed me."

"I do need you, Will. I do need you. And to tell you the truth, I don't understand why you're doing this. You were made for the field. Not a classroom. Not some university, even if it is Miskatonic."

"Rachel grew up without a mother," he said. "I don't want my child to grow up without a father. I don't say that to hurt you, but you've been lucky. There's no other word to describe it. People don't see the things you've seen and live to tell about it. Eventually, it catches up with them."

"William, I understand your sentiments. But that is all they are. You've got to leave your emotions behind and use your reason. I love my daughter, and that's why I do this. Someone has to. Someone has to be willing to do what must be done, whatever the price. Nothing else matters. Not our lives, and to tell you the truth, not anyone else's."

I watched him as he heard my words, watched as the look on his face become what one can only describe as disgust. "You can't mean that, Carter."

"I do mean it. I mean it without equivocation. It's not a deal we made. It's the hand that was dealt us, and we have to play it. Billions of lives, now and yet to be born, depend on us and what we do. That's no exaggeration."

"And you'd sacrifice my life, your daughter's life, for them?"

His eyes were pleading, and I know that he wanted me to deny it. But I could meet him with nothing but the truth. "Yes," I said. "I would. And if you wouldn't, then maybe you aren't cut out for this after all."

The silence hung between us for an instant that stretched on into eternity. Finally, William stood. He reached for the door and turned back to me as he opened it. "I'll see this one through, Carter. But then I'm finished. I'll understand if this negatively affects your decision to support my application for a professorship."

I probably should have said something then, probably should have stopped him from going. But in the moment, I was angry. It was a selfish reaction. I had put so much into him, I had invested so much time grooming him to take the reins when I was no longer able. So I let him go. When the door closed behind him, I was alone. And I felt it.

Chapter 14

Diary of Rachel Jones
July 24, 1933

When I was fourteen years old, my father took me to Walden Pond. "A place of inspiration," he called it in one of his attempts to educate me in the higher and finer things of life. Encouraging my intellectual curiosity was always at the top of his parenting checklist. My father was decidedly antiquarian, but when it came to me, he expected that I would have every opportunity—and every responsibility—of the boys my age. Perhaps he had always wanted a son.

In any event, we went to Walden Pond that summer. Walden—almost on the doorstep of Boston—was about as deep into the wilderness as my father was willing to go, particularly with me in tow.

"The wilderness," he told me, "belongs to *them*."

And it was in that aspect that my childhood differed most dramatically from those of children around me. I was never permitted to forget those cosmic forces at work in the dark places of the earth. Dr. Carter Weston's daughter would go into the world with open eyes.

At times, my father's eccentric views had gotten me in trouble. While my friends were taking first communion or learning the more esoteric points of the Old Testament, my father was teaching me about the *Necronomicon* and the *Incendium Maleficarum*, the *Clavis Salomonis* and the *Liber de Diabole*. Not that my father wasn't devout in his Christian faith; few men who've stood in the presence of God could come to doubt Him. My father simply believed that there was more in Heaven and Earth than are dreamt of in our philosophies, and he believed that the Bible held truths unimagined by ordinary churchgoing folk.

There were, of course, many in his field of study that disagreed, men who held that the forces we faced were not only cosmic in their nature but unfathomable in scope and power. The gods, they said, cared nothing for us. It was not hatred that drove them or evil that they personified, but simple indifference. We were not insects to them; we were bacteria, and they had no more compunction in wiping us out than we would in curing a disease.

I always thought that both factions were right in their own way. Maybe those beings that sought our destruction were not malicious in some philosophically dualistic good vs. evil sense. But when the survival of the human race is at stake, it doesn't much matter what you label the enemy that seeks to destroy us. All I know is that they must be stopped, whatever the cost.

It was during that summer trip to Walden Pond that my father explained to me so much of his wisdom, accumulated over a lifetime of haunting the wilds and the shunned lands. He told me about the war raging all around me. And like every war, there were more or less two sides. The openers, waiting till the stars come round right again, till the time comes to break the seal between this world and the next, throwing wide the door for the Old Ones to return. On the other side, and far fewer in number—for the allure of the forbidden was strong for anyone who has read the ancient books—are the closers. They stand in the breach for all mankind, with innocent bystanders caught in the crossfire.

"The Old Ones," I remember my father saying, "are chaos personified, and they wish nothing more than to bring chaos to this world. They oppose order, and it is for that reason that the *Necronomicon* says of them, 'They walk unseen and foul in lonely places where the Words have been spoken and the Rites howled through their Seasons. The wind gibbers with Their voices, and the earth mutters with Their consciousness.' The man who would seek them," my father told me, "walks in the shadows of this world, lurks in the cold waste of empty steppes, and sails above ancient cities of lost antiquity, long since sunk below the waters. The wind carries him where human voices have long ceased, to storm-wreathed mountain tops and endless, silent deserts."

It's probably a miracle that I related to the man at all. And yet somehow, his words have stuck with me for all these years. My father had a way with language, and it was those pieces of advice that I thought of as we made our way through Berlin, blanketed in a thick darkness that gave us our only comfort. It was a shallow comfort indeed. For if the agents of the Old Ones could establish a beachhead in the heart of one of the world's great cities, then we were already running out of time.

It was late, exceedingly so. We'd waited till after two in the morning to leave Margot's garret, hoping that the night and the deserted city would provide the cover we needed. As we approached the gates of the University of Berlin, it seemed as though our plan might work.

"Stay here," Guillaume said as we huddled in the trees and bushes beyond the gate. "I'll scout ahead." Before any of us could object, he was gone, swallowed up in the night.

"Can we trust him?"

I turned to Henry. I had not considered the question. In fact, doubting Guillaume had never entered my mind.

"He's proven true so far. Besides, I don't know that we have much choice."

"Quite a coincidence, don't you think? Him showing up at the ball? Him having seen your father?"

I hesitated. It was true; quite a coincidence, indeed. "Well… Zann is his professor. It's no surprise that he was there."

"And where, then, do you think his loyalties lie?" My eyes were drawn downward, and I noticed that Henry was clutching his pistol.

"Oh now, wait a second, Henry. We've no reason not to trust him." Henry was not one to be paranoid, but the situation was obviously getting to him.

"I haven't known Guillaume for long," Margot said, finally reminding us of her presence. "Still, he has shown himself to be trustworthy. If he says he will help you, then he will. You can count on that."

There was a rustling in the bushes ahead of us. Henry drew his pistol and pointed it into the night. Guillaume stumbled towards us. The smile faded from his face when he saw the gun.

"Whoa, whoa!" he said, a little too loudly. "It's only me!"

For a moment, it looked like Henry wasn't going to put the pistol down. "Sorry," he said, finally lowering it. "I guess I'm a little on edge."

"We all are," I added. "But we have to be careful. The last thing we need is one of us shot." I stared at Henry until he nodded, and I hoped that whatever doubts he held were forgotten. "What did you find?"

"Nothing," Guillaume said. "Nothing at all. There's no one on the grounds. Not even a guard. We are clear."

"All right, what now?"

"We'll head through the gate and follow the wall along the perimeter. It would be faster to go across the main yard, but we'd be in the open for too long. We can't risk it."

"Agreed," Henry said.

"The place we seek is more or less directly across from here, in an unused part of campus that the students call the Roman Court. Many years ago, when this school served the House of Hohenzollern, the area was a barracks and training facility for the Imperial Dragoons. There's a castle-like structure at its center. Completely abandoned now. That's why your father's appearance stuck with me. I was only there because I like the peace and quiet, the isolation; it helps me think."

"But it wasn't isolated then."

"No, and that was strange. He didn't seem as though he was under any duress, but there were two men, flanking him on either side. I guess if he had made any effort to escape, they would have stopped him."

"Is there anything special about this building? Anything we should know."

Guillaume shrugged. "There were always rumors. People talked, as people are wont to do. Some said it was built on an ancient ruin, from Roman times. That's where it got its name. But others said it was even older, and that the runes that marked its foundations were in no language that anyone—even the professors at the University—recognized."

My eyes met Henry's, and I saw an old fire burning within them. "Sounds like just the place," he said, "for a Thule Society coven. We're close now, girl. Close indeed."

"Well, gentlemen," Margot said, "perhaps the time for talking has passed, no?"

"My thoughts exactly," I said. "Lead the way, Guillaume."

We crept around the perimeter of the university, following the curving outer wall as it swept around those hallowed halls of learning. What we sought was a classroom of sorts as well. One where young men were indoctrinated into a society that sought the destruction of all things mankind holds holy. The Thule are not unlike many of the cults—both ancient and of recent vintage—that worship the old gods. Their particular catechism holds that the German people were created by the Old Ones as a master race, one meant to rule all others. It is as baseless and insane as any of the perversities that their ilk peddle to the weak-minded and the desperate, the hungry for power and those who would rule over others. Whatever a victim's sickness, the Thule and societies like them offer the cure. And thus they all march on to their destruction—and ours as well.

It wasn't long before we had finished our circuit. We hadn't seen another soul, and now the gothic-style castle of the Roman Court loomed above us. It seemed just as Guillaume had described it—utterly abandoned. The front door was chained, and hanging from the chain was a heavy padlock. I could hear Henry sigh.

"Locked up tight," he said.

"They didn't take Dr. Weston through the front." Guillaume whispered. "Come on."

We followed him around the side of the massive structure. Sure enough, there was a side door hanging half open that made a mockery of the security at the front.

"Eureka."

Guillaume gently pushed the door, and I was surprised that it opened without a sound. A black maw loomed before us. We'd brought flashlights, but to that point, we hadn't dared to use them.

"What do you think?" I asked.

"I don't think there's any danger in it," Henry said. "Something tells me that if they've got Carter inside, he's not on the main floor, if you catch my meaning. Still, let's stay as inconspicuous as possible. One flashlight."

He stepped into the darkness. When he turned the flashlight on, it didn't so much obliterate the night as cut it in half. A heavy shroud still hung over everything that did not fall within the beam.

"Now what?" Guillaume asked.

"We look for something unusual, something out of place. It's the foundation of this building that's important. Remember that. That's where they'll be. We just have to find a way down there. Margot," Henry said, "you stay just outside the doorway and keep watch. If anyone else approaches, warn us and then hide. You probably shouldn't have come, and I don't want you getting into any more trouble."

I thought she might protest. Instead, she simply nodded and moved to her post. Good girl. The rest of us fanned out. We were in the main chamber, a common area of sorts, with a great fireplace at one end and bookshelves on every wall. Some of the shelves were barren, while others were filled to overflowing with texts of every sort. I walked along, examining them in the dim light.

Most were military texts, histories of war, strategy, tactics, an exegesis on epic blunders in battle. There was also general philosophy, some mathematics texts, a copy of Tocqueville's *Democracy in America*. But it was one book in particular that caught my eye. It was a massive volume, a complete history of Germany, from ancient times up until the unification wars of the late nineteenth century. And unlike every other book in the library, it was completely devoid of dust. I smiled triumphantly, grasped the book, and pulled. I fully expected a latch to click, a door to open, a wall to slide away. Something dramatic.

Instead, nothing.

The book came away so easily that I almost fell when it ended up in my hands. Defeated, I slid it back into its place.

"Look at this!" Guillaume whispered, a little too loud for comfort. Henry and I hurried over as he pointed at the floor. At first we saw nothing, but the dust in front of this particular wall was different from everywhere else. There were no footprints or any obvious evidence that anyone had passed through, but something had disturbed the dust ever so slightly, leaving an unmistakable swept pattern. It was a subtle clue, indeed, and I was impressed with Guillaume for noticing.

Henry ran his hand along the wall, feeling every crevice in the bricks. He stopped when his finger trailed over a small hole. He shined his flashlight at the spot, and then it was obvious.

This wasn't a wall; it was a door.

"That's a keyhole," I said.

"Yes," Henry muttered. "But where's the key?"

It took me only a moment. I spun on my heel, walking back to the shelf of books. I removed the history of Germany, and this time I opened it. Sure enough, in a depression cut into the pages within lay a small key.

"Fantastic!" Henry almost shouted. "Bring it here."

He took the key from me, sliding it into the hole in the wall. He didn't even have to turn it. There was a click, and the panel popped slightly away from the wall. I returned the key to the book and slid it back in place. Maybe we could get out without being noticed after all.

Beyond the door was a ruin. A pile of rubble formed a rudimentary staircase down, while the rough-hewn, solid-stone ceiling showed that this structure—whatever its purpose and original design—was carved from the living rock. Modernity clashed with the ancient, as wires were strung along the wall, electric lanterns that hung at regular intervals casting a pale light over the cave. Nor were the walls themselves bare. As we descended, they grew thick with runes from the time of Arminius and perhaps even further back into the mists of the past. It was little wonder the Thule held this place as holy.

We proceeded with caution now. Whatever we sought, it was close. The air was thicker, warmer. It stank of humanity. Then we turned a corner and saw it.

We were standing on the second level of a great stone circle, a temple of titanic slabs of granite. Stonehenge might be its nearest cousin, though this place was complete, without the decay that centuries of exposure to the elements can wreak on even the hardiest of rock. It was a splendid find and would have been more so were it not for the garish banners that hung from every corner, black flags bearing yet more bastardized runes of lost antiquity, painted in a brilliant red. And lucky were we that we emerged on the second level and not the first. Otherwise, we would most certainly have been seen.

For Erich Zann stood in the middle of that great circle. And before him, in a chair with his arms spread wide behind him and one leg crossed over a knee—the image of perfect repose—sat my father.

Chapter 15

Journal of Carter Weston
July 24, 1933

I write this from the Alsace, on the border between France and the Ruhr Valley. That I ever left accursed Germany is a miracle, one worked by the hands of my oldest friend, Henry Armitage, and my dearest daughter, though I wonder if now she regrets my liberation.

This extraordinary day began with a rude awakening. A soldier barged into my room well after the midnight hour. It was not the first such late-night disturbance during my captivity, and thus it surprised me little. But there was something in the soldier's demeanor, something in his eyes, that said this time was different. When I saw Zann waiting for me in the central chamber of the ancient, Theodic temple, I knew that bizarre happenings were afoot.

"Why Dr. Zann, to what do I owe this unexpected honor? I always took you for more of the early-to-bed type."

Zann smiled flatly, that same icy sneer he always seemed to bear.

"I'm considering moving you, professor, but before I do, I wanted to talk to you one more time, here, in this most sacred place."

He walked around the stone circle, trailing his hands along the columns and their deep-set runes, caressing them almost lovingly. In fact, it might have been the tenderest moment of Zann's life.

"Don't you hear them, professor? The ancients? Calling to you? Whispering their secrets? Asking you for your help?"

"I hear only you, Dr. Zann," I said. "Yours is pretty much the *only* voice I hear these days. And I tire of it."

The grin faded. "And so it shall continue, my friend, until you give me what I want."

"I've heard that threat before, too."

"And I made good on it, did I not? You are here, aren't you?"

"But not for long, it seems. Tell me, if you love this place so much, why would you leave it? Getting too hot for you in Berlin? Somebody find out something they shouldn't have? About your little group, maybe? The government onto your cult, perhaps? Illegal, is it not? Occult dabblings were all well and good when you were in the wilderness, but in power? Well, then they can be quite the embarrassment. Not good for the Reich at all."

I relished the discomfort evident in Zann, for it was unusual to see him not in control.

"The Reich," he said, "has its eyes on this world, which I suppose, is fitting. It prepares for a thousand years of dominance, and it is even ready for whatever comes after. Did you know that all the new buildings in Germany are now being designed to make striking and impressive ruins? So that the glory of Germany will live forever, at least in memory? Quaint, isn't it? But I have my eyes on a higher goal. An eternal one. One that never fades, never decays."

"Then maybe you have a new torture chamber prepared for me? Going to beat the truth out of me? I'd like to see you try."

Zann simply glared. I wondered, as I often did, if I had pushed him too far. It was true I wasn't bound and Zann, visibly at least, was unarmed. But with only a word he could have me killed, shot down then and there. That he hadn't done so already was a testament to how much he wanted the answers he believed I possessed. Still, unstable men can be unpredictable—and dangerous.

"Dr. Weston," Zann began, "it seems always that you are full of questions, but so rarely full of answers."

I laughed, and the sound of it seemed to pain him. "Must be the professor in me."

"And there is the contradiction, or so it seems to me." Zann pulled a chair from in front of one of the stone pillars and sat down. "One does not see the things you have seen, learn the things you have learned, without wanting to know more. Help me, and those truths will be ours."

"You have the book, Dr. Zann. You can read it as well as I. What do you need me for?"

"I can read it, yes. But the book has secrets that would take decades to unfold. Decades that you have had. The book has chosen me, Dr. Weston. It speaks to me now. And yet even when you knew that it was a crime against nature to keep it, when you knew that it was not yours to possess, you refused to deliver it to me. In the past, men who have refused to relinquish *Incendium Maleficarum* have met with, how shall we say, *unusual* ends. And yet you live. It must have allowed you this respite for a reason. You must have a purpose as yet unfulfilled. I believe I know what that purpose is. You are destined to help me. The unknown calls to you. I know that it does."

I just shook my head. "There's nothing 'unknown' in what you want to do, nor is there anything altogether unique about it. It's been tried before. Dozens, even hundreds of times. Throughout history. Stupid, foolish men such as yourself who seek to control things they do not understand."

Zann grimaced. "You misjudge me, doctor," he said, false hurt dripping from his voice. "I am neither stupid nor a fool. I seek only what all great men seek—a brighter, better day."

"Then perhaps you are simply insane."

Now Zann laughed, and, yes, there was a touch of madness in it.

"Tell me, professor, you are a Christian, are you not?"

"I am."

"Ah, and what does your faith seek? What is its purpose, its goal?"

"The salvation of mankind. Quite the opposite of yours."

"Ah, perhaps, perhaps." Zann leaned back in his chair and crossed his arms, the smirk still in place. "But I would argue your premise, professor. The salvation of mankind? No, the destruction of mankind. That is what your god offers. The salvation of a select few, yes. The ones that follow him. And when your Christ returns? What is it that he has promised?"

"'But the day of the Lord will come as a thief in the night,'" I quoted, "'in which the heavens shall pass away with a great noise, and the elements shall melt with fervent heat, the earth also and the works that are therein shall be burned up.' Yes, Dr. Zann, I know my scripture."

"Then you know that we are not different, you and I. Except I do not seek the destruction of the earth; I seek its fulfillment. I do not seek the promise of eternal life, but its reality. Here, at the side of this world's true masters, those who ruled in the long ago, and those who will rule again."

"And how many would you kill to make it so? How many have you killed already? So that you and a chosen few can have your salvation?"

"Dr. Weston," Zann said, his smile quivering at the edge of his mouth, "you and I both know that the world is made of means and ends, of those who rule and those who serve. Salvation, after all, is for the elect. For men such as you, and me. To resist is a useless gesture. They will return. You know it as well as I. The only question is whether we will share in the cup of their victory, or whether it will be our blood that fills it."

"I wonder what your father would say about that."

Zann laughed again, but this time, it was genuine. It was probably the first honest emotion I'd seen him express.

"My father? What would you know of him?"

"I've heard enough," I said. "Enough to know that he was a great man."

"A great man," Zann spat. "Yes, I suppose you would think that. Let me tell you something about my father. One of my more vivid memories of him…I must have been five years old, if that. He was sitting in an upstairs room of our house, staring out the window. Our home, it sat on the banks of the Rhine River. Beautiful country. And he was gazing over the waters. I didn't know what he was thinking. I was only a child, but even at that tender age I knew well not to disturb my father when he was working. So I stood on the threshold of the room, hidden behind the door. But I could see him. He had his Stradivarius in his arms. *Mein Gott*, that violin was worth a fortune. It was two hundred years old if it was a day. He had it there, one hand on its neck, the other on his bow. Of course I thought nothing of it at the time but looking back—if Runge had been there, what a painting he could have made. The genius at work. The artist, deep in thought. That's what my father was, you know? A musical force of nature. And there he was, ready to play. That's how I would like to remember him. Yet, I don't even have that, do I?"

"I don't see why not."

"No, you wouldn't, would you? Do you know *why* I remember that image of my father so well? Because he left, the next day. He took his violin—and nothing else—and just went. Abandoned us, my mother and me. It didn't take us long to burn through the savings we had, substantial though they were. My mother, foolishly, tried to keep the house. She just couldn't accept that he wasn't coming back. That what we had was all we would ever have. From the Rhine to the slums of Berlin. That was the path I took. And I swore then that I would know what happened to him. I swore that I would track him down. I'm not sure what would have happened if I had found him. I'm not sure what I would have done."

"But you didn't find him."

Zann smiled mirthlessly, and for a moment, I felt sorry for him.

"No, no, I never found him. Which is not to say that I didn't come as close as any man ever will. I tracked his every step. From the train station in Mainz, where he bought a ticket to Paris. And from there to the neighborhood of Rue d'Auseil—which, I tell you, is impossible to find even with a good guide and the best map of the city one can buy."

"I know," I said, astonished. "I have looked for it myself, but never successfully."

"Yes, well, perhaps destiny led me there. I even located the peaked garret that he lived in until his disappearance. I stood where he must have stood, and I stared out over the city of Paris from his window, over the high wall that marks the border of Rue d'Auseil, and I must have looked to anyone watching like my father did, all those years ago."

I saw it then, as Zann's eyes were locked on some memory in the long ago. I saw the pain he had suffered, and even then, in that underground dungeon, I wondered if I might be able to reach him yet.

"But, doctor," I said, "you must know what your father did? You must know what he accomplished?"

"Oh, I've heard the story. I found him, the French student, the one who published the tale of my father's last days."

"Then you know that he stood in the breech, that it was only his music that kept the Old Ones at bay?"

"I know that he played, and I know that he dueled with another, one who would have opened the gate with his song, one who would have restored the Old Ones to their glory. Yes, professor, I know that. And it was then, when I discovered the truth, that I vowed that I would undo what my father had done. That I would throw open the door. That I would be restored to my rightful place in this world. Not a servant. But the master."

"So you would sacrifice the innocent, millions of them, for power?"

Zann's demeanor changed; his smile grew wider, his eyes, more fierce. It was as if he had caught me in something, as if I had said something that was to my own detriment. I shuddered, wondering what I had given him.

"Yes, you know something of sacrifice, don't you, doctor? And you know something of the power that sacrifice brings. The power that *only* sacrifice can bring?"

"I don't know what you are talking about." I had meant to state it boldly, to defy him, and yet, somehow it came out only as a whisper.

"Oh, I think you do, Dr. Weston. I think you know precisely what I mean. Yes, doctor. The Old Ones have sought a return before. *He* has sought it, the messenger, the harbinger of the doom of all things. And he almost had it. But you stood in the way. As you always do, it seems. But how to defeat him without the Oculus? How to stand against the crawling chaos with nothing to arm yourself? It must have taken quite a sacrifice to have banished him, if only for a time. Quite a sacrifice indeed."

I stayed silent, refusing to give him the dignity of an answer. Or perhaps fearing to do so. Zann's grin grew so wide that it threatened to split his face in half.

"Tell me, professor, when you killed your son-in-law, when you murdered William Jones, how much power did you feel then?"

From somewhere behind and above echoed a shriek, a pitiful "No!" as filled with sorrow and despair as any I have ever heard. And my heart sank to the pit of my stomach, for I recognized that voice.

Chapter 16

Journal of Henry Armitage
July 24, 1933

I should have acted more quickly. I should have seen it coming. But even as Zann set the trap, and even as Carter walked headlong into it, I did not think. Not until I heard Rachel scream. Carter spun around, and in his face I saw that the joy he should have had in seeing us, his liberators, was instead bitter sorrow. And then there was Zann, his eyes aglow with feverish light, with madness and hatred mixed into one.

"Well, well, well," he said. "I see we have company."

A sickening thud echoed through the room. The fire in Zann's eyes went out, and he collapsed to the ground at Guillaume's feet. If only he had reached him a few moments earlier.

"Let's go!" Guillaume whispered, as loudly as he dared. But his caution was in vain. The sound of hurried footsteps was already close. The soldiers had heard Rachel's cry, and they were coming.

"Rachel," I said, but she did not hear me. She and her father were in their own world. She, staring into the pit where he stood. He, gazing up to her with a look that had transformed from shock to resignation, an acknowledgement of guilt. But this was not the time.

"Rachel! We have to go."

I grabbed her arm and jerked her forward, veritably dragging her down the rough stairs of the temple into the pit below.

"This way!" Guillaume gestured to the tunnel opposite the one through which we had passed earlier. "They are coming. We have to find another way out."

We ran, and I was glad that Carter and Rachel had seemed to snap out of their trance, at least temporarily. We dashed out of the temple just as the Germans entered it behind us. It would take only a moment for them to figure out what had happened, so that was the time we would have for our escape.

Guillaume led, and I hoped that whatever sense of direction he was using to guide us was true, though I feared that we were running blindly. Who could know how far these tunnels extended or to where they would eventually lead? I had read once of explorers in the catacombs of Paris losing their way, desperately trying to conserve light as they wandered through endless chambers of ivory white bones. Some of them never emerged. Would that be our fate as well?

We'd been running for only a couple of minutes when we were undone. A soldier stepped from behind a wall and pointed his rifle at us. "*Stoppen! Hände hoch!*" he shouted, gesturing at us with the barrel of his gun. We threw up our hands, and I saw in my mind's eye an execution, bullets to the back of the head, all of us dead in a dark and desolate cavern.

Then something inexplicable happened. It seems that sometimes, Heaven shines on those that would do its bidding; and this time a small miracle was worked in our favor. The rocks above the soldier must have been loose, for his shouts seemed to shake them onto his head. He collapsed beneath their weight. It was a lucky break indeed.

Still, we could hear pursuit behind us, and I thought that perhaps our luck truly was about to run out. Fortunately, the tunnel ran out first. In the darkness and in our haste, we did not even notice when it ended in a short—but sharp—drop into the River Spree.

Down we plunged into its icy depths. Were it not for the adrenaline that burned through our veins, I have no doubt that we would have frozen to death that night. We made our way to the shore with no small amount of difficulty, fortunate to discover that we were not far from Margot's apartment. We found her waiting there, worried to distraction, having been forced to flee from her position outside the building when a garrison of soldiers arrived. She threw her arms around Guillaume and kissed him with a passion I have rarely seen. From his reaction, he had rarely seen it either. But yet again, there was little time for such revelry.

"I can't be sure that I wasn't seen," Margot said as we warmed ourselves in front of her hearth. "And while I doubt anyone would have recognized me—why would they, after all?—I would put nothing beyond the power of the SA."

"No," Carter said, "and in the end it doesn't matter. We have to go. We can't stay here."

"I'm coming with you," Guillaume said.

"So am I," Margot added. Guillaume started to protest, but Margot shot him a look that silenced him before he had said even a word.

Carter shook his head. "We've put you in too much danger already. I owe you my life. All of you." Carter's eyes met Rachel's, but she quickly looked away. A moment of truth would come. I hoped that she kept her head about her long enough for us to get out of Berlin.

"This is bigger than you," said Margot. "Bigger than all of us. Whatever this Dr. Zann is planning, it must be stopped. And with the resources he has, you need all the help you can get."

Carter sighed. "I'm afraid you don't know the half of it. Zann's only a small part of whatever is going on. I don't think Zann ever thought I would leave Berlin, at least not alive. He told me things during the interrogation. Or more often he just let them slip. Zann was looking for something. Two things actually. The Staff of Dzyan, and the Oculus."

Margot's eyes clouded with understandable confusion, but I knew all too well what this meant.

"Dzyan," I muttered.

Carter nodded. "It takes more than the Oculus to stop Nyarlathotep. The staff and the stone are one. Together, they can send him back to the void. That's why Zann wants them."

"Nyarlathotep?" Margot muttered, stumbling over the strange word. Carter waved it off.

"It's complicated," he said. "Just trust me when I say that he is bad news."

Margot shook her head. "But you said there was more to it than Zann?"

"It seemed that time was of the essence to him. Apparently, the devotees of Nyarlathotep are hard at work in Paris, trying to find the staff in the last place it was rumored to be."

"The catacombs…"

Carter looked at me and nodded. "Exactly."

Now Guillaume interrupted. "So you don't know where the staff is?"

Carter shook his head. "Unfortunately, I don't. But I know where we have to look."

"Paris."

"Exactly."

"And if someone else finds it first?"

Carter didn't answer. There was no point. I'm not even sure why I asked the question.

"Then we should rest," Margot said. "There's a train to Paris that leaves at 6 a.m. That's less than an hour."

"And I wish we could be on that train," I said, "but I think we should only move at night—as long as we are in Germany, at least. We'll lay low here until the sun sets."

And with that, we gathered our things and prepared for yet another journey.

Chapter 17

Portram Campbell Tobin, *A Guide to Spirits and Otherwordly Beings*, 2nd Edition (1907), Chapter 33

While the demon Pazuzu has received much scholarly attention in demonology for its tendency to possess virginal girls at the cusp of womanhood, there is another malevolent entity of far more dangerous potential, one whose name is obscure to all but the most learned in the hoary tomes of antiquity. I refer, of course, to the being known as Nyarlathotep.

Long shrouded in mystery, the name *Nyarlathotep* appears rarely in the ancient texts, absent altogether from the canonical books of the Holy Bible, Torah, and Koran. This absence is of particular note since the first recorded instance of the invocation of the spirit appears in the infamous scroll of Imhotep, discovered among the items in the eponymous sorcerer's tomb beneath the sands of the great Memphis burial grounds. As such, it would seem that reverence for, and indeed the fear of, Nyarlathotep would have been widespread amongst the denizens of ancient Egypt, and thus his name should have been well-known amongst all the peoples of the Mesopotamian region.

A possible explanation of this absence lies in the peculiar nature of the god often referred to as "the crawling chaos." It seems that the name of Nyarlathotep was considered a powerful curse, the mere utterance of which could lead to dire consequences both for the object of the curse as well as him who would cast it. Thus, Nyarlathotep came to be known by any number of epithets—the whisperer in the darkness, the black man (often evoked by European witch-cults), the haunter of the dark, the harbinger, the great messenger, he who strides in shadow, and the stranger, to name but a few. In fact, it seems that Nyarlathotep was but one of the proper names by which the god was summoned. References—in the Bible and elsewhere—to Moloch, Kesan, Zanoni, and Azazel have been interpreted as possible invocations of *Nyarlathotep*.[451]

Many scholars have noted the apparent dualistic relationship between the god Nyarlathotep and the Biblical Christ. Nyarlathotep is said to be the son of Azathoth—known simply as Chaos in the Greco-Roman pantheon—the slumbering god who sleeps at the center of all things. It is this Azathoth—chief among the Old Gods, the being whom even Cthulhu is said to fear—who gave birth to the swirling darkness, to the formless void of which the universe consisted before the present age. According to the lore of the ancient Ashmodai, when Azathoth awakens, the world will end, and the void will hold sway once more. And it is Nyarlathotep who will, one day, awaken his father, ushering in a second darkness of unending night. That he will do so eventually is seen as the inevitable end of all things, with echoes of Ragnarök in the Norse tradition.

It is perhaps not surprising, then, that early Christians viewed Nyarlathotep as the ultimate antichrist. This belief, once widespread, was considered a heresy of the first order by the clerics of the ascendant Roman Catholic Church. The first council of Nicaea decreed that the term *antichrist* referred to a minion of Satan—a fallen angel, and most certainly not a god of equal stature with Yahweh—and decreed it anathema to teach of the existence of Nyarlathotep or to promulgate any theories about his relation to Christianity or the Hebrew God. It is thus unsurprising that the name of Nyarlathotep is missing from the scriptures we possess today, even if it would have featured prominently in original sources now lost and presumably destroyed.

But some early-Christian references to Nyarlathotep do survive. The heretical sect known as the *fraternitatis oculus*—the Brotherhood of the Eye—were meticulous in documenting and protecting the

---

[451] Though some contend that some or all of these references refer to Azathoth himself.

early stories of Christ. Of particular interest to our study is an account of Christ's temptation in the desert, one altogether different from the tale that comes to us in three of the four gospels. According to their traditions, it was not Satan that appeared to Jesus as he fasted in the wastes of ancient Israel, but Nyarlathotep himself.

I quote from a translation of a fragmentary text recovered in a cave just outside of ancient Ephesus:

And in those days Jesus went unto Sinai, in Egypt, to the great desert through which he had passed as a child. There, for forty days and forty nights, he waited. The sun had not yet climbed high on the fortieth day when the stranger appeared to him, as Christ knew he must.

"Son of light," said the lord of shadow, "why do you come to this desert to perish? For you have debased yourself, clothed in the filth of this world. It need not be so. Forsake the light, for every day will surely end in darkness."

But Jesus answered and said, "It is written, 'The sun also riseth, and the sun goeth down, and hasteth to his place where he arose. For no darkness will last forever.'"

Then the harbinger lifted his hand to the heavens, and the day did turn to night. The constellations wheeled above, and the harbinger spoke, "Look to the abyss above, son of light. The stars are like dust, pinpricks on a funeral shroud, swallowed by the night that surrounds them. For it is the shadow that covers all."

But Jesus answered and said, "It is written, 'The light shines in the darkness, and the darkness can never extinguish it. For without light, there can be no shadow.'"

Nyarlathotep was enraged, and he took up a sword, saying, "Son of light, it is written, 'He was oppressed, and he was afflicted, yet he opened not his mouth: he is brought as a lamb to the slaughter.'"

But Jesus answered him and said, "It is written, 'He is despised and rejected of men, and of men will he die. For it is not your place to take me, and is not my time to go.'"

Then Jesus reached forth his hand and took up wood from a cedar and a pine and a cypress, weaving them into a staff. His other hand he swept across the dirt, and from the earth he formed a shining pyramid of stone which he pressed into the head of this staff. A flash erupted from it, and before the brilliance of the staff and stone Nyarlathotep fled, as all darkness must flee the light.

This story is remarkable not only for its failure to adhere to the traditional temptation motif, but also because of its inclusion of the Staff of Dzyan and the Eye of God—the combination of which is the only known weapon, according to legend at least, that can defeat Nyarlathotep. It is hotly debated among scholars whether this is the first depiction of the Oculus myth, or whether it predates Christianity altogether. In any event, the staff and Oculus, if they ever existed, have long since been lost to antiquity.

* * *

Carter Weston, *The Gods of Ancient Days*, (1920),
Chapter 6, Pages 85–86

While the mode and method of worship vary wildly across cultures and religions, there is one element that seems to be universal—sacrifice. It is sacrifice by which the adherents of the faith prove their devotion, and it is through sacrifice that the priest and the penitent harness the power of the gods.

Sacrifice can come in many forms and under many names. In the Buddhist tradition, personal sacrifice is necessary to achieve enlightenment, particularly through the shedding of *taṇhā*, or cravings. Similar acts of self-control are required in the three great religions to emerge from Mesopotamia—Judaism, Christianity, and Islam. Each of these faiths calls upon the believer to give up the carnality of the material world for spiritual enlightenment, to reject "sin," ordinarily encompassing hedonistic, sybaritic pleasures.

But while we have come to associate sacrifice in the modern day with personal strength and self-betterment, true sacrifice, as envisioned by the ancients, was often bathed in blood. The core tenets of these faiths was that the life-force was just that—a natural force as strong as gravity or magnetism, and one just as subject to exploitation. And through sacrifice, such energy could be released and harnessed.

Animal sacrifice was most common, though human sacrifice was also prevalent. Whether we look to the Aztecs and Incas of the Americas, the tribes of sub-Saharan Africa, the ancient Chinese and Greeks, the druidic faiths, or the ancient religions of the Fertile Crescent, the tendency to turn to human sacrifice in times of crisis was nearly universal. Even the Romans—who generally eschewed human sacrifice—embraced the practice when the armies of Hannibal threatened to destroy their ancient capital.

In some of these societies, human sacrifice was more thoroughgoing. The Aztecs were known to cut the hearts from thousands upon the festival of Acolnahuacatl, a god who was said to drink the blood of humanity. And his thirst was nigh unquenchable.

It is in Moloch, however, that we see the most dramatic example of sacrifice as a means to achieve power, and the cost that such power often entails. For not just any offering would please the dark god of ancient Canaan. He required the most precious gift of all—the life of the firstborn sons and daughters of his followers. In return for this devotion, Moloch was said to grant his adherents power and wealth beyond imagining. It is not surprising that many of the greatest nations among the ancient Fertile Crescent were known to worship him.

Biblical sources indicate that burning alive was the preferred method of conferring the offering to the god. There is, however, an interesting anecdote within the infamous *Necronomicon* that posits another theory of Moloch altogether. According to the mad Arab Alhazred, some followers of Moloch were known to practice a form of crucifixion. The *Necronomicon* speaks of fields of wooden *crux decussata*, the saltire of the St. Andrew's Cross, with children, from newborn babes to teenagers, nailed nude and spread-eagled, their screams and cries echoing across the plain. Only when their pain was so great that they began to lose consciousness was the final blow struck: the offering was slit from gullet to groin. Often, the internal organs were allowed to spill upon the ground. For special offerings, they were removed and ritually placed in esoterically significant locations.

This alternative manner of sacrifice described in the *Necronomicon* is remarkable as it mirrors precisely the method of worship employed by the followers of "he who walks in shadow," Nyarlathotep. Can there be any doubt that *Moloch* is simply yet another denotation of the Great Old One?

Chapter 18

Journal of Carter Weston
July 24, 1933

Rachel found me, as I knew she would. I was waiting for her in my cabin in the train, having sent Henry away when he came to check on me. Yes, I was tired, but I could not sleep on this. I could not let another night pass until my daughter, my only child, knew the truth. For better or for worse. So I was eager for her coming, even as I dreaded it.

I didn't say anything as she entered, and she didn't look at me as she closed the door behind her and sat down. A minute passed. Two. Still, I said not a word. It was not my place to speak. At least, not first.

"I never questioned you," she said finally. "I never asked why. Not when you were gone for weeks and months on end. I never had a mother and, bless Aunt Gertrude's soul, you were my world. My whole world. Until I met William." She looked at me, and in her sad eyes there was a wistfulness, the reflection of a soul that longed for days gone by, of a pain so deep that I could barely stand it.

"Damn it all, if you two weren't just alike." She laughed mournfully and shook her head. "Too alike." She looked down at her hands, rubbing the deep lines in her palms, and somehow my little girl had never seemed so old.

"And when he died," she said, and her voice cracked. The tears came then, the sobbing whimper of a cry. I reached to put my hand on her shoulder, but she brushed it away. When she looked up at me, anger had replaced the sadness.

"Still," she said, "I never questioned you. I never asked what happened. I never wanted to know. But never," and now her voice grew as sharp as the edge of a knife, "*never* did I imagine that you had something to do with it. That you might be *responsible* for it. You have to tell me, Papa. You have to tell me right now. What happened to William?"

I opened my mouth to answer, but she held up a hand.

"And if you love me, if you care for me at all, you won't spare a detail. You won't try to save my feelings. I just want the truth, every last bit of it."

I nodded, and in an instant, I was transported back a decade or more, to that day in the barren wastes of Siberia, when our world was saved and hers was shattered.

* * *

Tunguska Field Journal of Dr. Carter Weston, December 7, 1919

It took only two days for our train from Irkutsk, traveling at its maximum speed and making no stops, to reach the end of its line—the Siberian village of Vanavara. And a village it was. As we alighted, it struck me as something of a miracle that anyone lived here at all. Rostov answered my unasked question.

"When the railroad was built, it was the government's intention to colonize this place. What the area lacks in charm, it compensates for in natural wealth. Coal, silver, even gold. This line was finished not a month before the war. And now," he said, gesturing to the deserted area around us, "well, development will have to wait."

We followed Rostov to a town square where a handful of men were gathered around a roaring fire, smoking long wooden pipes and drinking from a single jar that was passed around the assembly. Rostov boomed a greeting in Russian, and the men answered back. I gestured to William.

"What is he saying?"

William shook his head. "It's impossible to say. It's Russian, I suppose, but some dialect with which I am not familiar. In a place like this, they might as well be speaking another language altogether."

For a while the conversation seemed wholly a mystery to us, but when Rostov started gesturing with his hands, I knew they were talking money. Then the old man who was apparently the leader of this group began to shake his head. Rostov raised his voice, but the old man remained firm. I didn't need a mastery of Russian to know that he had just given Rostov an offer he could either take or leave. Rostov sighed and nodded. The two men shook hands, and the Russian bear lumbered back to where we stood.

"Well," he said, "the old man serves his village as elder for a reason. He drives a hard bargain."

"But he'll take us to the site?" I asked.

Rostov shook his head. "Not exactly. He is the leader of the Evenki tribe, the people who call this place home. He remembers well that day, the day he says that 'Hell fell to earth.' An incredible story. He says that a column of fire descended from the heavens, that it devoured the forests on the banks of the Tunguska River. He says that in the weeks following the event, the sky glowed a yellow so bright that the night appeared like day. It left quite the impression."

"So will his men take us or not?" I asked again, growing impatient. Rostov frowned.

"He says that the guides will take us to the edge of the valley. But we must go the final few miles alone. I argued with him the best that I could, but on this matter he was definite. Apparently, at some point after the event, curiosity got the best of some of the braver or bolder or stupider men from the village. They went to investigate. Some stopped at the forest-fall, where the trees had been flattened. They came back. The ones who went into the fires and the smoke never returned. The old man," Rostov said, turning and gesturing to the gentleman who watched us from beneath a snow-covered, pine-bough roof, "he says that what he calls the 'Valleymen' patrol the region. Whoever they are, he is very much afraid of them. He told me that he will take our gold, but that he can promise we will not return. He was very clear. 'If you go there,' he said, 'you will die.' He says they call it, 'The Valley of Death.'"

At that Rostov roared out a thunderous laugh. He slapped William on the back and said, "Charming, eh? I love these people. So simple. So superstitious. We leave tomorrow at dawn."

Rostov left us to talk to the Evenki guides about horses. Once he was out of earshot, William turned to Henry and me. His smile, normally easy, was forced. "Well, that's quite the story, isn't it? Not exactly what one wants to hear on the eve of an expedition." He laughed, but it was no more honest than his smile.

"Yes," Henry said, and from his furrowed brow and the drop in his voice I knew he was pondering something, something he didn't like much at all. "You know this doesn't make sense," he said, turning to me.

He was right; it didn't.

"This should be a simple recovery mission. We go to the site, we find the Oculus. The hardest part should be digging it up. The most dangerous part, the damnable Red Army. But you take what the village elder has to say, and that's something altogether different. What do you make of these 'valleymen'?"

"Could be superstition. Probably is, in fact."

"No," Henry said. He shook his head against the idea. "You and I both know that superstition is all too often grounded in cold, hard truth. There's something to this."

I suppose I should have listened. I suppose I should have heeded Henry's warning. But we were so close. We were there, on the cusp of something great, on the verge of having the Oculus, one of the greatest artifacts man has ever known and a tool that we could use against whatever evils we might face in the future.

"Something to it, of course. But you must remember, Henry. Remember what these people saw. Fire falling from the heavens? An explosion, greater than anything they had ever seen? Is it any wonder that myth and legends have grown up around the event? The men from the village, the ones who never returned, they probably did die there. But not from any 'valleymen.' And we will be careful, as we always are. But this is something we cannot turn back on. We've come too far."

Henry hesitated, but he never could stand up to me. Finally, he nodded.

"I don't know, Carter," William said.

"If you wish to stay behind," I spat, still angry from William's betrayal of the night before, "then you certainly may. Some of Rostov's men will wait with the train. Feel free to join them."

William glared at me. "You know, a man once told me to use my rationality, to leave my emotions behind. That logic and reason were the only defenses we had against the madness of this world. Why don't you use that reason now?"

"No," I said, struggling to keep my composure. "The only person being unreasonable is you. We know why we are here. We know what we must do. I am willing to take the risk."

"You know that we are with you," Henry said. I grasped his arm in thanks, and then I looked at William.

"Yes," he said, "but we would do well to take every precaution."

"Of course. We always do," I said, looking William in the eye. He held my gaze a moment longer than I would have liked. In the end, it was Rostov that ended the tension.

"We have the horses," he announced. "It was extra, as I have come to expect. I suppose they thought that we would walk. The people here are adept at separating a man from his gold."

"We will reimburse you, of course," Henry said. But Rostov only shook his head.

"There is no need my friend. Money holds little value to me these days. After all, once the Bolsheviks take power, what will we need gold for anyway?" The same thunderous laugh followed. Whatever fate awaited Rostov, it was clear that he had embraced it in full.

"We leave tomorrow at dawn."

* * *

The sun had not yet broken above the horizon when we set out. A cold day, with mountains of ice and snow before us. I was glad for the horses.

It was the three of us, Rostov and one of his men, and two of the Evenki who would take us as far as the crest of the valley. There, in the deep cut in the earth made by the Tunguska River, we would find our quarry.

And yet, with every step, the tension seemed to grow. Our Evenki guides became more restless, more prone to panic, their hands shaking as they gripped the reins of their horses, their wild eyes scanning the forest, their voices gibbering endlessly about Chort and Baba Yaga. They weren't the worst. William's attitude had darkened with every step our horses took, the rift between us growing wider the closer we came to the valley's edge.

The sun was still low in the east when we arrived at the rim of that accursed valley. And what a sight it was. It seemed that we had been traveling through thick, frozen forests for eternity. That made the shock of what we saw all the more palpable.

The end of the trees was as abrupt as previously it had been unimaginable. But our eyes did not deceive us. The forest continued until it simply did not, and at that point a vast field of felled timber met our eyes—trees bent and broken, flattened and burned. Where there had been snow before, thick and unyielding, here there was none, as if the ground itself emitted some ungodly warmth. William murmured beside me, quoting from a foul text that I knew all too well.

"'They bend the forest and crush the city, yet may not forest or city behold the hand that smites.'"

I glanced at Henry, and he at me, but neither of us spoke. Speaking was left to our guides, who were not so silent. Low moans rose from the pits of their stomachs and turned to wails. Rostov shouted at them in Russian, and in his voice I could hear a pleading, a begging for them to stay. It was no use. They turned their horses from the face of this impossibility, this absurdity. Spurring them to action before Rostov could say another word, they were gone. Disappearing into the still-standing forest behind.

"And with that," Rostov said, turning back to the destruction ahead, "we are on our own. Though I must wonder if you still wish to continue."

"We press on," I said. I could feel William glare at me, and even in Henry's eyes I could see doubt, but now was no time to give in to superstition and fear. "I believe what we seek is there."

I gestured to a copse of still-standing trees some miles away, if trees they were. For while the forest around them had been pressed to the ground, they remained upright. But something was terribly wrong. It seemed as though they had been stripped of their limbs by some ungodly force, the trunks like sharpened pikes that waited, gleaming pale white in the morning sun. They stood as sigils to what had befallen this place, jammed into the earth like the bones of some long-dead giant, portents of an as-yet-undiscovered evil.

I can't say what drove me in those moments. I can't say what made me forget years of training and experience, to scoff at the superstitions and sixth sense in which I had always found truth. Perhaps the Oculus had become an obsession. Perhaps I wanted to grasp it so badly that I was blind to the signs, blind to the dangers, blind to the warnings. Or maybe it was something else, something foreign and alien that had captured my mind. Perhaps I was led by forces I could barely imagine, forces that wanted me to come to them.

In the end it mattered not. I could not be dissuaded, and William and Henry, no matter what their misgivings, would follow me into Hell. So we left our horses, tied to the trees that still stood, with Rostov's adjunct to keep them safe, and into Hell we descended.

* * *

Our path was not easy. Into the valley we went, but felled trees blocked us at every turn. The ground itself was loathsome—a cold, frigid bog that soaked our shoes and sapped our strength. If I have ever before been so miserable, I do not recall it. The very air was foul, and a thick, pallid, yellow fog covered the earth, making every step a dangerous adventure. An eerie darkness crept over us, although the sun had not yet reached noonday. We had entered a place where even the light dared not go.

Despite the horrid conditions, my scientific curiosity remained strong. When Henry knelt beside one particularly large tree, running his hands along its trunk, I felt that youthful rush of excitement that always comes with discovery.

"Look at its size," Henry murmured. "It must have been ancient. It would have taken an enormous force to knock it down."

"Not to mention all the rest of them."

Henry gestured to the underside of the tree. "See the burn marks? They're only on one side. An enormous explosion, somewhere over there," he said, pointing to the copse of naked trees. "It's almost unimaginable."

"It fits all the prophecies," I said. "The Oculus has returned." And yet, while I was certain, I saw doubt in Henry's eyes. For several moments he sat there, staring into the distance at those still-standing trees.

"Does it?" Henry said finally. "Does it match what we've been told to expect?"

"Fire and flame, Henry. That's what the book says. The Oculus will return in fire and flame."

He shook his head. "This is more than that, Carter. This is destruction. Look around. It's not just the trees. Nothing lives here. Nothing moves. There are no animals, no plants. It's death, Carter. Death. Is that what you expected? Is that what you associate with the Eye of God?"

I sighed, long and deep. I couldn't understand their doubt. Not William's, and certainly not Henry's. I felt a pressure building inside, welling up and threatening to fracture my very mind. "I don't pretend to understand how all this works. But if you have a different explanation for what happened here, I'd love to hear it."

A look of terror flashed across Henry's face. "Not an explanation," he said. "Just a fear of what might be out there."

I didn't bother to answer him. I turned and joined Rostov and William, who were standing at some distance, waiting on us with not a negligible amount of impatience. Henry knelt there for another moment, staring at what his mind either couldn't comprehend or didn't want to. William stepped behind Rostov as I approached. An involuntary shudder ran down my spine. I loved William, but now I loathed him, too. His rejection still stung.

"You know," he said after we had walked for five minutes in silence, "this place, it reminds me of a story I once heard, back in my first year at Miskatonic. In that folk-tale class that old Freeborn taught."

I grinned despite myself. Freeborn was a dear friend, and a professor of the highest order.

"It was a story from the South, from before the war. Nobody really remembered where it took place. Tennessee, Georgia. Alabama, maybe. It was about this old farmer, whose name was also lost. About the only thing anyone seems to recall is the name of his neighbor and rival, a planter called Wingate. Anyway, the farmer was poor. He owned enough land to get by, but not so much that he'd ever be considered wealthy, either in land or in possessions. Wingate held vast wealth, and his mammoth plantation dominated the countryside for miles. But Wingate wasn't satisfied. He wanted more.

"So he came to the old man and offered to buy his land. The man refused to sell. So Wingate offered him a higher price. Still, the man said no. He doubled the offer, and the old man told him that the land had been in his family since they'd come to America from the old country. That it had gone to his father from his father's father, and he would pass it to his son when he died. No price would buy it.

"Wingate, predictably, was infuriated by such a position, one almost as irrational as his own. He decided to kill the man and buy the property from his creditors before the son could take title. But he couldn't just shoot him, of course. No man, no matter how rich, can get away with murder. So he went into the swamps, to see an old woman who local legend held was a witch. He told her his problem. She said that for a price, she could make the old man disappear. Wingate agreed and asked her how much. She named a sum in gold, a tiny amount really, for such a deed. Wingate was ecstatic, so much so that he completely missed the old woman's warning. 'All power has a cost,' she said, 'a cost that cannot be paid in gold. But paid it must be.' Wingate handed over the money and returned to his house to wait.

"The next day, the old farmer went into his field. His wife, on the porch, watching him as he walked away. He turned to her, and waved. It was a ritual they had repeated every morning for all their lives. Waving to each other before the workday began. But then, in an instant as singular as a flash of lightning, the old man was gone. One moment he was in his field. The next, nothing. Now, that's the story the wife told, though she was so distraught with the horror of the thing that they could barely get a coherent sentence out of her. But the evidence was clear she believed it. Her hands were covered in dirt, her fingernails broken. When they went down to the field, they knew why. There was a hole where the man had been standing, a hole dug by the old woman's hands as she tried to save him, tried to figure out where he'd gone. She didn't find him, and neither did anyone else, despite the biggest search the county had ever seen.

"Wingate got the property, bought it from under the family before they knew what had happened. He built new barns for the extra harvest he expected from the newly acquired land. But then something strange happened. From the spot where the old man had disappeared, contagion started to spread. It was unlike any disease the local farmers had seen. It poisoned the ground, and nothing would grow. Not a blade of grass, not a weed, and certainly not cotton. It wasn't long before the old man's field was barren. But it didn't stop there. It spread to Wingate's property as well. The harvest came to the county, but none came to Wingate. With the added debt from the new barns on top of his other expenses, Wingate was a ruined man. He hung himself from the central beam of one of those barns. And the price for the old man's death was finally paid.

"Wingate's body wasn't even in the ground before life returned to the soil. His eldest son, a wealthy man in his own right, mortgaged all he had to keep the family's property. But he didn't keep that field. He returned it to the old man's family, free of charge."

When William finished his story, he swept his hand across those barren lands. "That's what I think of when I see something like this. Evil has touched this place. An evil as powerful as anything even you have ever seen. That's the only explanation for what has happened here."

"Perhaps," was all I said.

It was a good story, but not one I cared to hear. I had hardened my heart.

In the end, whether he was right or wrong, we didn't stop. Instead, we continued, crossing the seemingly endless plain of fallen trees, until finally we came beneath the eerie canopy of the dead copse.

It was then that I heard the voice.

I probably wouldn't have noticed it if I had been anywhere else, not at first. But in that silence, in that place devoid of life and sound, even the murmur of it was like thunder, even its whisper like a crashing wave. And that's how it started, as a murmur. But no voice of this earth ever made a sound like that. It was neither male nor female, neither babe nor crone. Or perhaps it was all of them, at the same time, the sound of all mankind speaking as one.

At first I could make out only one word—my own name.

"Carter."

I stopped dead, spinning in place, searching for the source of that voice. Henry and William looked at each other, concerned by my sudden, unusual behavior.

"Carter?" Henry said. I jerked around to face him, and I could see the madness in my eyes reflected in his.

"Did you hear that?"

"Hear what?" William said.

I told myself that the dead lands and the stress of the last few days were affecting me. "Nothing," I said. "Just the wind." But it's never just the wind, is it?

We continued, and as we advanced, I noticed that an unease had fallen upon my companions. Henry and William became apprehensive. They were glancing about, searching for something or someone.

"Carter Weston," the voice whispered again. I steeled myself, determined that no matter what happened, I would not add to the confusion enveloping my friends. "Long have I watched you. Long have I awaited your coming."

The trees surrounded us, and I began to wonder if whatever was speaking to me waited inside their shadow, even as I knew that the voice was within my mind.

"Now you are here, but what you seek is not. And still you will continue, for you have never turned from your appointed path. Never doubted the righteousness of your own purpose. Always assured that you know truth, and that in that truth you would find glory."

We continued forward, as if we were all pulled by an invisible force, pushed by unseen hands, as if we had no choice. The pale, limbless trees rose above us, covering us in their thin shadows, adding to a preternatural darkness far greater than any we had known before.

"What price would you pay, Carter Weston? What would you sacrifice to accomplish your ends? What would you give up? And what would you take? Soon, you shall know, for there is no turning back."

I stopped again, and so drawn in by that voice was I that I didn't notice that the others had stopped, too. But they weren't looking at me this time. They no longer thought that I had lost my good sense. No, they heard it. The voice spoke to them. And while I knew that the words told to me were for my ears alone, whatever power was acting upon us allowed me to hear their messages as well.

"Henry Ar...mi...tage..." it whispered. "You who had such promise. You who had such dreams. Do you remember? The heady youth in his first days at Miskatonic? When all seemed possible? Do you remember? All the things you would become? All the things you would accomplish? Before you met *him*. Before Carter Weston came to dominate you in a way you could not escape.

"And now you follow him, his loyal lap dog. Always second. Always the inferior. Henry Armitage, the librarian. Henry Armitage, the assistant of Carter Weston. That is your fate, the fate you chose. It need not be so. You can free yourself from him. You can still be the great Henry Armitage, but only if you act now. Only if you remove from yourself the burden of Carter Weston, once and for all."

I watched as the voice spoke to Henry, as my old friend's eyes went wide, his mouth quivered. He shook his head slowly, voicing an almost silent, "no."

And yet, there was truth there, no? How selfish had I been? So tied up in my "destiny." In my "fate." In my life's mission. Convinced that I alone was chosen. Henry had followed me, until the end. At that moment, I wondered if the end had come. The voice, though, was not finished.

"Viktor Rostov, son of Rus, he with the heart of a patriot. You stand at the grave of your mother. Soon, she shall be dead, and you with her. It cannot be stopped now. You know this. No power on this earth can save her. What would you give to turn back the enemy? Who would you kill to rescue your country?

"Win my favor, and I will turn the tide in this war. Do my bidding, and I will give unto you dominion over all the lands from the Sea of Okhotsk to the river Vistula. The price? Nothing so high my friend. Only one life. The life of Carter Weston."

Rostov turned, his huge frame spinning on an axis as if he were driven into the ground where he stood. His eyes fixed on me, and his hand tightened around the grip on his pistol. And still, the voice droned on.

"William Jones. Long have I watched you from afar. Not even you know the strength you possess. Not even you realize the power of your intellect, the man you might become. The things your mind might do. The heights mankind might reach on the back of your creations. And yet, perhaps it will never be. For one stands in your path. He seeks to destroy you. To punish you for not doing his bidding. Carter Weston will never forget your betrayal. He will never forget that you chose love over him, even if it was the love of his own daughter.

"But you have your chance at salvation, here, in this place. Would anyone question if Carter Weston never returned? Would anyone know what became of him in the desolate wastes? 'After all, these things do happen,' they would say. And you would be free."

William's gaze remained fixed on a spot on the ground, a swirling miasma of yellow fog. I could only wonder what thoughts were going through his mind. Wonder and hope that they were not of blood and death—my own.

It happened so quickly that I didn't have time to react. Rostov came at me and with one great blow knocked me to the ground behind a fallen log. He pulled his gun and cocked it. I looked up at him and saw a fire, the flame of a man consumed with an overriding purpose. Then he shouted, "Get down, you fools!"

Henry and William didn't move. They were, I think, as shocked as I. It wasn't until a rock crashed against a tree that they awoke to what was happening. William dove down beside me, and Rostov threw Henry after him. He raised his gun and fired three shots. A howl echoed through the dead forest, a scream devoid of life or humanity but unlike any beast I had ever heard. Rostov stepped back and dropped to one knee, swung the rifle he had carried on his back around, and took aim.

Silence surrounded us. The sun, which should have been directly above us, was gone; day had turned to night. Not even a pale moon lit the way, and whatever lurked in the shadows would have the advantage.

"You heard the voice," Rostov said, not taking his eye from the gun sight. "Something stalks us. Something not of this world."

"What did you shoot?" William whispered. All three of us now had our pistols drawn, though even so I felt as naked as a babe in a pack of wolves.

"Something," Rostov answered. "A man, perhaps. Or the image of one at least. He wore tattered clothes, but ones that I recognized nonetheless."

"The Evenki…"

All of us looked to Henry, whose face wore the frightened expression of a man who did not expect to see the next sunrise. He cleared his throat, and when he spoke, some of his courage had returned.

"The valleymen," he said, "the ones the elder warned us about. I think we know now who they are. Or were at least. The tribesmen who came to investigate the crash. They weren't killed. They didn't disappear."

"No," William said. "No, they didn't. And whatever it was that fell to earth all those years ago, it's not what we thought it was. There's nothing holy here. There's nothing good about this place. It took those men, and it will kill us if it can."

Rostov shook his head. "Perhaps," he said. He lowered his rifle and looked at me. "But I think there is one of us it wants more than the rest. Don't you agree, Dr. Weston?"

"I've made many enemies in my time."

"Enemies that make their home in the Russian waste?"

"Yes, Colonel. Enemies who are always to be found in the dark and lonely places of the earth."

A shadow moving between the trees caught my eye. A hulking beast wearing clothes that were tattered and ripped to shreds. That it was ever a man I could not believe. When it moved into the moonlight, I could see that its skin hung from its bones. It was as a corpse that walked, a dead man that had risen. My mind went back to years before, on a desolate island in a place in the Pacific that exists only in legend. The same dark power that had commanded ghouls in those days commanded this creature now. A shot rang out and the back of its head exploded. Rostov smiled.

"Another one down."

"I have a feeling," Henry said as he fired a shot at a dark mass that might or might not have been one of the beasts, "that it doesn't matter how many we kill. They're not the real threat."

Perhaps Henry was prophetic. Or maybe his words sparked the change. But at that moment, the forest fell silent. The creatures' roars died away. It seemed as though we were alone. Even if we knew we were not.

The sallow mists swirled around us, and then, as if a vacuum had opened in the middle of the forest, they seemed to withdraw. Faster and faster the fog flowed away, massing in the distance. As it grew, it began to glow, and a yellow fire burned within it. It formed into the image of a man, and my mouth fell open.

"We were wrong," I muttered. "We were terribly wrong."

"It was never here," William said. "The Oculus was never here."

"What does this mean?" Rostov asked, and even in his eyes I saw fear. "What does this mean?"

I turned to him. I turned to them all, to William who waited breathlessly, to Rostov who was utterly confused, to Henry who had his head in his hands. And guilt and shame and horror were all bound in one. "It means…"

I swallowed hard. How to explain what it was that was appearing before us? How to explain what it meant?

"No star fell from the Heavens to do this," I said, sweeping my arms across the plains. "Nor the Oculus either. Nothing from Heaven brought down that fire and death."

"You mean the prophecy was wrong?" William asked.

"No," Henry answered. He raised his head and stared at the jaundiced fire that roared before us. "We picked the wrong prophecy."

A flash of amber light burst through the forest, turning night to day, a roar shattering the stillness with the thunder of an avalanche. We were blinded and struck deaf, all of us. When our senses returned, we were no longer alone. A god stood in our midst.

Rostov and Henry both fired their guns. I didn't bother. The bullets passed through the figure as if he were nothing but the swirling brume. And yet he was so much more. He stood fully six-and-a-half feet tall, his angular face and aquiline nose held high and haughty, the princely visage of a tyrant king. But his sallow robe, his cowl and cloak, they told a different story. Tattered and stained, marked with blood and mud and the tears of the damned.

He spoke to us, though his mouth did not move. Still, the booming voice was not only in our head. It rang through the forest, echoed off the trees.

"The time has come," he said. "A time for choosing. Long have we waited, and the hour of our return is at hand. I am the harbinger, the one who walks before, a voice of one crying in the wilderness. I speak for Him who sleeps beneath the waves. I speak for Him who dreams at the center of all chaos. I speak for those whose names alone would shatter the minds of man. What is shall cease. What was will be again. Bow before us. Mark the way. Or burn with all that is waste, all that is filth, all that is corruption."

In answer, I drew my pistol and fired. The bullet passed through him as I knew it would, but the point was clear. His lips split into a wide smile.

"My friends," he said, holding his skeletal arms wide, "you need not die for him. He has brought you to this place, to your destruction. Now he knows that there is nothing he can do to save you. He has failed."

He turned to me.

"How many times, Carter Weston, have you stood in our way? How many times have you manipulated forces you do not understand to delay the inevitable? But there's no more tricks in your bag, no name of God will dispel me. No sigil or sign. Not the cross or the ankh or the pentagram can stay my hand. You know that, as well as I."

"Tell me he's wrong," William whispered. "Tell me you have a plan."

My mouth went dry, and my body began to shake. "There's nothing. He is the father of lies, but of this, he speaks the truth."

Nyarlathotep took a step forward, and the earth seemed to cry out with his footfall. The air grew hot, and everything his robe touched burst into flame. In the smoke that arose from the dying lands was pestilence, the end of all things.

It came to me then, the obvious. The truth that the messenger of the Old Ones had denied. There was yet one act that could be performed, one incantation that would banish him, if not forever, for time enough. But it required a power that only one thing could bring. Sacrifice. It all came down to sacrifice.

I stood. I would hide from him no more. I cocked the pistol that I held at my side. I raised the gun, pointing it at my temple. The smile faded from Nyarlathotep's face, replaced by a sneer.

"And so it is, Carter Weston. And so it is. The power of sacrifice, yes? So eager to give up your life. So eager to play the hero. So brave. You would exchange your own breath, but what else are you willing to give? No, Carter Weston. It will not be so easy for you."

I should have fired then. I should have said the words, and pulled the trigger. I should have ended it, before the strange, dark one could do whatever it was he intended. But I hesitated, and in that moment, Nyarlathotep had all the time he needed.

The fire erupted around him, his being dissolving before our eyes. We had not time to wonder about his aims; they soon became obvious. William's body went rigid, his arms flung wide. His eyes rolled back in his head, and his tears turned to blood.

"No," I whispered. "God, no."

Henry stumbled backward. Rostov's mouth fell open. An utter silence broke upon the forest. Whoever William was, whoever he had been, he was no more.

He turned to face me, and when he spoke, his voice was not his own. "This will do fine," the thing that had been William said. "A more than worthy vessel for my purposes."

That was when I had to decide. That was when I had to make a choice. I raised my pistol. I pointed it at William's heart. I said the words.

"*A ne a mai. Ma lei. Ma dooz.*" For an instant I hesitated. "I'm sorry."

I pulled the trigger, and time slowed down. The bullet struck William. The fire extinguished. The evil fled. And for one brief moment, what had been William was with us again. For one brief moment, before he died in my arms.

Chapter 19

Journal of Carter Weston
July 24, 1933

Rachel sat in silence. She didn't weep. She didn't scream or yell. Somehow, it would have been better if she had.

My story ended there. I didn't bother to tell her how we climbed out of that accursed place, how we wrapped William's body in a sheet and carried him to Irkutsk. There, we bid Rostov a sad goodbye. He would not leave with us, even though death was on his doorstep. Cannon fire from the Red Army rocked the city. When the last train pulled away from the central station, we were on it. Advanced units of the Bolsheviks arrived the next day. I never learned Rostov's fate, though I think it is known to all.

In the days that followed, the lot fell to me, of course, to tell Rachel that William was dead. She did cry then, falling into my arms, beating her fists against my chest, begging me to tell her it wasn't true.

And it wasn't true. Not, at least, as I told it, that William had been shot in a gunfight with local bandits. That he had saved all our lives. He had, of course. In a way.

As he had no family to speak of, we buried William in the Weston family plot at Christchurch Cemetery in Miskatonic. Rachel's son was due seven months later. Still-born, he was interred beside his father, and so my hubris claimed another.

I wish I could write here that in that train-car on the border of France we had some epiphany, that she broke down and forgave me, that I held her close and started to forgive myself.

That is not what happened. Instead she stood without looking at me, turned, opened the door, and was gone.

I gazed out the window of the train into the darkness beyond. I wished for a sign. I wished for something to come out of that eternal night, to tell me that my life had not been lived in vain, that the battles and the sacrifices and the unending quest to hold back another night—one far darker and truly endless—was well worth it. That I had, as the Apostle Paul of old once wrote, kept the faith and finished the course. That somewhere, somehow, a reward awaited me, one where Rachel and William would join me. And that in that day, they would say, "Well done, father. Well done, indeed." Yet, I knew those were the vainest of all hopes.

I didn't know how much farther we had until Paris would break into view, but I was sure sleep would not come. So when there was a knock on my door, I was thankful for it, even if I had long since ceased to hope that Rachel might be waiting in the corridor. The door opened, and Henry entered.

"Guillaume and Margot are growing restless. I think it's time to tell them more about what we face."

"Have you seen Rachel?"

Henry shook his head, with equal measures of pity and sadness. "No. She's in her cabin, but I don't think she's coming out anytime soon. Did you talk to her?"

I nodded.

"And it didn't go well."

It wasn't a question.

"No. It did not."

I could not bear the silence that fell between us, and neither could Henry.

"Be that as it may, our guests deserve answers. They've come a long way on faith alone."

"Bring them in then," I said. Anything to break the monotony of that lonely ride. "And Henry, see if Rachel will come."

"She already knows the story."

"I know. Still."

Henry sighed, something I did not hear from him often. He nodded once, wearily, and left.

When he returned, only Guillaume and Margot were with him. It was to be expected, I suppose.

"I know you're confused," I said as they sat down. "I can appreciate that. I don't know that I understand everything that's going on here myself. But what I know, I'll tell you now. Henry, can I have a piece of paper?"

Henry reached into his jacket pocket and removed a small pad. He handed it to me, and a pen with it. I took them both and began to draw. It took me only a moment to finish. "Take a look at this."

I handed the pad to Guillaume. Drawn clearly, albeit crudely, was the image of a pyramid, an eye wreathed in fire where the pinnacle should be.

"An unfinished pyramid," I said, "crowned by a single eye, one locked in a pyramid unto itself, inscribed in a circle of flame. This is the Great Seal of the United States, my friends. Now, if you ask the average historian the provenance of such an enigmatic and esoteric emblem, he would likely tell you that it is a legacy of the nation's Masonic roots. But he would be wrong. For this emblem is not part of Masonic lore. It has no basis in the teachings of that order. This is something far older, something far more important."

"The Eye of God," Guillaume whispered.

I smiled, more than a little pleased. "As perceptive as ever, my young friend." Perhaps this Guillaume has a bright future with us. Someone, after all, would have to take up our cause. And I no longer believed it would be Rachel.

"There is a group," I said, "one whose age is unknown to me— for who can say how long they have existed?—who has made it their duty to protect the Oculus. They are called the Tzadikim Nistarim. The history you know is incomplete. In the long ago, this world was not like it is now. It was ruled by something else, something not made of the stuff of this earth. In a time before time, there existed great beings, what some would call gods. Scholars spend lifetimes arguing about where they came from, what drove them away. They can agree on only one thing—in every culture and every society there are prophesies of their return. Ragnarok, Armageddon, the Frashokereti, all share one common thread. The rise of great beasts, kings that have come to seek dominion over this world. And always, there is the harbinger, the messenger, the one who walks before. He is the herald of their coming. He goes by many names, but only one that he claims as his own—Nyarlathotep.

"The order watches for his coming, for it is foretold that in that day, the one power that can stop him will also return." I pointed again to the image on the paper.

"How does it work?" Margot asked.

"There is an incantation, one contained in certain rare books— the *Necronomicon*, the *Incendium Maleficarum*. When the Staff of Dzyan and the Oculus are combined and the words are read, then he who holds the staff need not fear the old gods. Nyarlathotep cannot stand against him."

"And what does this have to do with you?"

"I had the *Incendium Maleficarum*. The man who captured me, Zann, believed that contained in the book was a way to use the staff, not to destroy Nyarlathotep, but to control him. Zann is no cultist. He doesn't worship the Old Ones. Not in his heart. If you are unlucky enough to fall into his clutches, then he'll bore you with endless speeches about building a better world or some other nonsense. I can speak to that from experience. But in the end, he simply wants the one thing he has never had—power."

"I'm glad we left him behind," said Guillaume.

"Not far enough I fear. He's heard the rumors. The staff of Dzyan is said to be in France, buried in the catacombs beneath Paris. That is why those who would see Nyarlathotep restored have gone to that place. They want to find the staff. Find it, destroy it, neutralize it, whatever they must do. Without the staff, we are lost."

"And the Oculus," Guillaume said, "where is it?"

Henry glanced at me, and Guillaume saw in that look all he needed to answer the question. "You don't know," he said.

"It could be in a thousand places. The last place we looked...."

I trailed off. I didn't want to go back there, back to the snows of Russia, Siberia, the Tunguska forest, even if only for a moment.

"We didn't find it, and there's no guarantee we'll find it this time. But we can't worry about that now. Zann will go to France. He will do what he can to find the staff before the followers of Nyarlathotep. We just have to beat them all."

Chapter 20

Diary of Rachel Jones
July 25, 1933

When I heard the knock on my cabin door, I told whoever it was to go away. I hoped it was Henry; if I heard my father's voice from beyond that wood paneling, I'm not sure what I would have done. My reserves were weakening, my ability to hold things together falling rapidly away. But when the person did speak, it was not who I had expected. Not at all.

"It's Guillaume."

Guillaume. God. My father might have been better. I was a mess. A blubbering mess. And yet, although my first instinct was to send him away, I needed company. I needed a shoulder to cry on. My pillow simply wasn't doing the job.

"Hello?"

"Just a second," I said.

I opened the door, and felt a physical pain when I saw his reaction to my sad state. His mouth fell open, and he looked me up and down like I was some visitor from Mars out of an H.G. Wells story. But then his eyes softened, and his face with it.

"Can I come in?" he asked. I didn't particularly like the pity in his voice, but I wanted it, nonetheless. I hated myself for that.

"Of course. Sorry my room is such a mess," I said, smoothing the blanket on the hard, unforgiving bed. The accommodations, though theoretically first class, left something to be desired.

He sat down beside me and, to my utter surprise, took my hand.

"Are you all right?" he asked. I stared at my fingers, clasped in his. His hands were much bigger than I had realized, and they seemed to swallow mine whole. They were warm, and they were comforting, and at that moment, they were exactly what I needed.

"Yes." I said. "Of course, I am."

"I don't know what happened, but from the little I heard, I can imagine. Your husband, he died?"

I shuddered involuntarily, and Guillaume flinched.

"I'm sorry," he said, "forgive me. We don't have to discuss it."

"No. No, I want to talk about it. His name was William. And yes, he died. It was a long time ago."

"But not so long that you've forgotten."

"I'll never forget," I said, looking up into his eyes, those sea-green eyes. I had heard others describe the look in another's eyes as stormy. Never before had I understood that term. There was something about Guillaume. Something older than his years on this earth, something that spoke of wisdom and understanding beyond what he should have possessed. I wanted to tell him everything. And so...I did.

It seemed to pour out of me. A decade of pain and loss and longing. But that was only the beginning. For my father had provided me more sorrow than most people were ever likely to know, more than I would have ever imagined.

God, what a fool I must have seemed, baring my soul, my darkest thoughts, to this stranger, to this boy, a student far from home, wrapped up in a mad quest that was not his own and that he could barely begin to fathom. And yet I could not stop myself. Not until the last word was spoken. Not until there was nothing left to give.

Finally, I fell silent. He didn't speak either. Only the steady drone of the train rumbling through a darkened French countryside kept us company.

Then he did something entirely unexpected.

Guillaume leaned across the space between us and kissed me. I began to pull away, but his strong arms wrapped around my shoulders and would not let me escape. Not that I tried all that hard. I was feeling something I hadn't thought possible again, things I hadn't felt in a very long time.

It was electric. It was amazing. I had heard others speak about a "spark" between two people, but I had never felt it like that, not even with William. It was palpable, and if the cabin had been darkened, I think the fire between us would have provided enough light to read by.

The kiss might have gone on forever had I not regained some semblance of composure, some semblance of myself. I pushed him away, and this time he let me.

"But Margot…" I said.

Guillaume blushed slightly, and then he smiled so sweetly at me that I almost felt guilty for asking.

"Margot, she is a good friend, and a wonderful girl. But…" He gestured with his hand, palm up, and I understood.

"She's clearly taken with you. Taken completely."

He sighed, long and deep. "Yes. She is. But that I cannot help. In fact, I had told myself it wasn't true for a very long time. But now, I suppose it can't be denied."

"No," I said. "No, it cannot."

"Look, there is nothing I can do about Margot, or how she feels. But I am not bound by that. She has been a dear friend to me when others were not to be found, and I treasure that more deeply than you can know. But still, there will always be a gulf between us. It's different with you. When I saw you, the very first moment, I knew that we had met for a reason. I felt something, unlike anything I had ever felt before. It was fate that brought us together, no? Fate that led you to me so that I could help you find your father. And I won't let anything, not even Margot, stand in the way of that."

He leaned forward and cupped my chin in his hand, lifting my lips to his. I did not fight him this time. I let him have me—all of me. And for the first time since William died, I felt like a woman again.

Chapter 21

Journal of Carter Weston
October 24, 1926

The legends regarding Nyarlathotep have always been of particular interest to me. It was his relationship to mankind that drew me, his antithesis to the Christ figure. For he was also a god who walked among men. But to destroy, not to save. Still, I found hope in that dependency, in that connection to humanity. If it were true that Nyarlathotep somehow needed men to accomplish whatever foul deeds he sought, then men could stand in the breech against him as well, even if we were always outnumbered by those who would do his bidding.

I witnessed them and their perversity only a few years ago. I'd attended a conference on ancient Sumerian religious cults at the Louisiana State University, in the city of Baton Rouge. The conference itself was a waste of time and money, but I did not leave empty handed. Not in the slightest. For there was another at the conference, one who did not belong. And yet he was the most important attendee of them all.

I met him in the bar of the Bellemont hotel. He wore a seersucker suit and white patent-leather shoes. But it wasn't his clothes that drew me to him. It was the fact he was reading my second book, *Witch-cults of the Ancient World*. Still, I probably would have let him be, not wanting to draw attention to myself or waste either of our time. But it was not up to me, for he sought me out.

"Dr. Weston," he said, extending his hand. "I had hoped you'd turn up here. I am Detective John Dubois, up from New Orleans for the conference. Two Sazeracs," he said to the bartender. The man nodded and went to work. Dubois had an easy smile and an innate charm, the kind that made you trust him immediately. I had a sudden feeling that he was very good at extracting confessions. The bartender returned with two glasses of a frothy white liquid I did not recognize.

"To freedom." He took a sip and then held a finger in the air. "I was hoping you would sign this," he said, sliding the book in my direction. As I did, I asked him what would bring a New Orleans inspector of the police to such a conference.

"Interesting you should ask, professor, for that reason sits before me." Dubois must have seen a hesitancy flash in my eyes, because he put a hand on my arm and laughed. "Oh, it's nothing you've done, professor. Nothing at all. In fact, it's something I wanted to do *for* you." It was then he began to relay to me the story of many of the strange things he had seen on the job in Orleans Parish. It seemed that one of the cults I had written about in my book—ancient, yes, but certainly not dead—had found its way to the Crescent City.

"Fifteen years or so ago, when I was fresh on the force, we broke up one of their meetings out in the swamps, some thirty miles from the city. Middle of nowhere, kind of place that honest people don't go if they can help it. Arrested a bunch of them, not that we could make the charges stick, even if we did believe that they were involved in some pretty nasty stuff. They left behind an artifact though, one I'm sure you are familiar with. The man in charge of my unit, Inspector Legrasse, spent the rest of his life trying to figure out just what he had."

I was indeed familiar with the artifact. Professor George Angell of Brown University was a dear friend of mine, and he had related to me the very same story that Dubois was now telling. Of how the inspector had discovered an eldritch and untraceable idol—a grotesque, ancient stone statuette—and he had sought scholarly advice on the object and the cult that possessed it, much as Dubois was now seeking from me.

"I was under the impression, detective, that you had succeeded in driving the cultists out of the city."

Dubois shook his head and scoffed. "Were it so, professor. New Orleans is not the kind of place that one can purge of such things. Oh, they've gone underground all right, but they are still there. Waiting. That's why I became so interested in your particular area of expertise," he said, gesturing to my book. "Obsessed, my wife says. But when you've seen the things I've seen, you come to believe that men, with the right motivation, are capable of just about anything. And as much as I'd like to believe it weren't so, my eyes don't lie to me."

"So they are active again, you say?"

"They are. It took us a while to get a figure on it. They hide in plain sight, cover their tracks with voodoo and such. The voodoo is harmless enough. Ancestor worship, protective potions, that sort of thing. Mostly hocus-pocus and cheap tricks. But there's one voodooeen who was different, one who had real power."

"Laveau."

He nodded once, throwing back the rest of his drink and ordering another with a nod at the bartender.

"Been dead thirty years at least, but they say she still walks the streets of the Old Quarter, still peddles her wares and her witchcraft. Still preaches her black masses. Sounds crazy, I know. But probably not to you, and certainly not to me."

"And you think there's more to this Laveau woman than voodoo?"

Dubois leaned back against the bar. "Tell me, professor. What do you know of the Ashmodai?" A grin flashed across his face as a shudder roiled through me. "That's what I thought."

The Ashmodai were, perhaps, the world's first great religion. The fires of their worship had burned through Mesopotamia, down into Africa, and out into the Far East. Their adherents slaughtered men, women, and children by the thousands in Gaul and across the channel in ancient Britain, locking them in towering wooden figures formed in the shape of a man, before burning them to the ground. It is said that the empires of antiquity arose from the maddened cries of savaged peoples, inspired by desperate souls that begged for anyone to save them from the hordes of the Ashmodai. And while the Egyptians and Greeks and Babylonians struck heavy blows against the old faith, it wasn't until the Roman Empire brought the sword and the cross to every known corner of the world that the flame of Asmodeus was extinguished.

And yet, even now, whispers of their continued workings float across the winds of time, and who can say that they ever truly disappeared?

"Surely," I said, "you don't believe that the Ashmodai have come to New Orleans?"

"You think they *are* dead, then? Truly dead?"

"Dead or not, there's been not one recorded instance of their presence for 1,500 years."

"But there have, haven't there? The nameless cults that exist throughout the world? Maybe not so nameless after all."

It was true that there were those who claimed that the ancient religions had not vanished but simply gone underground, disguising themselves in the garb of more modern faiths. I had seen evidence of such subterfuge, from the Esoteric Order of Dagon, which had spread from New England's own Innsmouth to port cities around the world, to the Circle of the Crescent Moon, which had debased mosques throughout Indonesia.

"Even so," I said, "it seems highly unlikely you would have them in Louisiana, no matter what you've seen."

"Perhaps," he said, staring down into his drink. "Maybe you should come with me to New Orleans, and we can find out together. We think we know where they meet, and I want you there when we break it up."

"Me? But why?"

For a moment Dubois was silent, but then he picked up the book that I had signed for him and pointed to it. "Because, professor. I've read your book, and I've read a lot of others, too. I know more than just about anyone out there about this stuff," he said, gesturing to the hallway where the conference-goers were gathered. "Call it obsession if you want, but I've learned that knowledge is power. And that's why you need to be involved. The Old Ones want chaos, and they thrive on ignorance. If we're going after them in the shadows, then we gotta shine the light of truth on them. That's what you do. 'Cause there can be no faith without seeing truth, and faith is what we need now more than ever."

I didn't need convincing. If even half of what Dubois believed had solid foundation, then the trip to New Orleans was well worth the cost in time and money. In the end, I was not to be disappointed.

* * *

The conference still had a day to go, but I was no longer interested in presentations and scholarly theories. Dubois and I were on the next train to New Orleans, watching the swamps speed by as he relayed what had brought him to Baton Rouge in the first place.

"We found her," he said, "in the cellar of an abandoned tavern on the outskirts of the city. It wasn't a pretty sight, professor. Not a pretty sight at all. Never seen anything like it. She was split, all the way down her body. Naked, of course. Most of her organs had been taken out and placed around the chamber, some burnt in front of crude alters. To what god, I don't know and don't care to find out. Coroner said she was alive through most of it."

"What do you know about her?"

"Well, nothing, at the time. But we were able to track down a name based on a locket that we found under one of the chairs in the cellar. Probably got ripped off when they were getting her ready. Her name was Janet Barboux, seventeen years old. Her father was a sailor, in and out of New Orleans most times. We've been unable to locate him, but we also can't find a speck of proof that he's aboard any of the ships that have left port in the last month. Sad to say, he's our prime suspect."

"His own daughter?"

The inspector shook his head, but not in denial. "Terrible thing, isn't it? Anyway, once we focused on Barboux, we were able to track down some of his less reputable associates. One of them, a man named Joe—doesn't have a last name that we can find—has a reputation around town as being mentally unstable. Spent some time up at East Louisiana, and they probably should have kept him there. He denied any involvement at first, of course, but we were able to break him. Can't say I'm altogether proud of our methods, but desperate times, right?"

"And what did he say?"

"Claimed he fell into some tough straits. Lost his job, needed money. Someone from his church said they could help. Said they belonged to something special, something that would change his life. They called themselves the *pòt an lò*, creole for the Golden Gate. Things turned for him. He had money in his pocket for the first time in his life. After about a year, they told him the time was right, that the stars had come round. Told him that a sacrifice was needed, the spilling of blood on the death of the moon."

"I assume there was a promise attached to this sacrifice as well?"

"Indeed, there was. If done correctly, the sacrifice opened a doorway on the coming of the next full moon. A gate through which might pass what he called the *bondye wa*, apparently some kind of ancient demon, a messenger of some sort." I must have blanched then, for a shadow of understanding passed over the face of Dubois. "You know of what he speaks? This makes sense to you?"

"I have heard the legends," I mumbled.

"In any event," he said, "the full moon is tonight. With the assistance of this Joe, we were able to track the cult to its heart. A place called La Salle. I'm not surprised. La Salle has quite a reputation, the sort of place that kids make up ghost stories about and old folks shun. It was one of the first permanent settlements in the territory, and would have been the capital, or so they say. The Catholic Diocese built this enormous cathedral in the center of town. Something else to see. But then the floods came. Some people say it was an Indian curse, that the settlers had disturbed old magic better left alone. But whatever the truth, the intentions of the townsfolk, no matter how grand, couldn't stand against the rising waters. Before long, the whole place was a ghost town. It's been that way ever since."

"And that is where we are going?"

"It is. Tonight. My men will meet us at the train station."

We rode in silence then, nothing but the sound of the engine and steel wheels on steel rails to interrupt our thoughts.

* * *

The inspector's men were waiting for us at the station, just as he said. There were ten of them, strong men with hard faces that I hoped reflected their hearts. The sun already hung low in the western sky.

"Time is running short," Dubois said, "and we have a ways to travel yet."

We climbed into a couple of pickup trucks. I rode in the cab of one with Dubois, while most of the men settled into their beds, checking and rechecking the rifles they carried.

"You expect a fight?" I asked. He nodded.

"Mmmhm. That's what we got last time. Can't imagine why this would be any different."

Our truck led the way, and we hadn't gone far before we left civilization behind entirely. The swamps and thick woods we had traversed aboard the train did not prepare me for the utter desolation of that world. And yet, even though the green jungle was thick around me, the stench of rotting decay was in the air as well. For this was a dying world, one struck with some disease that went beyond the ordinary realm. Something older. Something more foul.

We rumbled along the broken pavement until the pavement itself ran out. Now it was dirt and rocks, a one-way road that barely deserved the name, a trail that the swamp was gradually swallowing. It seemed that we were no closer to much of anything when we turned off the main path onto an even more perilous lane, but we had not gone far before Dubois pulled behind a copse of trees and killed the engine. "We walk from here," he said, turning to me. "Wouldn't want to give away our approach."

The twelve of us piled out, each man removing an electric torch and switching it on. Dubois addressed his troops briefly, telling them that they had his full faith, his full confidence. They had been with him the longest, and many of them had seen the cult's foul doings in the swamps more than a decade before. Today they would extinguish its flame, once and for all.

"Let's go."

We crept back to the main road, staying in tight formation on either side, ready to dive into the forest at the merest sound of an approaching vehicle. The night was growing thick, and it was only then that I noticed something peculiar. We were in the midst of a great swamp, surrounded by wilderness for a hundred miles, maybe. And yet I heard nothing. Not a bird, not an animal in the brush, not even the insects that normally teem about. No mosquitos feasted upon us. No ancient-eyed owls watched our approach. We were completely alone. It was as if they had foreseen some coming doom that we could only imagine, the maw of which we were now walking directly into.

We'd gone maybe a mile when Dubois held up his hand. "Do you hear that?" We all stopped, craning our necks to try to hear better, to catch some semblance of sound. It started off as a murmur, a thumping echo that I might have mistaken for the beating of my own heart. But it was too regular, even for that. Too deep. That throbbing rhythm, that howling bass. Conga drums, pounding through the night.

"Check your weapons," Dubois whispered. "We'll be upon them any second."

Suddenly the forest changed, and it was only when I peered deep into its depths that I saw why. We were in a town. You would barely know it, since the jungle had claimed it back for nature, but there were buildings in the gloaming of the swamps, covered in vines, long, green arms breaking through signs that read "Oldman's Apothecary" and "Village Café," all collapsing under the weight of kudzu and Spanish moss. The road was no longer dirt but rather cobblestone.

Dubois gave a signal, and we extinguished our lights. In an instant, we were plunged into a black darkness that swallowed us whole, and I had to fight with all my being not to go running headlong into the wilderness.

The moon was bright that night, though, and the sky clear of obscuring clouds. In only a moment, my eyes had adjusted and I could see as well as, if not better than, before. We continued on, and it was no time at all before we came to the empty city square, as dead as if it were the end of the world. And at the head of that square sat a towering cathedral, made all the more glorious by the vines that wreathed it in green. I almost didn't notice the flickering lights from within.

Dubois glanced at me before nodding to his men, flicking his hand left and then right. The detectives filed out, forming a rough cordon around the building, surrounding it. They were the hunters. We were the hounds meant to flush our prey. I followed the inspector as he made his way around the old church, searching for some weakness, some point of access. We swung wide of the door; a direct entry would not do. From within, the sound of discordant piping had joined the bestial thump of the drums.

I saw it before Dubois. A ladder, wrought iron, added to the side of the building for easy access, some time before the cathedral was abandoned forever. I tapped the inspector on the shoulder, disheartened by his startled reaction. If I was looking for a rock on which to lean during this journey, he was not it. I gestured toward the ladder. He followed my eyes, nodding back at me when he saw it.

We began to climb.

I was not entirely convinced that the rust-rotten iron would hold us, but it was our best bet. If I was to fall to my death in the midst of that swamp, then so be it.

Our target was an opening high on the cathedral wall, a window I suppose, meant to provide ventilation and light during happier times. It still might, if we could squeeze through it. I had my doubts about Dubois, raised as he was on the sumptuous fare of Louisiana, but he managed to pass with little effort. I followed him, and we found ourselves on the inside.

The sound which had been growing with intensity as we climbed boomed through the dank attic of the church. Light seeped through the wooden slats of the floor, illuminating motes of dust that swirled and danced around us. I found myself stifling a sneeze, knowing that such a mistake would be the end of us both. We crawled forward on our hands and knees, careful not to make a sound, though I wondered if our weight alone was raining down the accumulated dirt and detritus of many decades on the adherents below. Not that they would have noticed in the frenzy of their exultations. We were in luck, in any event, for, not ten feet from us, a great square had been cut in the floor, a veritable skylight through which we could peer without fear of discovery.

We crawled forward, every creak of every beam sending lightning bolts of terror into the pit of my stomach, and yet the sound of drums and pipes and now human voices was enough to drown out all sound, if not all fear. There was a smell too, a combination of burning smoke and something sweet I couldn't place.

And then we peered over that edge to below and looked upon madness made flesh.

The cathedral floor was a shambles of all that is holy. Rotten pews and prayer kneelers had been torn up and shoved into piles along the side, save where the boards would serve a purpose. The wood had been fashioned into crude St. Andrew's crosses, though I knew well that this ungodly crew had another name for the implements of death that surrounded the gathered mass in a large semi-circle.

"The mark of the harbinger," I dared to whisper to Dubois. "The sign of the cult of Nyarlathotep."

Would that they had been empty. The people—three men, three women, and worst of all, a boy who could not have been more than seven or eight years old—that hung, spread-eagled, from them were beyond saving. I knew then what the smell was; it was the scent of rotting flesh, mingled with the smoke from the torches that illuminated the room. The skin hung loose and low from the naked bodies, and in places—especially around the face—it had peeled off altogether. The stench was overwhelming now, and I marveled that I hadn't recognized it earlier.

The cultists numbered a couple of dozen. Their god was no respecter of persons. Among their ranks were men and women, young and old, rich and poor, black and white. At their front stood a single figure, its long, black robe decorated with strips of fabric in every color, head wrapped in a crimson scarf that seemed to climb into the sky. A priestess of Nyarlathotep, or so her bearing said, though there was nothing soft or feminine or motherly about her. She was the sword of the god, the bringer of his vengeance, the sower of his destruction. Lying before her on what must have been the cathedral's once-holy altar was a youth, a man of perhaps eighteen. He was nude, and no bindings held him down. He was either there of his own volition or, more likely, drugged for the sacrifice.

Dubois removed his pistol and a whistle from his pocket. Once he gave the signal, his men would rush the building, and in the confusion we hoped to take our prisoners without violence. But if they had weapons, Dubois was prepared to take down anyone who threatened his men. He put the whistle to his lips, but I stopped him with a hand to his shoulder. He looked at me, and without words, he knew I wanted to see more. The woman below began to cast her spell.

When she spoke, I was surprised that her words were not English or French or even Creole. They were much older—Sumerian—an ancient tongue from the ancient people who first wrote of Nyarlathotep, before the Egyptians gave him the name by which we know him best. I record her words here, as closely as I can.

The translation, though rough, conveys all the truth of those dread utterances.

Her voice started as a whisper, rising to a murmur, and then soaring to a roar. "Alal. Alla xul. Nisme! Ati me peta babka! Kanpa! Taru! Iksuda! Negeltu xul labiru ensi ersutu!" *Destroyer. Dark god. Hear me! Throw open the gate between worlds! Remember! Return! Conquer! Then shall the old gods awake and restore their dominion over the earth!*

A roar shook the foundations of the old church. It was below, above, and around all at once. The cultish fires flared, and yellow smoke poured from their flickering flames. The sallow fog gathered around the altar. Reaching tentacles probed upwards, wrapping the body of the boy, covering him in a blanket of golden mist. The youth breathed deep, sucking the yellow smoke into his lungs.

And I knew.

"This is no sacrifice," I whispered.

An explosion roared from Dubois's pistol and through the church. A bullet ripped off the back of the youth's skull. Another roar followed quickly, but of a completely different quality. And if I hadn't known better, I would have said that this hate-filled cry erupted from a demonic maw that formed in the midst of the now-dissipating fog.

What followed was chaos. Dubois was now firing wildly, as many in the cult had drawn weapons and were shooting toward the ceiling. The front doors of the church burst open, and in poured Dubois's army. With their guns added to his, the battle was short-lived. When it was over, a dozen cultists were dead, the same number in custody.

The enigmatic woman who had led them had escaped, seemingly vanishing into thin air. I had caught her eye, just after Dubois fired his first shot. She had gazed up through the portal that framed our faces. And when her eyes met mine, I would swear that a dark smile crept up the corner of her mouth.

Was that the end of the New Orleans coven? Who can say? But I think we had stumbled upon something far more significant than a simple cult, dedicated to some lost and forgotten deity. We had seen something much older, and much more dangerous. This handful of devotees had come within moments of calling forth the dark one himself, the black messenger of Azathoth. And if even they were able to come so close, then what hope do we have of stopping others in the future?

I visited her grave before I left New Orleans, the voodoo queen, Marie Laveau. I left the offering of bourbon and I made the three x's on her tombstone, as so many devotees seeking favor from beyond the veil have done before me.

But my wish was different. My wish was that neither she, nor the dark god she served, would ever return.

Chapter 22

Journal of Carter Weston
July 25, 1933

"Carter Weston. The last time we parted, I swore I would kill you if we met again."

He stood twirling his ivory-handled cane in his hand, glaring at Henry and me. For a second, I was concerned.

"Well, Marcel, I certainly hope you are as good at keeping your word now as you were back then."

Henry glanced at me nervously, but then the man at the head of the table where we sat burst into laughter. He kicked back a chair and fell into it.

"I was never able to resist your charms, Carter, even if you are a son-of-a-bitch." He called for a waitress and ordered a Beaujolais and three glasses. "I always preferred Beaujolais," he said. "Like men, it is better when it is young. Neither it, nor we, it seems, age well."

"I don't know about that, Marcel. You seem as though you are doing quite well for yourself, despite the years."

"Yes," he said, lighting a cigar. Marcel offered one to Henry and me. He declined. I did not. "It took me awhile to get over our last encounter. You cost me a fortune."

"Well, that artifact you discovered and I...disposed of...would have been quite dangerous in the wrong hands. And it tends to be from those hands that the largest sums will pass. You always did believe in the philosophy of the highest bidder."

Marcel smiled. "I didn't get in this business to lose money. But you are right, my friend. You are right. I realize that now. Not much comes with age, but maybe wisdom still does. That little trinket was a score that was too big for me. Too big for anyone, I suppose. Still, it was worth a lot of money."

"Perhaps I can make it up to you today."

The young woman, the only other person in all of the Café du Marché—what one might call a "rustic" establishment well off the beaten Parisian paths—arrived with the wine. She uncorked it, pouring three full glasses. Marcel raised his. "Well, to making up old debts then."

He took a sip and gestured with his glass toward me. "I'm not surprised you had something in mind. I didn't suppose you wanted to talk about old times. You never struck me as the sentimental type."

"No," I said, smiling. "Straight to business then?"

Marcel nodded, and I knew that, whatever he might say, he still remembered what I had cost him a decade before.

I had known Marcel since we were both much younger men. Marcel had been a French lieutenant in the Great War, and after watching most of his friends and countrymen cut down in a conflict that shattered the world and slayed a whole generation with nothing to show for it, he decided he had given enough of himself. From then on, fortune and glory—with an emphasis on *fortune*—were his watchwords. He became a procurer of rare antiquities. A grave-robber to some, but a good one. Our paths had crossed many times over the years, but it was when Marcel came into possession of a rare and exquisite diadem which he procured from a questionable trader on the Massachusetts coast that we had our little disagreement. It was fortunate that we were able to intercept Marcel and "liberate" the artifact from his possession before the Walpurgis moon shone down on Devil Reef.

"We need a guide, an expert to take us down in the catacombs."

Marcel arched an eyebrow. "The catacombs? That's dirty business, Dr. Weston. Dirty business, indeed. The catacombs are the resting place of my countrymen, my brothers." He grinned broadly. "To violate their sleep would be a desecration."

He had always driven a hard bargain.

"Come now, Marcel. You and I both know that quite a bit of your empire is built on lost treasures you've dug up from that same ground. There's no man in Paris, no man in all the world, who knows those tunnels better than you do. Your reputation precedes you."

Marcel shrugged and leaned back in his chair. "I said it would be a desecration. I did not say it would be impossible." Then he grinned again. "Nor did I say it would be cheap."

"Good thing you know that I'm good for it."

"It's hard to say what you are good for these days. Last I heard, you were dead."

Now it was my turn to grin. "I suppose I should be flattered that rumors of my demise made it all the way across the Atlantic. But as you can see, they were greatly exaggerated."

"Of course, Carter. And yes, I do know that you are a man of your word. So about that, I am not concerned. What does concern me is that trouble seems to follow you like a storm cloud. And whatever you seek in the catacombs? I can only assume that it will bring some of the worst trouble of all."

I grabbed the bottle and refilled our glasses. When it ran dry, Marcel gestured for another. We sat in silence until it arrived. "Have you heard of the Staff of Dzyan?" I asked. His brow furrowed.

"Ah, the Staff of Dzyan. So that's what you seek? You *do* look for trouble."

"What do you know about it?"

Marcel stubbed out his dying cigar and exhaled a last cloud of smoke. He leaned across the table, resting on his elbows, and clasped his hands together. "In its early days, a thousand years or more ago, Paris was known for its mines. Limestone, gypsum, what-have-you. And then the city grew," he said, waving his hand across the table. "As it did, it covered the old mines, burying them beneath the city's glory. And perhaps that would have been the end of the story, but the mines did not want to be forgotten. When they started collapsing, with streets and people and buildings disappearing below, everyone was reminded. The old mines had to be reinforced, lest the entire city fall into the depths.

"And then someone hit upon an idea. No one knows exactly who it was. You see, the city had an overcrowding problem. Not of the living, but of the dead. Bodies were stacked one upon another in their graves, four, five deep. The stench of decay and the smell of disease were ever-present. Finally, a use for the miles of limestone caverns carved beneath our feet. Paris's dead were disinterred and entombed, this time forever, in the catacombs.

"It's a beautiful irony, I think. Paris, the city of lights, the crown jewel of Western Europe. And yet, like a beautiful and supposedly virtuous woman, the truth she hides underneath is quite different."

Marcel leaned back in his chair and sipped his wine. He cocked his eyebrow and swirled the burgundy liquid gently. "At least, that's the official story."

"Precisely," I said.

"There were always rumors that powerful interests used the opening of the catacombs to hide certain valuable and…how do you say…sensitive items where only they could find them. For their protection, I suppose. I can confirm that the first rumor is true. As to the protection…" He grinned wide. "Well, I'll just say that in these difficult times, people will go to great lengths to ensure that buried treasure does not stay buried for long."

"And the staff?"

Marcel had now transitioned to cigarettes. "Of all the gifts of the new world, tobacco is certainly the one that I prefer the most. Yes, Carter. I have heard of your staff, but it is one relic I have never found. A certain religious order is said to revere it."

"The Tzadikim Nistarim," Henry said.

Marcel merely nodded. "And the story I have always heard is that they themselves deposited it in the catacombs. Buried it, deep below the main tunnels. Unless you knew where you were looking, finding it would take an army. One that was dedicated, and highly motivated."

He grinned again, and it was evident that he was toying with us.

"All right, Marcel," I said. "You've had your fun. Clearly you know something you're not telling us."

"Well the thing is, my dear Carter, you are not the first person to enquire into the Staff of Dzyan. In fact, it seems that any number of people are interested in its whereabouts. Including some unsavory characters of Teutonic descent."

"Germans?" Henry said more than asked, as if there was any question.

"Indeed. In fact, they were here yesterday. We met in this very restaurant."

Henry and I glanced at each other. Suddenly, this charming hole-in-the-wall bistro took on a more sinister atmosphere. I half-expected a division of SA to burst from the kitchen at any moment.

A sly smile crossed Marcel's face. "Lucky for you, I hate Germans. So I told them to go back to Berlin. To eat a sausage, as it were. But I wouldn't count on them listening."

"No," I said. "They are rather persistent."

"In any event, I am at your disposal. Personally, I rarely go into the catacombs anymore." He patted his stomach, it having grown much larger than the last time I had seen him. "It seems that time has been kind to me, and I have grown weary of tight spaces. But I will send one of my best men to guide you. He will meet you at your hotel. I hope you find what you seek, particularly before the Germans get to it."

"Thank you, Marcel," I said, taking his hand. "I promise you that I will make it worth your troubles."

"I know you will, my friend. But Carter, one other thing. It is not only the Germans who seek the staff. Rumors persist in the Latin Quarter of unsavory goings-on in the dark corners of the city. Tales of unsavory men about, strange tidings and strange portents. Beware the Yellow Sign."

Marcel rose, grabbing his cane and throwing a few francs on the table. "That should cover it. Next time, it's on you. My man will meet you tonight in the lobby of your hotel at eight o'clock, sharp. Don't be late." He tipped his hat to Henry and me, and then he was gone.

"The Yellow Sign?" Henry muttered.

"We knew it would come to this," I said. "It seems the Germans are the least of our problems."

Chapter 23

When I told Rachel that we were going into the catacombs—and that I wanted her to stay behind—she was not pleased.

"Absurd. That's what I think. We came here to get you, to save you. And now you expect me to wait behind while you risk your life? You know what could be waiting for you down there."

"And I am sure that Guillaume and I can handle it."

"Guillaume?" she said, and I could have sworn the blood drained away from her face. The young man stepped forward and took her hand. Margot inhaled sharply.

"I spoke to your father about it earlier. I promise I will keep him safe."

Rachel jerked her hand away. "You can't promise that," she said, but her voice was weak. "You can't promise that at all."

"Rachel, darling," I said, "I won't tell you it won't be dangerous. But I assure you, we will take every precaution."

"And if something happens? If you run into something you can't handle? What if Zann shows up? You know he's here. You know he's looking for you."

"All the more reason for you to go with Henry and Margot. I don't want you to be in more danger than you have to be."

The look on Rachel's face combined shock and disgust. "You have some nerve. Some damn nerve. You're feeling guilty about something that happened thirteen years ago, and now you're taking it out on me?"

"Now Rachel, that's not fair," said Henry.

Rachel would have none of it. "You're damn right it's not fair. God, Henry. I would have thought you of all people would understand." She rounded on me. "The only reason you are even here, the only reason you are even free is because of me. Because of us. And now you want to go off on your own."

Guillaume put a hand on Rachel's shoulder. I half expected her to bite it off. Instead, she instantly softened.

"Rachel, it's okay," he said. "Your father knows what he is doing. We'll be fine."

Now it was Margot's turn. "I don't appreciate being left out of this decision. I didn't come all the way from Germany to tag along while you two fools risk your lives."

"You're right," I said, holding up a hand. "And the truth of the matter is that I have something important that I need you to do."

"All right," Rachel said. "I'm listening."

I sat at the table and spread out a map of France. "There is a monastery between Paris and Orleans, one of the oldest in the country. It is called Abbaye d'Crosse."

Guillaume furrowed his brow. "The Abbey of the Staff?"

"Precisely. The most reliable stories point to the catacombs as the hiding place of the Staff of Dzyan. But the catacombs are not all that old, in the grand scheme of things. Legend has it that the staff was kept at the abbey and revered as a relic for the better part of a millennium before it was moved for safe keeping."

"But if the staff was moved, what is the purpose of going there?" asked Rachel.

"Legends can be wrong. We must be sure. It may turn out to be a dead end, a waste of time. But it's an avenue of inquiry that we cannot ignore. I wish that I could go with you, but I fear the hour is short. Rachel, I need you to do this for me. I need you to use those investigative skills you were renowned for and learn what you can at the abbey. Who knows? Perhaps the staff remains there yet, or maybe the priests will know its resting place."

She fixed me with her eyes, staring hard. I feared she didn't believe me, that she would assume I was merely trying to keep her busy and that she would refuse the errand. It was true that I did not want her venturing into the catacombs. But at the same time, we needed to know what the masters of the abbey knew, and I trusted no one more to find out that information than my daughter and Henry.

"Fine. I'll go."

"Good. I've purchased three tickets for you, Henry, and Margot on a train that leaves in an hour."

Henry didn't like the fact that I was sending him away. But he didn't say a word.

"It's all right," I said. "Last week you thought I was dead. Now I'm alive. I don't intend on that changing anytime soon."

Rachel looked from Guillaume to me, and then she sighed, long and deep.

"Just be careful," she said. "I can't bear to lose you. Either of you."

Perhaps I was the only one to notice how Margot glared at Rachel, and I began to wonder if there was much I did not know going on between them, among all of them.

"Then it's settled. We meet back here tomorrow night."

* * *

Rachel gave me a hug before she left. There was little warmth. I believe the only reason she did it was in case I didn't make it back. After they were gone, Guillaume and I wasted away the day as we waited to meet our guide. "That could have gone better," Guillaume said. I suppose he was right, but my only thought had been that it could have gone much worse.

The man Marcel had sent was waiting for us in the lobby. He was tall and slender. A black man, probably from the Algerian or Tunisian colony. Perhaps Morocco. I had dealt with men of his nation during several of my expeditions along the African coast of the Mediterranean. I had found them to be reliable and efficient, and I hoped that he would live up to my expectations.

"Gentlemen," he said, bowing slightly to us both. "I am Nassim. Monsieur Dupont sends his regards."

"Thank you, Nassim," I said. "You can give him ours when we return."

He bowed again slightly and we followed him out the door.

"Monsieur Dupont tells me that you have a rather unusual request," he said. "It is not often that outsiders visit the catacombs."

"Outsiders?" said Guillaume as we stepped out into a cool Parisian night. "Surely it's not that often that anyone visits the catacombs, outsiders or not."

Nassim chuckled lightly. "You would be surprised, my friend. There are some in this city that have a peculiar obsession with death. A legacy of the war, I suppose."

We followed in silence while he led us deep into the warrens of Montparnasse. The casual visitor knows Paris as a city of broad boulevards and open space, a city of light. But off the beaten paths that tourists travel lie darker, older places, where furtive eyes stare from towering tenements to the artificial canyon floor below.

It was there that we went, stopping at a café that had no name. Nassim signaled to the man behind the bar, who nodded once in return. Then, without a word, we were led into a back room, empty but for a table and a single lantern that swung lazily from the ceiling, providing the only light. Nassim reached inside his coat and removed a roll of papers, which he spread out on the table.

"The catacomb system is vast," he said. "More than a hundred miles worth."

"Oh God," I said, "and we don't even know where to begin."

"Then perhaps your God favors you," Nassim said with a smile, "for I do. My youth was spent in Marrakesh, selling baubles to wealthy sons of the aristocracy with more money than they could spend in a lifetime. I learned quickly how to tell the difference between a treasure and a trinket. Monsieur Dupont found me, recognized my talent. Through him, I came to know the catacombs like most men know the streets around their home."

"And you think you know where we should begin our search?"

Nassim nodded. He pointed on the map to a square that meant nothing to me.

"Much of the catacombs are unremarkable. At least, as unremarkable as a city of the dead can be. But this area here, it is different."

"Different?"

"There are...whispers. Stories. They say things lurk within those tunnels. Things that walk when they should crawl. When I was a boy, my father told me that the wastes of the desert were to be feared. He told me that Allah dwelt with men and in the land of men. But the wilds, the deep, the tunnels beneath the earth, the places where human voices are stilled? That is where *they* dwell. The catacombs are the same. The remains of the dead keep men at bay, but that does not mean that nothing walks those halls. And in this area in particular, one can feel their presence. It is for that reason that those who have something to hide often hide it there."

"According to the information I have received, the staff would be buried beneath the catacombs themselves. Have you heard of anyone digging?"

Nassim leaned back and stroked his beard. "There are always stories, but about several months ago, word spread among those who work the trade that it would be ill-advised to venture into the catacombs for the foreseeable future. Others spoke of large groups of men descending into the tunnels. And then, of course, there were the murders."

I glanced at Guillaume and saw the same fear in his eyes that I was trying to hide in mine.

"Murders?"

"Killings of the most devious kind. The police have done everything in their power to keep information out of the press, but the street has many ears. Sacrifices. Women, cut from stomach to throat. Gutted alive."

It is a cliché, I suppose, to say that I felt my blood run cold. But I can think of no other way to describe it. The signs were clear. The cult of Nyarlathotep was not only searching for the staff, but they had attempted to raise their master, to bring him into our world, once again. And unlike that day in the Louisiana swamps, there was no one to stop them. Our mission had become all the more critical, and all the more dangerous.

"Whatever is going on in the catacombs," Nassim said, "it is no coincidence that it began at the same time as these murders. You are taking your lives into your own hands, my friends."

"Well," I said, "I suppose we had better get started then. Shall we?"

Chapter 24

The train carried us from Paris into the bright countryside of endless French fields and blood-red poppies. Away from the danger my father was facing. Away from Guillaume. I'm embarrassed even to write it down, but my heart aches when I think of him. This schoolgirl crush is maddening. But at least the feelings are returned.

The tension with Margot has reached a level of discomfort I have rarely experienced. It is palpable. Even poor Henry feels it, though he, of course, is utterly unaware of the source. Though I have known the girl only a short while, the sense of friendship I felt with her had grown to a quiet intensity, sealed by our shared encounters with danger and possible death.

That bond is broken now. She knows. As surely as if someone had told her. Call it intuition. Call it paranoia that happens to be right.

I'm not sure exactly what I should do. I know that I owe her nothing, that she has no claim over Guillaume, whatever her feelings towards him might be. And after waiting so long for happiness, I cannot surrender it because of misguided courtesy. Besides, Guillaume made things clear to me. She is a friend to him, and a friend only. Though I am beginning to wonder whether such a friendship can last. It would have been better for her if she had remained in Berlin.

We arrived in Abbeville-la-Rivière a little after five o'clock. The station was no more than a depot, and I was sure this tiny, idyllic village rarely saw visitors. In fact, there were no cars to be had.

"I suppose we walk," Henry said.

And walk we did, down the narrow, paved lane from the station. It did not take us long to find the town, not that there was much to find. Just a few shops and a government office, where Henry asked if anyone could direct us to the abbey.

"It's a mile down the road," Henry said. "Unfortunately there doesn't seem to be much in the way of cars for rent, so I guess we walk some more."

At least it was only a mile. If we'd had to go any further, Margot's eyes might have burned a hole in the back of my head. I tried to think of something to say, but nothing seemed sufficient. And so silence it was.

We reached the Abbey as the sun had already begun to set. Behind a simple cottage stood the remains of an ancient monastery that, in its day, must have been a majestic monument to the living God. But now it was a ruin. The central nave more or less remained, but other than that, there was only one great, towering wall that bespoke the glory of its past.

An elderly man was on his knees in a garden in front of the cottage, pulling weeds and tying off vines. He glanced up as we entered the abbey gate and smiled.

"Bonjour," he said. "Bienvenue, mes amis."

Henry spoke a greeting to the man in French. His smile never faded.

"Ah, my friends. You are Americans? We don't get many visitors this far from Paris."

"Oh, you speak English?" Henry said.

"Of course. I spent five years in a diocese in Maryland. I speak it passably well, if you will forgive my stumbles. My name is Father André, and it is my pleasure to make your acquaintance." He stood, wiping his hands on his apron, and we introduced ourselves in turn. "So," he said, "what brings you to our corner of the world this evening? The sun is setting, and it is not wise to travel rural roads at night, even in a place such as this."

The gathering shadows were indeed lengthening, and for the first time I considered that we would be making the short walk back to the village in darkness. It shouldn't have bothered me. Not at all, really. But there was much truth in the words of the priest, which also seemed to contain more than a bit of a veiled threat. But there was no such threat in his pale blue eyes or in his smile.

"Come, my friends. I was just about to make supper." He held up a bag of vegetables from the garden. "It is rare I have guests."

I glanced to Henry and then Margot—though she immediately looked away. There seemed to be little reason to say no. Perhaps we would learn something of the staff. "Of course," I said. He nodded once and walked into the abbey, the rest of us following behind.

The interior was sparse, with a modesty befitting a man of God. And yet there was a certain beauty in its simplicity.

"I apologize for the lack of accommodations," the priest said as he brought an extra chair in from another room. "As I said, it's not often that we receive guests. I have some soup on the stove, but it's not yet enough for us all..."

"Oh that's all right," I said. "We don't want to be trouble."

"No, no, no," he said, holding up his palms. "It will only take a moment. Please, just wait here."

"So," Henry whispered as the man disappeared into the kitchen, "what's the plan?"

"I don't know," I said. "I hadn't really thought it through."

Margot rolled her eyes. "It's obvious," she said, "that this was once a place of great honor. But that was a long time ago. There is a story to what happened here, and he will want to talk to us. He will want to share with us the history of this place. It is only human nature. He is like a man whose child has died. If you ask him, he will talk. But respect him. Don't play games."

I don't know if Margot and I will ever be on friendly terms again, but I certainly couldn't argue with her. There was something about the priest that spoke to me. He was a stranger, and yet he seemed as though he had known me all my life. If there was one thing my father taught me when I was young, it was to always trust my instincts. And my instincts told me that this man was a friend, not a foe.

He returned with a smile, a tray, five bowls of soup, half a loaf of bread, and a bottle of wine. "Please, my friends, gather around. So, tell me about yourselves and your travels," he said as he passed the soup around.

Margot and Henry both turned to me, and so it seemed the duty of explaining was mine.

"We were hoping that you could help us with something. Have you ever heard of the Staff of Dzyan?"

My words froze the old priest in his place. He looked at me with an intensity that I would not have expected from a man of his age. He seemed to be studying me, studying all of us, looking deeper into our souls than should have been possible. After what seemed like an eternity but couldn't have been more than a few moments, he nodded once. Then

Father André sat down and began to stir his soup. "You should eat," he said. "Then we will talk. I find in such matters it is better to have your strength before you begin."

The soup was delicious. Hearty and earthy, like something my grandmother made when I was a child. The wine was dark and rich, and I felt its potency from the first sip.

"From the vineyards beyond the old abbey," Father André said. "As there is power in the blood, there is also power in the wine. Treat that one with particular respect, and it will respect you as well."

I smiled. "Indeed."

It wasn't until our bowls were empty and our stomachs full that he spoke again. "Now," he said, as he gathered up the dishes and arranged them on the tray, "I suppose we can talk."

The sun had long set on the French countryside when the four of us gathered in the sparsely furnished main room of the cottage. Father André looked at each of us, but now with a caring, almost concerned, visage. "I can hardly imagine," he said, "what would bring ones such as yourselves all the way here, looking for the staff. And I wish you would turn away now from your quest and go home. For few who seek the staff find it, and all who find it leave it with a heavy heart."

"So you do know of the staff?" Henry asked. The priest merely nodded. "Then let us assure you that we do not seek it for our own ends."

"Then why seek it at all?"

"To protect it," I said. "From those who would use it to do evil."

"There are already men who have sworn themselves to that sacred duty," he said. "From beyond the shroud of time and memory, the Tzadikim Nistarim have protected the staff. And, when need be, used it to hold back the darkness." He sighed. "But if what you say is true, you certainly bring ill tidings. If agents of the strange dark one seek it, much blood will be spilled before this story is done."

I looked at my companions, but I found no comfort there. Margot had fixed the priest with her gaze and did not look away. Henry's eyes were downcast. In his experience, what the priest had promised would undoubtedly come to pass.

The priest's kindly, blue eyes turned to me. "And tell me, my child, what do you know of the staff?"

I shrugged my shoulders. "It's hard to say, I'm afraid. Legends, mostly. Rumors. Nothing concrete. My father told me once that some believed Christ Himself made it."

The old man laughed. "Yes, I've heard that story. That he twisted it together in the desert from cedar and pine and cypress wood. The same construction, incidentally, as the true cross. It's not surprising, really. Holy scripture," he said, gesturing to a beautifully illuminated Bible that sat open on the table, "tells us that those who believe without seeing are truly blessed. And yet, mankind wants proof, don't they? So whether it be the Holy Grail, or the Spear of Destiny, or the Shroud of Turin, the believers look to something concrete to cling to. For the men who wrote that legend, the staff was just another relic, something else to prove the divinity of Jesus."

"So you don't believe the staff really existed?"

"Oh no, no, no, my dear. I know the staff exists. I just believe it had existed for centuries before Christ was even born."

He reached over and picked up the Bible, flipping through it, almost all the way to the beginning. "Ah, yes," he said. Then he turned the book towards us.

There was an illuminated page, an image, as exquisitely rendered a piece of art as any that might find a place of honor in the finest French museum. It showed a great column of people trailing into the distance. They carried all their belongings with them on rickety carts pulled by beasts of burden. The great caravan traveled through a mighty canyon, but its walls were not made of stone. They were sheer cliffs of churning water, a sea piled upon itself in defiance of all laws of nature. And in the foreground stood a man, his arms raised high, holding a staff above his head.

"Moses," whispered Margot. The old man smiled.

"Yes, at the parting of the Red Sea." Then he began to read. "'And the Lord said to Moses, "But lift thou up thy rod, and stretch forth thy hand over the sea, and divide it: that the children of Israel may go through the midst of the sea on dry ground.'"

Henry leaned forward in his chair. "But how did Moses come to possess the staff?"

"The Bible tells us it was given to him by God when he charged Moses with leading the Israelites out of Egypt. But Moses was a Prince of Egypt, so it's certainly possible that he found the staff among the treasures of Pharaoh. Whatever the case, the staff would become the emblem—and perhaps the source—of his power. It was the staff that turned the waters of the Nile into blood. It was the staff that served as the sign of authority in the Kingdom of Israel for a thousand years, until it was lost when the Romans invaded Palestine."

"But not lost to you?" I said.

There was a twinkle in the priest's eye. "No, my dear. Not to me. And not to my order. When Rome fell, the staff was taken here, to this abbey, for safe keeping."

Henry gasped. "Then the staff was here? All this time?"

"Perhaps if you had visited a few centuries ago. For all things that rise must fall, even a religious order. So when the Revolution swept France, the rationalists launched a crusade, if you will, against religion. This was one of their targets. The ruins you see behind this cottage are all that remain of the old abbey. It was burned to the ground, the brothers who lived here, slaughtered. No, I am here to tend a small flock in the village, not to guard a precious relic. When the crown fell, the staff was moved once again, hidden beneath The Directory's very nose."

"In the Catacombs."

"Precisely."

"So that's that then," said Henry. "The staff is in Paris." Father André chuckled and shook his head.

"You should have learned by now, my friend, that the staff rarely remains in one place for very long. In the Great War, when the Germans came within sight of Paris, my order decided that it was no longer safe buried beneath the city. And thus, it was moved again."

"But," I said, "if the staff's not in the Catacombs any more…"

I looked at Henry and he at me, and our voices rang as one.

"They're digging in the wrong place!"

Chapter 25

Journal of Inspector François le Villard (Translated)
8 May 1933

There is a memory, one from long ago, when my daughter was very young, that goes with me every day of my life. It was from that time when her mind was opening, when she was beginning to see the world as it is, and from this new vision untold numbers of questions were born. She wondered, I suppose, why I left every day very early, only to return at night, often very late. It stuck with me, and I remember it exactly as it happened. She asked me, "Papa, where do you go to work?"

"I'm an inspector of the police."

"What does that mean?"

"Well," I said, surprised, as many a father has been, at how difficult it is to answer the simplest questions of a child, "I keep bad people from hurting good people."

Her little eyes grew wide in amazement.

"That's what you do every single day?"

"Every day," I said.

"There must be a lot of bad people in the world."

"Not so many," I said, not wanting to leave her in fear. "It is just that it is hard to do the right thing, and easy to do the wrong. And when people do bad things, it takes a lot of work to make it right."

"And that's your job, to make it right?"

"It is, *mon chéri.*" I kissed her on the forehead and led her off to bed. I have little doubt that she slept the sleep of the innocent that night, unaffected and undisturbed by the dark forces that move in the world. After all, she had her father to protect her.

But there are so many, it seems, that I cannot protect.

For six days, we have pursued what the Press has dubbed the "Butcher of Cour du Dragon." But in all their wildest imaginations, no journalist in Paris could conjure the truth of what happened that May-eve night in the Latin Quarter. I am scarcely sure I believe it myself.

The case began to break yesterday when I received a letter. It was unsigned, and how it came to be upon the desk in my office was as much a mystery as its author. In all of my days, with all I have seen, I have never felt my blood run cold in my veins, but as my eyes scanned that cursed missive, all the warmth seemed to drain from the world. It was only by some force beyond my knowing that I kept myself from destroying the letter, then and there. Instead, I have recorded it here, for posterity, though perhaps there are some things that mankind is better not knowing.

Inspector Villard. Do not look for me, for you shall not see me. Do not seek me, for you shall not find me. Hear me, if you have ears to listen. Only then will you know the truth, and only then will you know what you face.

This world is not ours, inspector. It never was. All cultures call for a conclusion to this existence. Every holy man who has ever put chisel to stone or pen to parchment has written of the end of all things. Or, at least, all things human. And if it were to happen, if we were to vanish from this earth, leaving nothing but our ruined cities and dark tombs behind, and if in the ages upon ages that followed, the epochs of time that passed the world by, a vastly inferior being that had never known man were to rise from the muck and the mire and stumble upon those stone necropolises, would it not go mad in the offing? Would not the cosmic truth be so great that its mind would simply break, dark insanity falling upon it?

We need not wonder, Inspector, for we stand upon the brink of the endless abyss, and the truth of the ages shall soon come to us all. Man was not the first to rule this earth, nor is he the greatest of her masters. There were others that came before, beings of such immense intellect and boundless hate that our minds are ill-equipped to comprehend them. And although they are gone, they left behind a promise to return.

For ten thousand millennia they have lain undisturbed, but the world has not forgotten them. They sleep. But they do not rest, and their slumber is not peaceful. They speak to us in our dreams. They are the voice in the night, the shadow that walks, the madness that haunts the broken mind. And although they reigned long ago, they are not diminished. They are the gods of old, the demons of religion, the haunters of the dark. And the nameless cults of lost antiquity worship them.

They worship one above all others.

If it is through the god of light that all things were made, it is through the god of darkness that all things are unmade. At the center of all chaos, across the fathomless void of eternity, in the swirling center of endless darkness, he waits, sleeping. And when he wakes, there will be worlds nor gods no more. Only he and those who serve him.

He has many names, the most-high god, though only one that is his own. The Canaanites of old worshiped him, believing that it was his will that his adherents were to offer the blood and burnt flesh of humanity—in the form of their firstborn. At the summit of lofty ziggurats, at the center of mighty cities, the screaming children of Sumeria were made to pass through the fires for Moloch, for Kesan, for Zanoni, for Azazel, for Chaos.

For the great god Azathoth.

For 30,000 years we have waited. For 30,000 years we have shed our own blood so that Azathoth might wake from his eternal slumber. And finally the time of his return is upon us.

But for him to rise, first must come the harbinger.

I am writing you this letter, Inspector, in the hopes that you can bring an end to that which I have helped set in motion. In the hopes that you can stop our order before it is too late. Even now, they search beneath your feet, digging into the earth, scouring the land of the dead for a grave. Not one of man, but of legend—of the eye of truth and the staff.

You have seen our work, how we opened the gate. You have seen the price we must pay. I cannot live with the cost.

You see, Inspector, it was I who bled her dry. It was I who sliced her open. It was I who cut out her eyes. It was I who tore out her still-beating heart, till the screams of my first-born daughter died away in my ears. Till her voice was silenced forever.

It was I who made the way for the return of He Who Walks in Shadow.

The letter ended there, as too, I believe, did the life of the fiend who wrote it. Whatever madness possessed him is not his alone, I fear. And so I must search the city of the dead that lies beneath this, the city of the living. I pray I find the answer to this riddle before more lives are lost, before more innocents are sacrificed.

Chapter 26

Journal of Carter Weston
July 26, 1933

Under the cover of night, we followed Nassim out of the nameless café, each of us clutching a knapsack containing canteens of water and two electric lanterns.

"The first man to explore the catacombs," Nassim had told us, "died of thirst after searching the dark for an escape for days on end after he lost his light. They found his body not ten meters from an exit. The catacombs are the city of the dead, and they will add to their kingdom from the ranks of the unwary."

We would be better prepared.

Entrances to the catacombs were many, but we were going to one that was little known and little used—better to avoid any unwanted confrontations. It was located in the Cimetière du Montparnasse, in an abandoned crypt. The theory put into practice by its creators was simple in its cold logic. How better to shuttle the dead into their new grave than through a tunnel in the midst of the cemetery? Untold multitudes were dug up and cast into that pit. It had been bricked up when the morbid task was complete, but Nassim and his fellow cataphiles had broken through and now used it for their nightly activities. We would be following in their footsteps.

It was a strange thing, creeping through Paris at night. Oh, how different a city feels when it is lit by the moon instead of the sun. How different when the night rules instead of the day. When Guillaume began to speak, I was happy to have something to break the tension. But then his words made me wish for silence.

"So Rachel's husband…"

His voice trailed away.

"He died," I said. "It's hard to say more than that."

"You know you weren't responsible, even if you did pull the trigger. Even in the short time that I have been with you, I have learned enough to understand that."

"I know that," I snapped. I was immediately embarrassed. I had not meant it as an attack, but I knew that was how it sounded. Or worse, as a defense. I sighed, and in the silence of a Parisian night, the magnitude of my sins seemed to overshadow all. "But Rachel feels differently. And maybe she's right."

"What do you mean?"

"There's so much about this world we don't understand," I said. "But one thing we know for sure is this—there is power in sacrifice. When it happened, when William died, well, we needed that power. We needed it for reasons far more important than ourselves. We had to decide. And what is the life of one man put against the fate of the world?"

Guillaume didn't answer me, and I found that even I was appalled at what I had just said. For many years, I had told myself that I had done what I must on that icy Russian steppe. That I had no choice. But now even I wondered if all those years ago I had seen it not as a necessity, but as an opportunity. If I had welcomed the chance to sacrifice the man my daughter loved, to harness the power of his death against my adversary. That was the thought that weighed upon me as we walked.

The streets were all but deserted, and few honest citizens ventured out. In fact, we met only two others—a man and his dog. As they passed us, the dog stopped, gazing up to study us. I caught the beast's eyes and had an uncanny feeling of recognition. But it was only for a second, before the gentleman said, "Come, Snuff," and they were gone.

All the while Nassim continued his steady pace. If he heard our conversation or noticed the others, if he even cared, he never showed it. His focus was on our destination, which we soon reached.

The gates of the cemetery were closed and locked, but there would be no midnight ascent up and over the walls. Nassim had a key, a benefit of keeping a close—if somewhat financially costly—relationship with the groundskeeper.

Upon our entrance, seemingly limitless lines of tombstones met our eyes. The granite sentinels shone white in the moonlight, keeping watch over the dead. Between the rows we crept, and even though the chance of capture or interference by the authorities was negligible, we stayed silent and we stayed low.

An abandoned crypt lay at the heart of the graveyard, and to any of those who passed it unawares, there was nothing that bespoke its sinister purpose, this gateway to the land of the dead, the empire of the shade. Only the name above the portal—or should I say the lack thereof—provided a clue. Whatever family crest had once graced that slab of stone had long since worn away, and I wondered what extinct line of French nobility had built this monument to last forever, to trumpet the glory of their name until the end of time.

Nassim pressed another key into the lock, and the great iron doors opened with a sound of metal grinding against metal that made the fillings in my teeth hurt. A black maw opened before us, a cold rush of air chilling me despite the warm night.

"I hope you're ready," Nassim said. He reached within his bag and pulled out an electric lantern, turning it on and shining its feeble beam into the tomb. Where once the sarcophagus would have sat was the beginning of a crude stone stairway descending into the depths.

"A week ago I was in a beer hall in Berlin. And now this," said Guillaume.

"It always ends up like that," I said. "You hunt your quarry where it lives. And this particular beast resides in the dark places of the world." I thought back to all the times I had found myself in this position, standing on the precipice of some great descent, or preparing to wander off into a forbidden desert, or set to climb a shunned peak on a demon-haunted steppe. If it weren't so serious, it would almost be comical.

"Stay close," said Nassim. I had no intention of letting him get away. Everyone is afraid of something. For me, ironically perhaps, it was the dark.

Like Dante of old, we began our descent, down into a deep place where the sun was silent. The roof above us was one of rough-hewn granite, and even in the pale light of the lantern I could see the dark stains left by burning torches from a century before. What brave men those must have been, walking into shadow with nothing but a flickering flame for comfort.

The air was still and cold, growing more so with every step we took. Before long, the outside world was but a memory. We were entombed, encased in a coffin of stone.

The stairwell ended in a low archway. We ducked underneath and into a larger chamber that ran off in two directions, one to our right and the other our left.

"This is the first of the old granite quarries," Nassim said. "There are hundreds of miles of tunnels down here. If you take the tunnel to the left, you hit the vaults, larger spaces where the Parisian youth like to go and drink absinthe. We go to the right."

I could not help but wish we were going left.

Nassim led on. In that dark, dank underworld, minutes seemed to stretch on for hours. One turn followed upon its brother, and we passed from one unremarkable corridor to another. Were it not for Nassim, we would have been hopelessly lost, doomed to wander until we fell dead of dehydration.

It was after one of a seemingly hundred turns that we first saw them. They filled the corridor, piled to the ceiling. Yellowing bones, moldering. How many thousands of souls did they represent? How many lives lived and lost, laid to rest only to be wrenched from the earth and piled like trash to be left behind forever?

"Come," Nassim said. "Our path takes us through there."

It was foul business. Again Nassim went first, crawling on his hands and knees over the bones, femurs rattling off the pile like stones as we went. More than once my hand sank to the elbow into the crumbling remains. Forward we slithered, my back scraping against the roof of the tunnel. I was as a man buried alive, a hundred feet below the streets, living what would have been most men's nightmares. But it was when I came to the end that I made a horrendous mistake.

The worst was over, and the pile of bones began to drop away. But as I was making my way, haste overtook me. I lost my balance and tumbled to the stone floor. A crack rang through the corridor. It was not a broken bone—either my own or one of the many others. It was almost worse; my lantern was shattered.

Nassim cursed in a language I didn't understand, but I joined him in the sentiment.

"You two stay close," Nassim said. "And be careful. The darkness is thick here already."

And he was right. With only two lanterns, it seemed that the shadows had become living beings that might swallow us whole. As we walked, it only worsened. I was beginning to suspect we might wander forever when Nassim came to a dead stop. Before I could ask why, he turned to us and put a finger to his lips. He leaned forward and whispered in my ear.

"I smell freshly turned earth."

He turned off his lantern. Then he gestured for us to do likewise. In Guillaume's eyes, I saw the same fear that was surely reflected in my own. That narrow beam of light was a life-preserver for my sanity. To imagine it shuttered was almost too much to bear. Nassim gestured again, and Guillaume hit the switch.

I have been in the dark places of the world before, and I have heard tales of men plunged into a Stygian night just as black as that which descended down upon us. But I had never experienced it myself. Never experienced the utter madness of the abyss. Not until then. I nearly screamed when I felt a hand on my own, and I prayed to the God above that it was Nassim.

He pulled us gently ahead, and I could feel rather than see Guillaume moving beside me. We tried to stay silent, even as we stumbled awkwardly forward. It was obvious, of course, that he wanted to make sure our lanterns didn't give us away to whoever was ahead. Still, I hated every moment of it. So when his light flashed on once again, it was like a thunderclap.

We were standing in a vaulted chamber. A dozen open holes were before us, the dirt having been recently turned. Tools, shovels, other equipment lay around the room, abandoned.

"It appears your speculations were correct," Nassim said. "Someone was digging for lost treasure."

Guillaume reached down and picked up a shovel. "And whoever it was left quickly. Wait, look at this?"

He held up an object that glimmered in the light of Nassim's lantern. It was a shell-casing. The light from my lantern glinted off a dozen more spread around the room. And then patches of earth, darker than the rest.

"Looks like whoever it was didn't go down without a fight."

"The Germans?"

"Actually, we were just about to ask you the same thing."

A half-dozen or more lanterns illuminated at once, and even before the blinding flash had cleared I had drawn my pistol, with Nassim and Guillaume doing the same. The sight of our weapons only made the grin on Zann's face grow wider. He gestured to the men who stood beside him, every one of whom was holding a sub-machine gun.

"I think, Herr Professor Weston, that you are outnumbered and out-gunned."

I pointed my pistol in his direction. "It only takes one, Dr. Zann."

"Yes, yes," he said, with a wave of his hand as if to dismiss it. "I suppose that is correct." Zann sauntered around the room, and we might well have been at an evening soiree, albeit one with guns trained on every participant. "But you would die, of course. And then what? What of your quest? Who would save the world, my dear Carter, if you were no longer around?"

"I suppose that means we are at a standstill."

Even that was a stretch. The Germans with Zann—military men dressed in suits that didn't fit them and did little to hide their true intent—were better trained and better armed. They would cut us down in a moment.

"It's a pity, really," said Zann. "All your knowledge, all your experience. Wiped away, and for what? Just think what we could accomplish together."

It was an exultation I had heard from him time and again. I found it no more convincing here, beneath the streets of Paris, than I had beneath the streets of Berlin.

"Does that mean you aren't surrendering?"

He barked out a laugh. "No, not quite. Just think, Carter," and his voice took on a feverish tone, a desperation that did not befit him nor his position. "Together we could find the staff. And the stone. We could bring this threat to our world to heel. We could both have what we want."

"So I take it that means you haven't found it then?"

"No, not yet. But we will. Do you think you can say the same? Look at yourself, Carter. You, a student, and your Negro. What were you planning on doing? Where were you going to dig? What if the members of the cult had still been here? My companions and I are civilized men. You are fortunate we found you first. But that's always been your way, hasn't it, Dr. Weston? Throwing yourself headlong into things? Without a thought or a plan? Without any idea what you will do when the moment of crisis comes."

"It's always worked before," I said.

Zann grinned. It was like a wolf showing his fangs.

"But it seems your luck is changing, doesn't it? It wasn't with you that day in Siberia. And it is not with you now."

He reached behind him, and one of the soldiers handed him a book. But not any book. *The* book.

"I suppose I should make it a habit of never letting this leave my sight," he said, "lest someone take it from me."

He stepped forward, flipping through page after page. I considered shooting him dead then. If nothing else, it would conclude his part in this sad story. But I knew to do so would end only in tragedy. Another would simply take the book, and no one would be there to stop him from doing whatever foul deeds it desired of him.

"Since you left me so unceremoniously before," he began, rubbing his hand across the back of his head, "and with a nasty bump I might add." He gestured toward Guillaume. "Was that your doing, young man?" Guillaume said nothing. "Pity, too. You were quite the student. In any event, I have been studying your old book, and I have learned quite a few things, things that I suppose I knew before and yet still did not quite understand. And one of those things is the power of sacrifice."

My face dropped, and Zann seized upon the expression. "Oh, yes," he said. "I know you are quite experienced in that area."

He gestured at the same soldier who had bought him the tome. But this time the young man returned with something very different.

She cried out as he dragged her into the chamber, even though her hands were bound and her mouth gagged. She had been weeping, as I suppose anyone would. For the briefest of moments, my heart sank into my stomach; I had thought it was Rachel. But no, she was someone else's daughter.

"My God, Zann..."

The darkness seemed to ebb and flow like the roiling sea.

"There is more than one god, Dr. Weston. You know that. Not all of them care for your sense of morality, but there is one thing they do have in common. They all demand sacrifice, and there can be no sacrifice, no power, without the shedding of blood."

We should have acted then. We should have done something. But we were frozen in place, as if the wisps of black smoke that had begun to coil around us were iron chains.

Zann opened the book, and the *Incendium Maleficarum* seemed to whisper to us all. In one hand he held the devil tome; in another, a knife. Words poured from his lips—German of course, for the book always took the language of its master—and the knife glowed with a pale luster.

Lanterns dimmed. I felt weak and sick, and bile rose in my throat. It was as if the blade was draining the energy from the room—including, and perhaps most importantly, the life-force of us all.

The blade went to the girl's throat. Her eyes went wide. Zann wasted no time. Metal sliced through flesh. Blood arched from an artery, painting the ancient soil and polished granite of the catacomb floor, and the acrid smell and taste of copper filled our nostrils and our throats. It was over as quickly as it began. Zann's man released her, and she slumped to the dirt, her life pooling in an expanding crimson circle.

"You should have taken my offer, Dr. Weston. There is no limit to what we could have done together. But it does not matter, not in the end. You see, Carter, I don't need you anymore. The book answers to its master, and that master is me."

Zann held out his hand, and we could sense the energy pulsating through the room. I felt suddenly empty inside—thin and hollow. But not simply empty. *Emptied.* Like I'd been carved out and poured onto the floor.

The feeling rolled over us like a wave, and then we could see the cause of it. The air shimmered with an alien force. Zann flicked his wrist and a column of hot, putrid air roared by my face. Nassim stumbled backwards as if struck. I started to reach out to him, but when I saw his face, God help me, I recoiled. His eyes rolled into the back of his head. His ebony skin burned away, flaking off his skull like burning paper. It was a blessing when he fell to the ground, dead.

Zann's cackle shook rocks from the ceiling, and I knew that whatever good had once been left inside of him was gone, whatever soul he had, lost. There was no bringing him back now. Not that it mattered. We would die in that tomb. Whether struck down by bullets or his power, the end game was the same.

"Such a pity. No one will ever find you, Dr. Weston. No one will ever care. You will die, and I will rise."

Zann held out his hand. My vision blurred. My chest tightened, and I felt as if his fingers were coiled around my heart. What happened next came in the blink of an eye.

The room dimmed. Then there was a flash and the sound of shattering glass, and I was plunged into night. I wondered if this was what death was like. Then I heard Zann's roar. Only then did I realize that the lights—all the lights—had burst as one.

"Carter!" I heard Guillaume cry. "Run!"

The words had not but left his mouth when the flash of gun fire and the bark of angry rifles filled the chamber. I stumbled backwards, falling on my back as a bullet nearly clipped my scalp, slamming into the wall and raining broken granite and choking dust upon me. I couldn't see. I couldn't hear. Where Guillaume had gone, I didn't know. I rolled onto my stomach, firing my pistol wildly in the direction of a muzzle flash. A pained scream told me my aim was true. Using the shots that answered back as my only illumination, I crawled in the direction of the archway that marked the chamber's exit, daring to stand and run only when I reached it. I was followed out by Zann's mad cries.

"You'll die down here, Carter! You'll never find your way out of the dark!"

Of course, I knew he was right. But that was a concern for the near future, not the immediate one. I stumbled into the darkness, driven by fear and horror and the same thing that spurs all men to desperate action—a fool's chance at survival.

I ran until I'd made so many twists and turns that I no longer believed that Zann still pursued, if he ever had at all. That's when the darkness truly closed in on me. Thick and eternal, in those endless passages that never would see the light of the sun, not even a thousand millennia after mankind had passed from the earth. I thought of the man Nassim had told us of, the one who had gotten lost in these same catacombs, who had shambled through the night until madness and hunger and thirst took him.

I stumbled upon the mound of bones we had passed hours before. If the passage through the moldering remains of those long dead had been unpleasant before, it was a nightmare now. I crawled through the skulls and mandibles and femurs, made somehow more horrifying because I could not see them. But at least there was reason for hope. If I had come upon the bones, then perhaps I might still find a way out.

That hope was soon dashed, for there simply were no other landmarks to guide me. I clung to the wall, creeping forward, even in my desperation wondering what had become of Guillaume. Was he already dead? Or was he, like me, cursed to a slow demise in this unlit tomb? But still I struggled on. There was nothing else to be done.

It seemed that I wandered for hours, but in truth, it may have been no more than a handful of minutes. In that titanic shade, I could imagine eternity. Then there was a moment when I wondered if I had truly gone mad. In the distance, I thought I saw a shimmer, a flash of light. I ran towards it, and if it were a demon of the pit waiting to devour me, so be it.

It was no mirage. The light grew brighter, clearer. I ran as hard as my tired legs could carry me. I heard voices that seemed to call me. I fell forward, bathed in, and blinded by, light. My vision cleared, and I was staring into the barrel of a gun held by a man, tall and yet elegantly built, a thick mustache defining his face and a bowler hat sitting on his head. Another man held Guillaume, his arms bound tightly behind his back. At least he was alive. The man who held the gun looked down at me and smiled. In thickly accented and yet impeccable English, he said, "Ah my friend, it appears God has answered your prayers. You will have plenty of time to thank him in prison."

Chapter 27

Journal of Carter Weston
July 27, 1933

Once again, we are on the move, headed north by train to Normandy. I write today with an officer of the law seated across from me. The circumstances by which he came to be here and those surrounding our departure from Paris—like so much of this journey—are worth recording for posterity.

The gendarmes who took us into custody in the catacombs were, in fact, inspectors with the La Sûreté Nationale. As always it seems, we went from the pan to the fire.

For a long while we waited underground as they debated whether to delve deeper into the tunnels to seek what they assumed were our compatriots and collaborators. My pleas and protestations of a German infiltration fell on ears that, while not deaf, certainly were unwilling to hear. When I mentioned the infernal power that Zann possessed, well, I lost whatever credibility I might have retained.

Finally the man with the mustache, the one who was obviously in charge, walked over to where Guillaume and I sat and squatted in front of us. He removed a silver case from his pocket and cracked it open. He pulled out a cigarette, offering the two of us one as well. He shrugged his shoulders when we declined, snapping the case shut. He lit the cigarette, breathed deeply, and blew a column of smoke towards the cavern ceiling. The process seemed to go on forever.

"So you say there are others?"

"Yes," I said, "for God's sake, that's what I've been telling you."

"And you say they are Germans."

"Yes."

"I saw them as well, Monsieur," Guillaume said.

The man nodded several times. Then he took another draw on his cigarette, this time breathing out the smoke through his nose.

"And one of them was a wizard, correct?"

I frowned. I was sick of being in this place, afraid that at any moment Zann and his henchmen might come around the corner and kill us all, police or not, and I was not well pleased with this Frenchman's lack of faith.

"We're wasting time. The longer we wait the closer they get to accomplishing their goal."

"The Germans."

"Among others."

He began to laugh. "Yes, my friend. We've noticed an unusual amount of activity in the catacombs over these last several weeks. Just last night, we rounded up a small army of your companions. They didn't go as easily as you, I must say. They certainly didn't run right into our arms. But now we have you, too, and you are going to help us get to the bottom of whatever is going on down here. Now come on. I tire of this place."

For the first time, I agreed with him.

* * *

The clacking of typewriters and the ringing of telephones drowned out all thought as I sat and waited in a holding cell to speak with someone who could release us. My requests to be put in contact with the American consulate were met with laughter and French curses. Guillaume, himself a citizen of the Republic, lay on a cot in the corner of the cell. He seemed as unconcerned as one could be in such a place.

"The wheels of justice grind ever so slowly here," he said. "And there's nothing you can do to quicken them. When they are ready, they will come. Until then…"

There was nothing more to be said. So we sat, and we waited.

It seemed hours before the detective who had interrogated us in the tombs returned.

"I trust you find the accommodations up to your expectations?"

"Quite," said Guillaume, who did not bother to rise from his repose. The detective simply ignored him.

"Come with me, *professor*." He opened the door to the cell, and I followed him down an inner hallway to a windowless chamber.

"So does this mean you believe me?" I asked as I sat in the only chair.

The detective lit a cigarette and leaned against a wall. "About your identity? That's a funny thing, monsieur. If you are indeed Professor Carter Weston of Miskatonic University, then you are most assuredly deceased."

"It wouldn't be the first time."

"And with all the strange things we have seen in Paris these past weeks, I admit I am inclined to believe you." The door opened and a man appeared with another chair. The detective thanked him in French and took it. As he sat, he said, "It's a tactic, you see," gesturing towards the chair. "Normally during an interrogation we make the accused sit while we tower above them. It adds to the intimidation factor."

"But this is no ordinary interrogation."

The man shook his head. "No. Though I do need to find out everything you know about what's going on in my city." He held out a hand. "Inspector François le Villard." I took it.

"The late Carter Weston."

"Something tells me your demise is related to the incident in the catacomb. Care to share that story?"

"You won't believe it."

"When you finish," he said, "I will tell you some of what I have seen, and I think you will agree that I am ready to believe quite a number of things."

So I did tell him. I told him about the *Incendium Maleficarum*, about the power it possessed, and of Zann's desire to have it. I told him about my kidnapping, and my rescue in Germany. And finally, I told him of the ancient beings who once ruled this earth, and of those who would return them to power. He listened in silence, his countenance never changing. If he disbelieved me, he did not show it. In fact, I was quite certain that he put his faith in every single word.

By the time I finished, his third cigarette was nearly gone. He snubbed it out in an ashtray, but not before he lit another.

"Earlier this year," he said, "in the spring time, there was a terrible murder in the Latin Quarter of the city. Officially, it is unsolved, though I believe I know who was responsible. It was a horrible crime, even as these things go. But what made it even worse was that it was a sacrifice of some kind, a ritual killing."

"Was the victim a girl?" I asked. He nodded. "Killed with a knife?" He nodded again. "And how was the body arranged?" He seemed to age a decade in that moment, as his mind turned back to the scene of the crime.

"She was sliced from her throat all the way down, her internal organs removed. Her arms were spread apart and tied down, like so." He illustrated with his own arms, holding them as wide as he could. "The same with her legs."

"Like a St. Andrew's Cross?"

"Yes," he said, apparently thinking of it for the first time. "Yes, exactly like that."

"Were there any markings, any writing?"

"The room was covered in symbols and runes, all in her own blood, none of which were familiar to me in the least."

"But were there any that stood out, any that you noticed?"

Inspector Villard gazed down at his palms and furrowed his brow. I knew that he was transported back to that place, that he saw it as clearly as if he stood in the darkened chamber once again.

"There was one," he said. "I remember it for several reasons. It was drawn beneath the altar on which we found the body, but in chalk, yellow chalk, instead of blood, which made us suspect that it had been made first. And it was very large, and very strange."

"Can you tell me what it looked like?"

He reached into his pocket and removed a sheet of paper and a pen. He began to draw, describing what he saw as he did. "It was a great circle," he said. "Unbroken, but for a single point at its base. In the center was something even stranger. An object that appeared to be three spheres melded together, as if one circle but with three lobes. It was an unnatural thing, and for reasons I cannot fully explain, it hurt my eyes to look upon it. Actual, physical pain." He ceased drawing, studied the image for a second, and then nodded. "Yes, I think this is it. Very close indeed." He held up the page for me to see. I recognized it instantly and gasped, for it was the stuff of legends.

"The three-lobed burning eye…" I whispered.

"Then you know it?"

I shook my head. "I know of it. But I've never seen it, at least in anything other than obscure writings and legends, even in all my years and all my travels. To tell you the truth, I never thought it was real." I picked up the paper, and it seemed to vibrate in my hands. "I'd like to send this to a colleague at Miskatonic, just to make sure I'm right. A second opinion you might say."

"Of course," Villard said.

"But you should know this," I said. "If the people we are dealing with have completed this ritual, and if this is the sign that marks them, we are in far deeper danger than you could ever have imagined."

Chapter 28

Journal of Henry Armitage
July 26, 1933

We arrived at the headquarters of La Sûreté Nationale early in the morning, having departed Abbeville-la-Rivière on the first train out. While we returned to Paris empty-handed, our journey had been far from a waste. In fact, I had learned several important pieces of information. Obviously, the knowledge we gained as to the location of the staff was critical to our quest, and we were desperate to alert Carter who, even at that moment, was deep beneath the surface of the city, risking his life in a search that was entirely fruitless. But I also became painfully aware of a deep rift that had developed between Rachel and Margot. What drove it, I could not say. All I knew for certain was that if we were to divide our forces again, I would not suggest sending them off together.

When we returned to our hotel, neither Carter nor Guillaume was there. Rachel was beside herself, as was Margot. For different reasons, most likely. Or perhaps for the same, at least in part, which might explain the hostility. We debated our next move. Pursuing the men into the catacombs was madness. We would never find them, and we would likely become hopelessly lost ourselves. And so the only options that were before us were to wait or to go to the authorities.

"Carter and I have seen many things, gone on many adventures together. And I can tell you this, the police were never our friends.

They don't take kindly to treasure hunters or troublemakers, and we fit the bill for both."

Rachel paced the hotel room from window to door, her hands clasped in front of her as in prayer. "Yes, I understand that," she said, "but I don't think I can stand to sit here and wait, either."

"This is not about you." Margot veritably spat the words.

"No, it is about my father, and about Guillaume. And right now they could be lost in the darkness, with no light to guide them and no hope of escape. Or perhaps worse, Zann could have found them. So you tell me, should we sit here and do nothing? Hope for the best? Or should we go to the police?"

So we went to the police.

What we found, we did not expect, even if perhaps we should have. The police had indeed heard of Carter Weston. In fact, they had him in custody at that moment. And to make matters even more interesting, he was in the process of being interrogated by the lead detective for that precinct on suspicion of murder.

At least he was alive.

I demanded to see him, and the man behind the counter turned to his compatriot and snickered. He said something in his native tongue that I did not understand, the words apparently not part of a classical French education. He looked back to me and said a single word in English—"No."

"But I am his lawyer," I lied.

"His lawyer?"

"Yes. And unless you allow me to see him at once, you'll have a diplomatic incident on your hands!"

It was bluster and bull, of course. The officer looked me up and down as if he was studying an alien life form, but I suppose I can strike an intimidating figure at times, though less so perhaps than in my younger days. He tore off a sheet of paper and picked up a fountain pen.

"Name?"

"Henry Armitage," I said. "Esquire."

He wrote it out with a flourish and then disappeared into the back room. A few excruciatingly long minutes later, he returned with another man of evident authority.

"Dr. Armitage," he said, holding out his hand, "a pleasure to make your acquaintance. You know, in some jurisdictions it is a crime to impersonate an officer of the court." I blanched, and his amusement was evident. "Do not worry, doctor, I have no intention of arresting you. Come, you and I and your friend have much to discuss."

I followed him into an interior office where Carter was leaning over a table, his arms spread wide, examining a number of photographs. He looked up at me as I entered and said, "You're going to want to see these."

They depicted a crime scene, one as horrific as anything I had ever before seen, in war or in peace. Carter moved a large photo of the victim to the middle of the table.

"See the precision of the cuts," he said, tracing his finger down what had been the center of her body. "At first glance you might say she was ripped apart, but that's not right at all. This was a cold, calculated dissection. Opening up the skin and the abdomen, breaking the sternum, and pulling her ribs apart so they could get to the heart. And of course, all of it while she was still alive."

"And how do you know that?" the detective, whose name I had learned was Villard, asked.

"A ritual like this requires a living victim. Blood is critical, as is the removal of the organs. But just as important are the less tangible forces that are unleashed. Fear. Pain. The inevitability of death. Only the living can provide that. No, she felt every minute of it, right until the end."

"I wish I could say you were wrong," Villard said. "But our expert concluded the same."

I had picked up several other photographs, if for no other reason than that I could not look at the dead girl anymore. They were pictures of sigils, runes, and other strange forms of writing that had not been seen for a thousand years—and never in the civilized world. But one in particular chilled me to my core. I glanced at it, just from the corner of my eye. The photo was underneath a pile of others, and I might not have noticed it at all were it anything less significant. I slipped the photo out, and horror replaced curiosity.

"Oh, my God. It's exactly as it was described."

"Indeed," said Carter. "I sent a copy to Dr. Foster, back at Miskatonic, to see if it could be anything else. I'm not sure what will surprise him more. Seeing that, or seeing a letter from me."

"Not to take anything away from you, my friend, but frankly, resurrection is less remarkable."

Villard cleared his throat, and we were stirred from the stupor of our own fascination. "Obviously, we knew that the murder was related to a ritual of some kind, but your Dr. Weston claims to know this cult, and he claims that they are responsible for the excavations in the catacombs. Do you agree with that opinion?"

I let the photo fall to the table. "I do. There can be no doubt of it." I pointed to the arcane image. "The three-lobed burning eye can be the sign of no other."

"Does this cult have a name?"

"It does not. Nor has it ever. It was nameless and forbidden long before Stonehenge rose on the plains of Salisbury or your ancestors entered Chauvet. And what they seek to bring about is no less than the end of the world and the beginning of a new one."

"Or an old one, depending on how you look at it," Carter said. "Which is why it is critical that we get back into the catacombs and find the staff before they do."

"The staff's not in the catacombs." Carter and the detective both turned and looked at me, and in Carter's eyes was nothing but dejection.

"What?" he said.

"But I know where it is. Our trip south, it turns out, was not a total waste."

"Then where?"

"An island, off the coast of Normandy. In a monastery of some sort."

Laughter interrupted us. "You mean Mont Saint-Michel?" said the inspector.

"Yes, you know it then?" Carter asked.

"Of course, my friend. It is as famous as it is beautiful. But beauty can deceive. It is a fortress, an island surrounded by the sea at high tide and quicksand at low. If they possess what you seek, they will not give it of their own accord. Which means you will have to steal it. And that is impossible."

"Alone perhaps. But not with your help."

"Me?" he said. "My friend, I am an officer of the law, not a thief."

"And a man who has served as long as you knows well that sometimes the only way to save the law is to break it. You won't be able to stop Zann, not officially at least. You won't catch him, and if you do, he'll hide behind his diplomatic shield long enough to be our undoing. And he has ears everywhere. If we know that the staff has come to this place, then he will know it, too. We have the advantage of time, but it is one that is slipping away even as we speak."

"You speak of this staff as if you think it is not only real, but has real power. And this cult as if you think they could actually accomplish their aims. We have been treating this as a case of madmen."

"And that is why you haven't found them. They are mad, but they are not blind. They see the world as it is, and as it will be—if they succeed."

"What if you are wrong? What if you are just as deluded as they?"

"I pray every night that is the case, inspector. I am far more worried that I am right than that I am wrong. But either way, if you help us, you will find the men responsible for your murder. They are after the same thing we are."

Villard weighed Carter's words, and I could see the balance shifting in his mind. He stepped forward and picked up the picture of the woman, the girl really, and I knew that his eyes had fixed on her face, on the expression of unimaginable pain and terror that was etched upon it and would stay etched upon it until the conquering worm had eaten it away.

"I want to tell you something, something I have never shared with another. Something I thought I never would. I thought it was my own madness, my own personal insanity. But now, for the first time, I think I understand it."

Carter looked from him to me, but he said nothing. Villard did not notice. He was somewhere else, altogether.

"When I was a younger man, I went into the field with my brothers to defend my country against the invader. I was with the XXX Corps on the banks of the Meuse, at a place they call Verdun. It was there that I learned that civilization is a lie, a mask that we wear to cover our own savageness. There I learned that men could do unspeakable evil to other men, that there was no limit to our callousness, to our hate. But I tell you this, and I tell it true, it was no mud-filled shell hole or tangled mass of barbed wire where I saw the true darkness that surrounds this world. As awful as the war, I learned then that there are things far worse."

Chapter 29

Letters from Lieutenant François le Villard to Mademoiselle Marguerite Deraismes (Translated), February 18 – March 21, 1916

My dearest Marguerite,

How I wish that I could see you again, if even for a moment. I know you are with me always, and when I close my eyes, it is your face I see. Sometimes I think that I catch a glimpse of you, walking amongst the fog and iridescent mist beyond the trenches, as if your spirit has traveled from Étretat to be with me as you sleep safely in your bed. But then the cannon fires and the earth quakes and my reverie is chased away.

The battlefield is no place for a dreamer.

There are those who would tell me that I should not so freely share with you the things that I have seen, the things that I have feared, the deaths I have almost died and may yet face. With the deepest respect, they are fools.

I know you worry for me. I know that it eats you away inside. Is it better to lie to you, to deny to you the truth? You have seen the death notices in the papers. You are no fool. And that is why I love you. So until that day comes when you tell me you wish not to hear of the things I see, I shall deliver them to you.

As clearly and truthfully as I can.

* * *

When I dream, I do not dream of war. I do not hear the cannonade. I do not see the arcs of fire. I do not feel their heat. Their crash does not shake me. I do not know where I go, precisely. Only that I am away. That I am absent. Without leave. Where there is no muck and mire. Where blood and stagnant water do not mix and mingle. Where the mud does not flow like a narrow sea, where death does not guard the shore.

That is my dream. Life is my nightmare.

* * *

There are rumors circulating among the men. I hear them, even though they speak only in hushed tones which drop to silence when I am nearby. There are times I wish I was an enlisted man. Soldiers may follow a lieutenant into fire and death, but they will never truly trust him. Still, I hear what I am not meant to.

They say that the Germans know they cannot win, that these endless lines of torn earth will never break. One might mistake this lack of confidence as a positive development, but such rumors seldom are. The men whisper of a new plan, to bleed us white. To deal death in such numbers that our will to fight is broken, even if our lines still hold. And they say that is why we have been sent here, to this place called Verdun.

To be bled.

* * *

The rain came down in torrents. The fog that rose up from the bog that lies between the lines was so thick that if the Germans had marched a division across the mud-sea we would not have known it until they were driving bayonets into our chests. But nothing moves out there. Nothing marches in the howling wind. Still, we wait and we stand guard. The rain pouring, soaking uniforms and men's souls. The water pools at our feet, eating away at them. Rotting them from the inside, while the rats are forced from their holes, scurrying along the edge of the parapets, grown fat and slow from the flesh of the dead.

My eyes have become accustomed to the darkness. To move in daylight is to invite death, and we have become creatures of the night. The pacifists and the philosophers say that war turns men into animals. They are wrong. War makes monsters of us all.

* * *

The Germans hold the high ground. Our aerial reconnaissance reports that they have placed artillery upon those heights. From there they will rain down fire upon us. And we will try to take those hills to stop them. Against that insignificant mound, the flower of France shall dash itself until we wash it away in our blood.

* * *

They came for us at midnight, rising up out of the mist, fire like dragons' eyes. We had been expecting them, and yet we were not ready for expectations to turn to that horror.

Every evening we had waited, eyes peering into the shrouded night, wondering much, seeing little. I had command of a three-man Hotchkiss crew, and all of us peered over the barrels of our machine gun, certain that what the mud slowed and the barbed wire stopped, we could kill.

That was the plan from command, at least. Let the Germans come. Let them weaken themselves. And then we would counter, break their lines, take the hill.

I wonder how many such flights of military fancy were formed in the bowels of command bunkers along the front. How often generals and colonels pushed imaginary units across imaginary lines to imaginary goals with a sureness that the real men they represented would somehow turn that fancy into fact. Would turn chalk symbols on a blackboard into gains on the ground. Would turn a pin pushed into a map into the end of the war.

The Germans had maps, too. And they were just as careless.

So we waited. Some might think that the waiting would dull the senses, that day after day and night after night of anticipation would lead to complacency. Not so, not there, not in the trenches. Every night, our nerves bristled, electric with the coming fight. We stared out over that endless dead plain and longed for daylight.

Tonight, though, should have been safe. The rains had fallen all day, and we doubted, in our hearts if not in spoken words, that the enemy would come. The fog was thick upon the field of battle. Nothing moved there in the swirling mists, at least, nothing we saw.

But they were there. Creeping along. Crawling, when they should have walked. Beneath the death-shroud gray fog.

Then they rose as one.

At first, we did not see them. We had stared so long into the darkness that our eyes were masked, as if covered in scales. Then we saw the light, and the scales fell away.

I'll never know, of course, what the others saw in that moment. No doubt that vision was for each man's eyes alone. All I know is this—in an instant, No Man's Land erupted in fire.

There were several hundred of them, perhaps a thousand feet from the parapet, spread down the line as far as the eye could see in either direction. They stood like Prometheus, each with one arm above his head, fire in his hand. Or that is how I saw them, at least, as gods come to earth, to illuminate the night and cleanse the battlefield of the muck and the filth with which we had covered it.

Every man in the trenches stood dumbstruck by what we witnessed. But it was no angel, no god, no deliverer. It was death.

"You fools!" I shouted, as much at my own stupidity as at my men. "Kill them!"

But it was too late. From the hills above, German artillerymen had zeroed in their guns. The flares the soldiers held above their heads gave them the ultimate marker. I didn't even get off a shot before the first shell fell. Instead, I grabbed my machine gunner and threw him to the ground.

The first shell exploded a hundred yards down the trench. Close enough that I saw men torn to pieces, close enough that I could hear the screams of the dying. But not so close as to put us in danger. That would come later. The first shell was the last one I really saw. There were too many that followed too quickly.

They crashed down like bolts from the thunder god, ripping apart our lines, bursting eardrums, shattering bone, shredding skin. A man cannot think in a moment of horror like that, and in my mind's eye I saw a kaleidoscope of images, flashes of my past, both familiar and unfamiliar days. A field behind my family's home on a summer eve. A girl at the Exposition Universelle, a flower in her hair. The sun half-obscured by clouds. A wooden stick, swirling in a whirlpool. Around and around and around. But never down. You, on the night of our wedding, your skin glistening in the moonlight, the half-smile on your face filled with love and lust in equal measure.

Thunder was our world, and in the maelstrom men screamed. Some called to their God, to their mothers, while others shouted words in tongues primeval, left-over languages long forgotten by the conscious mind.

How long did the shells fall? Was it minutes? Hours? Perhaps days, for if the sun had risen and fallen in that mind-shattering span I would not have known it, nor felt its warmth upon my face. You will never know, thank God, what it feels like to believe that every second could be your last and to expect that the next one will be.

But I did not die, and like a storm that rolls across the plain and into someone else's future, the thunder ceased. Of the men who lived, some cowered in the trenches, unwilling to believe that it had really ended. Others pulled themselves up, their eyes void of all understanding. But most started to celebrate. They had survived, and their cries of joy might have reached all the way to Heaven.

Fools.

I grabbed my gunner up from the pit in which he lay. He shook in my hands, and I am ashamed to say that I struck him across the mouth to calm him. I could think of no other way, and that act of violence brought him back. "Man your weapon," I said. Then I blew the whistle hanging from my neck. Even in their reveries, to that unmistakable signal they responded. Many turned to me, so conditioned were they to answer to that sound.

"Prepare for the attack!"

I saw it in their eyes, the recognition—the bombardment was only the beginning.

The racket of rifles clacking along the parapet filled the air. From the rear came reinforcements, men pressed into action as the generals realized what was coming. With them, the stretcher carriers, Charons of the battlefield, the bravest men I have ever known.

The trenches had become smoking pits. For as far as I could see the left line was shattered, and men were working to rebuild the walls in the precious few moments we had. The right was secure; the guns had overshot. It was a blessing, but I knew those further back in camp had suffered for our good fortune.

We gazed into the smoke and the haze and the darkness. The only sounds were of picks and shovels, of shouts of men to dig faster.

In the end there would be no time. The roar of shouting erupted before their guns did.

Then it was chaos and sound and shooting and blood and death and fire and madness. A man in battle is no longer a man. He does not think as a man thinks. He does not fear as a man fears. He becomes a machine, an animal that acts on instinct and training, that kills without regret, that dies without knowledge or consideration.

The storm-driven sea of Germans crashed upon the rocks of our lines. My gunner fired without ceasing, as I fed him belt after belt of ammo and poured the contents of several canteens upon the barrel that glowed red-hot. I threw back grenades without thinking. I killed men at point-blank range. I faced death more times than I can recall or could ever have imagined. Hours became as minutes, and it was only when the sun broke above the plain of dead and dying that I knew how much time had passed. The attack was over.

* * *

I have heard the most remarkable story, and I must share it with you, even as I now question the wisdom of our agreed-upon candor.

As is custom, those of us who survived the attack were rotated off the front line for a few days of relative relaxation in the city of Verdun, if one can rest with the sound of the guns always in one's ears. It is perhaps unsurprising that the only place where one might find a reprieve from the battlefield is the local tavern.

One night, when a storm hid the noise of cannon fire with heavenly thunder, I stumbled upon the story which I now relate. I had entered the tavern, intent upon nothing more than a glass of wine before I retired. It was a rustic place, the ceiling blackened by decades of pipe smoke and oil lamps that still hung from rafters. They swung gently, as if softly touched by the tremors from the fall of each shell miles away. Shadows danced upon the walls, and I followed them to a gathering of men, all of whom I knew well.

They were surrounding a sergeant, Nicholas Couchet, a man whom I had come to know as not only a fine soldier but as a loyal friend. And yet there was a feverish look about him that I did not recognize and did not like. The fire in his eyes burned with a quiet intensity, the lines of his mouth quivered, and I knew that whatever he spoke of now to these men was not something he would have so freely shared with me.

As I approached, he fell silent, and the men about him began to scatter, as those caught in imprudence are wont to do.

"No, stay," I said gently, "I didn't mean to interrupt." Something of my words or my demeanor must have calmed them, for I saw the tension relax in their shoulders as they allowed themselves to fall back into their seats. Only Nicholas still seemed nervous.

"Lieutenant," he said, "to what do we owe the honor of your presence?"

I pulled out a chair and slid into it. My glass of wine was full, but their tankards of ale were empty. I turned to the bar and ordered another round for them all.

"That's very kind of you, sir, but the night has grown old, and I best be making my way."

"No, no, Nicholas, please. Stay at least until you finish your drink. Besides, I noticed that you were regaling the men with some tale, and I thought I might hear it myself."

He glanced to either side of him, but if it was in supplication to his fellows, none of them stepped forward to save him.

"It's nothing that would interest you, sir," he said. "Just gossip amongst the enlisted men."

"And since when have you and I stood on rank? Let's have it. I could use a distraction."

He drew in a breath and sighed long and deep. That fire came back into his eyes, but this time I recognized it as fear.

"I've always respected you, Lieutenant Villard, and I suppose I've taken the notion that you respect me too, as much as a gentleman such as yourself might have such feelings toward a man like me. And I hope, after I tell you what you want to hear, that you'll still respect me."

I nodded, now both unsure of what was about to be revealed to me and somewhat unsettled by the possibilities.

"There are rumors spreading amongst the men," he said, almost in a whisper. "Stories, mad ones I would say, did I not know the sort who have related them, had I not seen some of the evidence with my own eyes."

He must have detected a look of concern flash across my face, for he paused then, and I had to urge him to continue.

"Go on."

"Something walks in No Man's Land," he said. "Something that the bombardment awoke. Something that shouldn't be, but is."

I was, of course, incredulous, but the look on Nicholas's face—his eyes wide, his skin blanched, his eyebrows raised high—cut off any thought that this might be a jest. More serious concerns presented themselves, that perhaps Nicholas had been broken by the bombardment, that a career spanning decades and dressed in the highest honors might have come crashing down around him.

"I know what you must be thinking, sir," he said, "but in my days I have seen enough to believe that there are things beyond our ken. Things that neither you nor I can understand, that they do not teach in universities and that cannot be found in books. At least, none that any Christian would dare to read."

"All right," I said. "Just what have you heard?"

"It started after the first bombardment, the one that you so honorably endured. They say that there has ne'er been one of its like, not in this war or any war to ever scar the face of earth. Something was uncovered, or awoken, or some door opened that was always meant to stay shut. But whatever the cause, strange things have started happening all along the lines."

"What sort of things?"

"It started with a mist," he said, "a fog unlike any that the men had ever seen. It crept across the broken fields when the battle was over, but it glowed green with its own light, even on a night when there was no moon and the stars were shrouded in cloud. They thought at first it was a weapon, some gas the Germans had released. But it came and did no harm to man nor beast. But it shone with that devil's fire, lying thick and putrid on all the land."

Of this one thing, I could not argue, for I had seen the green fog before our unit was relieved. "I assume there was more to it than unusual weather," I said.

"Aye," he said, "much more. Private Étienne, tell the Lieutenant what you saw."

A rosy-cheeked lad who could not have been more than sixteen if he was a day stepped forward, his cap clutched in his hand.

"It's all right, lad," Nicholas said. "Just tell it true."

"The day after the battle," he began, his voice cracking as he spoke, "two German officers came to headquarters under a flag of truce. They wanted to know what we did with the bodies."

"The bodies?"

"Yes, the Germans who had been killed in the fighting."

"I don't understand."

"They were missing, you see. When the German stretcher bearers went into the field, they only found a handful of men, far fewer than there should have been. Far fewer than they had expected, given their losses. And some of the ones they did find were, well..."

He looked down at his hands, and I noticed for the first time that they were shaking. Nicholas slid a tankard of ale over towards him, this child. He took it and gulped it, almost greedily.

"They were mutilated," he said finally. "And not like you would expect. Not from bullets or even bombs. From something else they couldn't explain. The Germans were very angry. They said that we had violated every law of war and human decency. The commander denied it all, of course. He threw them out, and told them that the next time he saw them he'd have them arrested."

"Which is understandable," Nicholas said. "Who would believe such a thing? But three nights ago we launched an offensive against the heights, to take the German guns. The results were..." Nicholas glanced at the men, mostly boys, who surrounded him and remembered his place, "a good beginning. But our losses were also steep."

The young man piped up again. "The stretcher bearers went out as soon as the ceasefire was called. Most of them were very busy. All but the ones in Quadrant C. In C, there was no one."

"No one?" I said.

"The commander thought it was the Germans, retaliating for what they said we had done with their dead and wounded. He said that they had done it on purpose to spite us. But I'm not so sure."

"Why not? Would you put anything beyond them?"

"No," he said, "of course not. But there was no time. Not to carry that many men away. Whatever took them did so quickly and quietly. Like a spirit."

"Or a demon," someone chimed in from the back.

"Or a monster," said another.

"Oh, come now," I said. I was unnerved, but I have seen many things in this war to unnerve me, and I have come to understand that the only real job of an officer is to never show his fear to his men. "This is a German ploy. They know they cannot break us with arms, so they will break our spirit instead with tricks and stories of ghosts in the darkness."

"Perhaps," said Nicholas, and I could tell that I alone truly believed it. "But watch yourself out there, Lieutenant. There's more to fear in No Man's Land than German bullets."

* * *

I must be brief. Our unit has been ordered back to the front lines to prepare for an attack on the heights. I don't have to tell you, my darling, what that means. I love you. I love you with all my heart, with all my soul. And if this is to be my end, then I will die with your name on my lips.

* * *

I have seen the darkness that haunts men's dreams, and I pray for the dawn.

I am writing from a shell crater deep within the dead zone, halfway between our lines and the Germans'. A boy named Joseph once lay beside me, shot through the throat. He is dead now, but it wasn't the bullet that killed him.

The army arrayed at dusk, miles of men and guns, bayonets gleaming in the dying light of the last day for so many. Row upon row of helmets, like corn in a field, stretching forth forever, awaiting the thresher.

The attack began at twilight.

We poured across the broken field, the mad shouts and hurrahs of boys fresh from the cities cut short by the *rack-y-tac-tac* of German machine guns. Sappers cut barbed-wire and blew hardened positions. Artillery shells filled the sky and crashed down ahead of us. Rangers hit machine-gun nests, and raiders dropped into forward trenches and slashed and stabbed and lobbed grenades.

Forward we pressed, as bullets passed and men died and the ground grew sodden with the tramp of a thousand feet and the gentle rain of blood. We reached the German heights. We went no farther. All of man's greatness, all of his genius, all that he has harnessed and achieved, distilled into the fragmentation grenade and the 8mm cartridge and the Big Bertha heavy-artillery gun.

Our lines faltered, then stopped, then broke. The bugles sounded. The retreat began. We fell away, a receding wave. Back, back, back.

Halfway home, between Heaven and Hell, I caught a round in the shoulder that spun me like a top before it passed through my flesh to bury itself in the dirt. It carried me forward with it, throwing me into the shell crater where I now lay. Joseph, bless his foolishness, turned to me. He started to say something, to check on me, I suppose. But a German somewhere pulled the trigger on his gun a split second earlier, and the words were drowned in lead and gore. Joseph's throat exploded. The artery within pulsed, and a stream of blood arched through the darkness and splashed into my face, stinging my eyes. Joseph collapsed beside me, his hand to his bleeding neck.

I was covered in it, Joseph's blood. I could taste the metallic tang deep in my throat. I staunched his wound as best I could, and we waited, his life slipping away and me trying to hold onto it. I prayed for daylight. The sun would rise, the battle would end, and the stretcher men would come. We had only to survive the night.

The sounds of war faded, save for the occasional crack of a sniper's rifle. Enough to keep us down, even if Joseph weren't bleeding to death in my arms. Eventually, even the sniper fire died away. It was just Joseph's ragged breathing and the sound of my own heart.

Hours passed. I could not help but notice that the same strange, green fog I had witnessed days earlier had grown thick and unyielding on the battlefield. I had little time to consider it, though. With every passing moment, I worried that help might not make it in time for dear Joseph. And then something happened that made that fear seem like the obsession of a child.

It began with a sound which I am not certain can be described, but I will do as best I can. It was a clicking sound, like claws on a tile floor, or scales sliding across each other. I tried to tell myself it was some kind of weapon, something we had not seen before, but it was a lie. I knew better. And whatever it was, it was coming closer.

I peered over the edge of the shell crater. Something moved in the mist.

I blinked, wishing it away. And yet it was there, and inching toward us. It stayed low and tight to the ground. It slid across the earth like the shadow of a Nieuport flying above at mid-day. But there was no light to cast that shade. It was a thing, like a man lying upon his belly, slithering, the blackest cloak ever put through the loom trailing behind.

I stared at it, stupidly, unable to take my eyes off of that specter, that ghoul. And then what I perceived to be its head tilted up, and it looked squarely upon me.

I dropped, sliding down the slope of the crater wall, praying to God that it had not seen me. The silence closed in. My heartbeat thundered with such violence that I was afraid whatever was out there could hear it. When Joseph moaned beside me, I am ashamed to write I drew my pistol, though what I intended to do with it I cannot say. To hush him perhaps? Even if I were so selfish, I would have been equally foolish. In that hell-quiet my gun would have sounded like thunder.

In the end, it didn't matter.

A moment later, it was upon us. It rose above the edge of the crater, a thing like a man in form only. Its hands were claws, skeletal and ragged. I might say that its face was something like a corpse, but even that would not do justice to the horror I beheld—noseless, its mouth a gapping maw, what passed for eyes burning like flames in its skull.

It swept down the ledge, and I did fire my gun then, though the bullet either passed through it or simply did nothing to stop it. It fell upon me, and the stench was such that I could not draw a breath. It crawled along my body, slithering like a snake. It seemed as though it breathed deeply of me, its face mere millimeters from the wound in my shoulder. Then it drew away sharply, and, fixing me with its gaze again, I would swear, were it not madness made manifest, that it said something.

Joseph, poor Joseph. It noticed him. It spun away from me, sliding across the ground. It breathed deeply again, but this time it did not hesitate. It fell upon the boy. He screamed only once, but even that was quickly stifled. I could not move. I could do nothing to save him. And I could not look away. I watched as this thing seemed to suck him dry, as blood and viscera and God knows what else splattered across the shell crater.

As quickly as it began, it ended. The thing slid over the top of the crater, carrying Joseph with it. Then it was gone.

I sit here, waiting, alone, for dawn to come. I know I made a solemn vow to you that I would hide nothing from your eyes. But in writing this letter, I know that this is too much. I will take this story with me to my grave, and if anyone finds these words here in this field, know from their telling that No Man's Land is not empty, but that it is no man that walks upon it.

* * *

Journal of Henry Armitage, July 26, 1933

Long we sat, listening to the inspector's words, and the sudden hunger that struck me as he finished spoke to the hours that had passed. But in that time, Villard had become one of us.

"They found me the next morning, of course. Delirious, gibbering about things that walked in the mist and devoured the dead and the dying. No one ever believed me, but I know what I saw. I spent a few weeks in a field hospital and then was promoted, for gallantry. I bided the rest of the war at headquarters, away from the front, away from the fighting.

"So I can tell you one thing for certain, gentlemen. I do not know if what you say is madness or prophecy. But I do know this. Evil is real, and it is horrible, and it must be confronted and defeated. So if you go forth on this crusade, then I will march with you, even if it is to our own destruction. It is a march I have made before."

Carter stood and clapped him on the shoulder. "Then we go together to Normandy, and we go now. Once more into the breach, and we will either return with the staff, or we will not return at all. On those shores, the fate of mankind will be decided."

As we stood to leave for the grand station in the heart of Paris, I turned back to the inspector, for I had one last question.

"You said that the creature spoke to you, before it took your friend."

"Yes."

"What did it say?"

The inspector glanced at his hands, and I suppose I was surprised that they were not shaking. Then he looked back at me.

"I can't be sure, of course, for I only heard the barest whisper. But I thought it said three words...

"'Not...yet...ripe.'"

Chapter 30

Excerpt from *A History of the Mont Saint-Michel* by Dr. Alan Ulfman,
New York: Columbia Press, 1875

...The Mont was, in fact, uninhabited for much of prehistory. When the Romans arrived on the coast of what they called *Gallia Lugdunensis Secunda* in the century before Christ, they found nothing but a rocky outcropping, some kilometers from shore, surrounded by water at high tide and great, barren salt flats in the eventide. Roman engineers quickly recognized its strategic value. In addition to the island's formidable natural ramparts, the churning seas provided a deep and impassable moat during daylight hours.

When Julius Caesar consulted with the local tribes as to why the island remained void of human dwellings, he was met with stories of superstition and dark lore that matched anything he had encountered during his conquest of the known world. In his *Commentarii de Bello Gallico*, Caesar wrote the following[29] —

---

[29] This particular passage was most difficult to locate, as it is not included in extant original Latin texts of *Commentarii de Bello Gallico*. Why it has been excised, I do not know. The existence of a record of Caesar's visit to the island that would become *Mont Saint-Michel* was widely known among historians, but thought lost. I was able to locate the following passage in a rare translation produced by a Dr. Charles DeWitt of Cambridge University in the early years of this century. I cannot, of course, vouch to the accuracy of the translation. The footnote contained herein describing the translator's unfortunate prudishness is his own.

The elders of the tribe would not dare venture to the island, nor would they send guides to accompany us. In fact, they would barely speak of the place. Bribes of gold were utterly ineffective, and even threats did not suffice to move them, not until we swore an oath that we would burn their village to the ground—with them in it—if they did not unveil the mystery to us.

The tale they told was one of black magic and dark artistry that even the great god Pan would have found debaucherous and unholy.

The island was sacred to the tribe, as it was the place where they believed their god, Nyarlatorix, would one day descend from the heavens to reclaim lordship over the earth. This would occur on the festival night that their holy men called Belenos, which came every year at the midpoint between spring and summer. The villagers, however, apparently feared their god far more than they loved him. In fact, they had made it their custom to build huge bonfires on the night in question, as it was their belief that the god could not abide the light.

But once every nineteen years, when Belenos fell on the death of the moon, the greatest fears of this primitive people were realized. For on that darkest of nights, the black ships would arrive.

The villagers were intolerably vague on this point, and even the mention of the black ships seemed to drive them into a frenzy that bordered on madness.

The ships were manned by a crew unlike any that dared ply the wild waters of the northern sea. The strangers came clad in strange raiment, faces hooded and cloaked. They spoke no language, at least no language that the tribesmen could discern or ever heard uttered. But words were not needed. It was simply understood on some primal level what must be done, what was required.

When the black ships came, a sacrifice was due, a girl chosen. The cruelty of what was described to me that night curdled my blood—and I am a man who has seen and dealt my share of cruelty. The villagers believed that the power of the sacrifice was directly proportional to its depth. It was not enough that one should die. The girls of the village were gathered, all those who had never known a man. This group was gradually reduced. First, to those who were already betrothed. Then, to those who were the only children of their parents. Then to those who were born of a mother too old to produce another child. The greater the sacrifice—the greater and more irreplaceable the loss—the greater the power.[30]

Once the girl was selected and night had fallen completely, she would be taken across the narrow reach to the rocky prominence, while the villagers huddled in fear behind the flimsy walls of their hovels, lest they look upon a sight not meant for human eyes. But the walls of their huts would not, could not, hide them from the shadows that danced in some unnatural violet light that seemed to roll in waves from the island, could not close their ears to the tenebrous beating of drums and maniacal piping that floated on the wind, could not shield them from the all-seeing, unblinking eye of Polaris as it shone down hatefully above it all.

Their description of the sounds in particular troubled me, for they were not at all what I expected. I inquired as to whether they were ever buffeted by the screams of the girls they had so willingly given up to sacrifice. On this point—unlike so many others—there was complete agreement. They had never heard a scream, nor a moan, nor so much as a word from the poor girl, whatever her fate may have been. Such a mystery gave me pause.

When the sun rose on the day that followed the sacrifice, only smoke and dust remained. I asked the elders if the god Nyarlatorix ever returned, if they had ever looked upon him. Wide eyed and haunted they shook their heads. "The stars were never right," they said. "But if they were, the seas would boil, the rock would melt, the great city of

---

[30] Caesar recounts various methods employed to disqualify the girls at the time of this reaping, including examples of incestuous debauchery which, for propriety sake, I do not include here. Those who wish to inquire into the matter further are invited to study the text in the original Latin.

old would rise from the depths, and mankind would be extinguished...or worse."

During this discourse, there was a boy standing at the edge of the firelight. In my previous travels, I had often seen the look of a man who knew more than he was letting on, and his was clearly such a case. When the elders had finished I allowed them to disperse before I slipped away to meet the boy in a more private location. I found him standing at the water's edge, as if he had been waiting for me. He spoke freely and without coercion. He divulged a story, the horror of which I could not have imagined.

He had snuck out the last time the black ships had come, when he was but a child, his curiosity overriding his good sense. Upon the island in the distance he observed a great and strange light, one unlike any he had ever seen. A raging fire was the only comparison he could make, but one of purple flames that undulated and pulsated instead of flickering. One that gave a cold, harsh light that sucked the heat from his body, even at that distance. It illuminated the night, and he could make out shadowed figures, dancing and throbbing wildly about the circle of flame. The stars turned to blood, and the sky changed. The boy had no knowledge of the heavens, no names for the constellations that wheeled above. But from his words, I had little difficulty divining what he saw, and such was the power of his story, I saw it, too.

Gone were the familiar, the comforting, the shimmering diamonds that I had come to know and love, that had guided me in my many conquests in the north. But there were stars. Oh yes, there were stars. Just not the pin-points of light I had come to expect. No, these were great orbs of fire.

The boy's words painted a picture of the impossible. According to him, some stars shone clear and bright as the sun, and yet their light gave no illumination. Others seemed to pulse, to beat like the heart of some great beast. Still others seemed to dance together, twirling in great pinwheels as he watched. And yet more would fade in and out, disappearing completely, only to return a few seconds later.

Of one thing he was certain—there was nowhere on earth with that sky. Nowhere.

Somehow, he told me, it was not the sight of such things that was the worst. For while he stared upon them, above him came the sound of massive beating wings, and the wind ripped at his body as a great shadow passed over him. I wish he could have told more, but in that moment, as whatever foul beast soared above the boy, he recounted that he had slipped into oblivion. He had fallen into a stupor. When he awoke, the sun had risen, and only lingering smoke remained on the island to confirm the presence of the visitors.

The black ships were gone.

The bravest of my men scoffed at these tales, as we had all scoffed at a thousand lesser myths in days gone by. Two of them set off across the salt marshes at low tide, determined to uncover whatever treasures the frightful tales might be meant to hide. One moment, they were laughing and singing. In the next, they had vanished beneath the shifting sands. Despite our best efforts, we could not save them. They were taken, unintended gifts to whatever dark power ruled that accursed island.

And so we abandoned that place, leaving it and its infernal legends to the mists of time.[4]

---

[4] While the best available sources transition at this point to other aspects of the Gallic campaign, there are some—of questionable authenticity—that maintain Caesar did not so easily abandon his assault on the myth-haunted island. In one likely apocryphal tale, Caesar is able to discern a path through the shifting sands by way of consultation with another local, an outcast shunned by his tribe for his ability to commune with dark spirits. Upon setting foot on the island, Caesar is then confronted by Nyarlatorix himself. This entity, whom Caesar refers to as "He Who Walks in Shadow," makes unto the ambitious general a proposition—he will give him dominion over all the world as well as the eternal glory that comes with it if he will but perform one task—take his legions to Egypt and burn the library at Alexandria, destroying an ancient artifact sheltered therein, one of some esoteric power. Caesar agrees, and thus ends the story.

History tells us that the terms of the agreement were fulfilled. Alexandria burned, and Caesar's name ascended to the heavens. And yet, the great man was struck down, on the eve of his complete triumph.

* * *

DeWitt's translation ends here, at least as regarding the Mont. No other record of Caesar's writings, extant or partial, is known to contain this fascinating excerpt. It is believed that if such a chronicle ever truly existed, it is now lost. Most scholars have concluded, however, that DeWitt fell victim to an elaborate hoax.

In any case, the small island remained desolate and unoccupied for another five centuries, whatever tenebrous stories that hung about its shores cloaking it in a seemingly impenetrable shroud of mystery and foreboding—that is, until the arrival of the Merovingian kings heralded a new dawn for that benighted coastline.

The Merovingian were fervent devotees of the cross, but their pagan roots were not so distant that they did not still know much of black magic and its nameless antecedents. So when the great king Clovis sought to conquer the isle—and perhaps harness its power— he would do it not with armies and swords and shields, but with the emblem of his God. So Clovis built upon the Mont a holy temple, a Christian abbey that grew into a monastery, and also grew in power and influence, until finally it came to be the majestic spired mountain of God we know now.

And yet, while the monks do not speak on it, it is rumored that to this day, the men who dwell upon the rock face have never forgotten the island's dark history…

Could it be punishment for some failing on his part? Indeed, one source records that before the great library was put to the flame, Caesar removed one item—a simple wooden staff that he intended to be an heirloom of his reign and his line. Perhaps this was the relic that Nyarlatorix sought to have destroyed, and thus also became the cause of Caesar's ultimate downfall. But what became of the staff? Sadly, the texts are silent on this point, the answer lost to antiquity.

Chapter 31

Diary of Rachel Jones
July 27, 1933

We arrived in the tiny hamlet of Beauvoir as the sun was fading to darkness. The great orb dipped into the sea, and the outline of Mont Saint-Michel burned in the sky, its pinnacle pointed at the celestial heavens like a flaming spear driven into the waters.

I had been eager to arrive, for in a moment of naïve stupidity, I had cornered Margot in an empty cabin, desperate to ease the tension that was growing between us. How foolish could I be?

"We didn't ask you to come into our lives," she told me. "We were happy. I was happy. As happy as I have ever been. The day I met Guillaume was the best of my life. The day I met you, the worst."

What does one say to that? Protestations of love, of the hole in my own heart filled, they all seemed so pointless. Insulting even.

Ugh, rereading what I've written so far makes me ashamed. The men out to save the world while the women bicker over a boy's love. How clichéd.

Yet there's no time for such emotional trivialities now, as our assault on the Mont is due to begin before the sun next rises. Inspector Villard has proven quite resourceful. We had not been in Beauvoir for more than a half hour when he led us to a small pub in the center of this quaint and picturesque town. There we were to meet a man, a sheep-herder by the name of Alain. He apparently knows the salt marshes well.

"He says he grew up here," Villard translated, as the man spoke only the barest amount of English. "That he and his brothers would play on the flats at low tide when they were younger, much to their parents' distress." Both men laughed at that. "Now he herds sheep that feed on the grass that grows in the salt marshes. He says we should dine on some, that it has a unique flavor." Alain made a gesture meant to convey the gastronomic delights we could expect to experience.

"Maybe later," said my father. "Can he take us across?"

Inspector Villard nodded. "Yes. He says that the high tide has only just passed, two hours or so ago. The next low tide will come early tomorrow morning. At 2:30, 3:00 A.M. Perfect for us."

"And what then? After we cross the marsh, how do we enter the fortress?"

Inspector Villard turned to the man and said a few words in French. Alain listened and then began to nod vigorously.

"He says that there is a back stairway, one that is used by the men of the village to deliver supplies. It leads to an elevator, a sledge of sorts."

Alain smiled and began to make hand over hand motions.

"Apparently, we will board the sledge, and he will pull us to the top using a rope and pulley system."

Henry groaned. "Sounds safe."

"So that's it then?" my father said.

As if in answer, Alain leaned back in his chair and took a deep pull from his pint.

"Yes," said Villard, "that's it."

"Well, there's no reason for us all to go. We'll divide up again. Villard, you and I will go up with Guillaume. Henry, you stay behind with the girls."

"Now wait a second," I said, in no mood to be treated like a child— or worse, consigned to the periphery because of my sex. "I think we have proven ourselves more than capable over the last few weeks. And besides, you are going to need all the help you can get on this one. I'm coming with you. And that's that."

My father began to object, but then Guillaume, sweet Guillaume, interrupted.

"As much as it pains me, I have to agree with Rachel." Margot rolled her eyes. "We don't know what we will face. She can fight; I've seen it. And Margot can be a terror." Of that, I was certain. "We need them."

Henry nodded in agreement. My father looked to Villard for support, but he only held up his hands. "They are in your charge, monsieur. You must decide. For my part, I wish only to see this thing done, and in that I believe they could provide invaluable assistance."

My father audibly groaned. "All right," he said. "All right. We all go together. But for now, I suppose, we wait."

And so there we sat. Customers came and went. Regulars all; in fact it would not surprise me if the entire populace of that tiny village visited the pub at one time or another during the night. We watched them, were entertained by them as the minutes seemed to crawl by. Or some of us watched them, I should say. Villard, Alain, my father, even Henry had drifted off to sleep in chairs or on the floor in the dark, somewhat quieter corners of the place. The three of us—Margot, Guillaume, and I—we could not even begin to think of rest. I suppose it speaks to the darkness those men have seen in their lives that, in the face of a momentous event such as the one before us, they are able to attain peace.

Margot, for her part, did not stay in our company long. She drifted away from us to be alone with her thoughts. I wish there was something more I could do. But the simple fact of the matter is that there is nothing for it. Nothing at all. And as much as I hate to admit it, annoyance is rapidly replacing pity, no matter how guilty I should feel about what has transpired.

"Are you scared?"

Guillaume broke me from my omphaloskepsis, just in time too, lest I had fallen into a state of such self-obsession I might never have escaped.

"No, not at all," I said, but before I had even gotten it out I saw the doubt in his mischievous eyes. "All right, perhaps a little."

"I suppose it does come with some danger. But I have faith we will come through."

I smiled at him, but then his countenance darkened ever so slightly, and so too did mine.

"Are you all right?" I asked.

"I just want you to know," he said, his eyes downcast as if raising them would have simply required more strength than he had ever possessed, "if anything happens, that I love you."

"Oh, Guillaume," I said, taking his face in my hands and lifting it so that his eyes could meet mine. But then I hesitated. I'm not sure why. Something came over me, some moment of brutal honesty that had to escape. I found myself searching the room for Margot, until finally I found her sitting in the shadows at the end of the bar. "Guillaume," I said, "I care for you, and when I think about the possibilities for the future I can barely contain my joy. One day I may love you, as you say you love me. But right now, that girl over there cares for you more than you know. So if you are speaking from your heart tonight, just in case it is your last opportunity to do so, perhaps you should talk to her, as well."

Guillaume looked from me to her, while I searched his eyes for the rejection, the hurt, that I did not intend but he might have suffered nonetheless. I did not see it. In fact, I saw something else, something I could not quite place, as if the gears of some machine were in motion. I admit, it confused me. But then it cleared, and I felt foolish for my over-analysis of a man who must be awash in a sea of conflicting emotions. I leaned forward and covered his hands in mine.

"It will be all right, Guillaume. Everything will be fine. I promise."

A shadow flickered across Guillaume's face. It was nearly imperceptible, so fleeting that I wasn't even sure it was real. Then he smiled. "I know, Rachel. I know." And I believed him, for that was the look I perceived, an almost mocking sneer of utter confidence. "Now I think I'll take your advice," he said, gazing at Margot. He patted me on the leg and rose. My eyes followed him, and my heart went with him.

The night fades away, and I should rest. I feel that the next few hours will determine the course of not only my life but perhaps the lives of us all.

* * *

I cannot write. Even though I know I should. I cannot. I see it when I close my eyes.

I am undone.

Someone else will have to record what happened in this accursed place. For the future, for posterity. For something greater than me.

But perhaps there won't even be a future. Not anymore. Not after what we have done.

Chapter 32

Journal of Carter Weston
July 28, 1933

The monastery is quiet as the sun rises over the channel, but even the first rays of morning cannot lift the gloom that has descended upon us all. I shall record what happened on this accursed rock as best I can, for whatever posterity may remain.

We left the pub in Beauvoir under the dark of a dying moon. None moved in the streets of the hamlet, as the hour had long since struck when good people would be upon the roads. We crept through the shadows. What did we fear? Perhaps we already felt the crawling fingers of evil spreading around our throats.

We reached the salt flats at low tide, and even in the dim light of a bare crescent moon they shimmered in the darkness, beckoning us to come to them, like the sirens of old. Tricking us into believing that we would find sure footing there. Fortunately, Alain knew better.

"Follow him closely," Villard said, interpreting both Alain's words and his gestures. "Step where he steps. And be very careful. The sands are treacherous, and they will seize you in an instant."

It was an admonition we were in no mind to ignore. So we followed, each footfall landing where the person in front of us had just strode. Were anyone watching, could anyone see, we would have made for a macabre spectacle. I could think only of the lines of wounded in the War, blinded by German gas, hand clasped on the shoulder of the poor fool in front of him, trusting that wherever he led was somewhere that they all wanted to go. Such was our faith in Alain. If he was not true, if his skills were less than he had led us to believe, then a suffocating death awaited us all.

The wind whistled across that desolate plain, and the sting of sea-salt and sand threatened to blind us. On those winds rode a storm, and we had not quite reached the half-way point in our journey when roiling clouds joined the great mountain of stone before us in blotting out the sky. With the moon and the stars—feeble lights though they might be—obscured, and the village of Beauvoir having long ago snuffed its candles and electric bulbs for the night, the shroud that fell upon us then was as complete as in the days before God said let there be light.

The occultists speak of the full moon as something to fear, believing that the orb at its most luminous commands the minions of evil. I must imagine that those who hold such views have never huddled in utter darkness, prayers for a single spark of illumination going unheard and unheeded.

Alain, however, must have the eyes of a cat. For even as we stumbled blindly, he remained true. When we reached the stone walls of the citadel, it seemed I breathed for the first time since we had stepped upon the flats.

"The sledge is in the rear," said Villard. "We must go around."

Even though our path took us scrambling across moss-covered boulders, this part of the journey went quickly. The sledge broke into view, a mass of hulking wood that at first I mistook for another large stone. My eyes followed the rope that ran up and into the dark void above. Hundreds of feet above. I thought to myself—how truly desperate we are to do this, to look into the face of such ultimate madness and go forward with it anyway.

Alain said something in French and Villard nodded. "He says for us to climb into the sledge's basket and he will pull us up. We should come out in the store room beside the kitchen. From there, we are on our own."

"He thinks he can pull us all the way *to the top*?" Henry said. The doubt in his voice reflected what we were all thinking.

"Faith, my friend," said Villard as he climbed aboard. "The pulley is designed to carry much heavier cargo than us. Besides, we have faced worse dangers, no?"

It wasn't the most reassuring thought, but with our prize so close, there was nothing else for it. I followed behind him. The rest joined, even Henry. We seated ourselves, backs against the shallow walls of the sledge, and all said our silent prayers.

Alain began to pull. Hand over hand, and we started to rise, foot by foot. The sledge climbed the wall. The angle grew steep, and gravity pulled us toward the earth below. Rachel, who had avoided me so studiously before, could not help but slide towards me as the climb continued. I held her tight, and she did not fight against me. Fear had overcome anger.

Our steady rise continued. Even as our height increased, I could make out no lights in the total darkness beyond. It was as if we were diving deep beneath the waves even as we ascended, into some abyssal sea of endless night.

And yet still, we rose. My eyes were fixed upon the walls of the monastery above, and within them there seemed to be an area of darkness somehow less solid than the rest. It was only when we came within reach of that black square that I realized why; this was the opening into which we would pass.

The sledge lurched forward one last time and slid to a stop in front of that cavernous darkness. Villard reached up and flipped down the locking hook to hold us in place. From his jacket pocket he removed a revolver with which he gestured at me. Henry and I pulled our weapons as well. Guillaume, Rachel, and Margot followed suit. On this adventure, we were traveling well-armed, care of the French police.

Villard led the way, and the sledge rocked gently like a boat on the waves as he stepped into the castle-monastery beyond. He stood on the edge, peering inside. When he signaled for us to follow, the girls and Guillaume entered, with Henry and me following behind.

A low fire died in a hearth in the wall, its glowing embers providing the only light to this room that appeared to double as both a kitchen and a storehouse. Villard turned to me and said in a whisper, "If we can avoid the monks and have your prize, all the better. I have no desire to engage in a confrontation with them."

"Nor do I. The staff is a relic of great significance, both historical and ecclesiastical. It would be kept in a place of honor, likely at the summit of the monastery. I think we will know its resting place when we see it."

"I certainly hope you are right. We don't split up. We stay together, even if it takes more time."

"Understood."

Villard took point. He moved forward in the orange glow of the firelight, towards a staircase that wound upward. Where it ended, none of us could know, but the general direction was correct. And in times like those, that is all one can hope for. The staircase ended in another open room, also deserted. Along the walls, which rose to a high vaulted ceiling, were bookcases; this was the library.

Gilt lettering on well-worn leather shimmered in the flickering firelight. There were names I recognized, and a shudder, a thrill of anticipation even, coursed down my back. These were ancient books, most thought lost before the great library of Alexandria was even built, much less put to the flame. *De Vermis Mysteries, Cultes des Goules, Ars Magna et Ultima.* On a table by the fire sat a scroll, held open by shards of obsidian. I caught only the merest glimpse of the angular writing, the jagged text, but enough to know it was the forgotten script of Hyperborea. This was the lost *Book of Eibon,* in its original form, unadulterated by countless clumsy additions and excisions over the centuries—the millennia—since pen was first put to paper on the plains of Antarctica. It is a testament to the urgency of our quest that I did not stop, even for a moment, to look upon those pages, to feel them against my fingertips. Instead, we rushed across the barren expanse and reached yet another stairwell.

To this point we had met no resistance, seen no other living soul. I began to harbor hope that we might yet succeed, steal the staff, and be gone, before the brothers or anyone else with more nefarious plans would know the difference.

One by one we ascended the stairs, Villard leading the way. We moved in total darkness, but our steps were true. We were as silent as the night was black, and no one could have known of our advance.

Such was my focus on the next step ahead that I barely noticed the dawning light breaking over us. For indeed, as we ascended, the night seemed to lift. It was not until we rounded the final turn and saw the firelight in its fullness that I even realized the effect had been more than my just eyes adjusting to the darkness

We had reached the courtyard, the cloister that crowned the Mont. Here our prize awaited us. And someone, it appeared, had been kind enough to leave on the lights. A great number of torches burned, and the vast expanse was lit from the doorway where we stood to the far wall overlooking the sea below.

"Do you think this is normal?" Villard whispered. "Do the torches always burn?"

"I don't know," I said.

"The ancient texts tell us that the haunter of the dark fears the light," Henry said. "Perhaps this is a way to guard against him. The ultimate protection for the staff."

"Perhaps," I said. I wanted to believe it. I wanted to think that we would not be stopped now, so close to our goal. But what I wanted to believe was largely irrelevant. We had come this far, and we would go farther. My ancestors on my mother's side were of Scottish descent, MacDougall blood. Their motto was a simple one— "Victory or Death." I have carried that same motto into battle every time I have ventured forth to conquer the forces of darkness. Tonight, we all carried it, whether the others knew it or not.

We stepped from the shadows of the archway into the open plain that formed the cloister. Silence greeted us. If anyone waited and watched, they did not make their presence known. I saw our destination almost immediately.

"There."

At the far end of the cloister was a vault, what might to the untrained eye have appeared to be a narrow coffin. But I knew immediately—this was the resting place of the staff. Henry put his hand on my shoulder; it was a momentous occasion for us both.

We fanned out around the stone sepulcher. The slab that covered the top did not appear to be held in place by mortar or sealed in any way. I thought this strange, but perhaps the speed with which it had been moved in the days of the last war had led to a less than fulsome approach to the staff's care.

Henry and Villard went to one side, while Guillaume and I approached the other. We grasped the slab and lifted, sliding open the reliquary with the sound of stone upon stone, which in the silence of that place echoed like thunder.

Inch by inch it opened. Light from the burning torches filtered inside. The slab slid away. I gazed inside and saw...nothing.

The sarcophagus was empty.

"What is it they say, Herr Weston? There is nothing which you can possess which I cannot take away? Or, in this instance, secure first."

I did not need to turn to look upon its source to know that voice, so filled with mockery and dripping with hate. Zann had beaten us to the prize.

Chapter 33

Journal of Carter Weston
July 28, 1933

He stood at the far side of the cloister, a pistol in his hand, his cold sneer somehow magnified by the flickering firelight. We all pointed our weapons, but as German soldiers fanned out from the surrounding doorways, armed each with machine-pistols, it become apparent that we were once again hopelessly outgunned. The last of Zann's guard brought out an elderly man in a cassock and threw him down upon his knees. This, I was certain, was the head of the order that had vowed to protect the staff. My heart went out to him, even as our own predicament remained most dire.

Zann gestured to another of the soldiers. The man disappeared into the same darkness from which the priest had been dragged. He returned with an object, wrapped in a long white cloth. Zann nodded, and the soldier tugged on the cloth, sweeping it away.

It was everything I had dreamt it would be. Three individual pieces of wood, each long and slender and polished to a shine, wrapped around each other as if they had grown that way, so tightly bound that I could not tell where one began and the other ended. Three, forming one. And at the crown an opening, the perfect place to slip a jewel the shape of a pyramid. There it was, and I had lost it.

"Oh, don't look so disappointed, my dear Carter. You had to know that it would end like this. We have been one step ahead of you throughout this quest. We have eyes and ears in every city and village in France, not to mention La Sûreté Nationale."

Villard tensed beside me. I thought I might have to restrain him if he made a move, but his control was better than mine. He took the insult in silence.

"The staff was always to be mine. You should have known that. It was my destiny. From the moment the *Incendium Maleficarum* sang its song to me, I knew that I was fated to do this great thing. And ever since that moment, you have done nothing but interfere with fate, with destiny, with God's plan, if you will."

"God's plan?" I said. "No god did this. You alone are responsible for what will happen if you take the staff."

"And what will happen? If the gods of old seek to return, I will stop them, just as you would. And should I not be rewarded for my efforts? Should the world not bow before its savior?"

Even in the calamitous straits we now found ourselves in, I could not help but laugh. Zann's madness was well beyond the absurd.

He lowered his gaze and scowled. "You laugh in your ignorance. Your inability to see beyond the lies you have been taught, all your life. But I am offering you another way. Tell me this, Herr Doctor, have you ever considered Judas Iscariot, and why he betrayed his Christ?"

"Can't say that I have."

"Well I have," said Zann. "I believe Judas was simply misunderstood. He looked around the world that he inhabited and he saw pain and disease and suffering and oppression. And here was a man who could cure the sick, who could raise the dead, who could call down ten legions of angels as easily as speaking a name.

"Think of it. Why should people go hungry when this man can feed five thousand with a couple fish and a loaf of bread? Why should people watch their bodies wither away from leprosy if he can cure them with but a thought? Why should the Jewish people suffer under the Roman whip when the Lord of Hosts stands ready to do the bidding of this man called Jesus?

"And yet, what did he do? Nothing. He spoke in riddles. He promised a kingdom not of this world, even as on every street and in every hovel the people of Israel suffered and died. Here, today, now. So I ask you this—given all the power that Christ supposedly possessed, who betrayed whom?"

"I have no idea what you are getting at."

Zann flexed his jaw as he always did when my obstinacy finally got to him. "I will use the staff for good. I will heal this world. I will earn my place on the earth's throne. The power I have will be denied to no one.

They need give me nothing, pay me nothing, offer me nothing. All they need do is bow."

Guillaume edged to the side. I saw it, but Zann was so wrapped up in his megalomania that he did not. There was a broken pillar not five feet from where Guillaume stood. It was obvious what he intended. He was armed, as were we all, and perhaps if he had some cover he could hold them off long enough to give us some time to find a defensive position of our own. But it was a long five feet.

"There was a time I thought you could be saved, Erich," I said to Zann, wanting any edge to keep his attention, even though what I said was very true. "When I thought there was some good left inside of you after all. But whatever was there is gone. Replaced with madness."

Guillaume took another step to the left.

Zann's face twisted in anger. "Mad? I am not mad, Carter. I stand at the crossroads of time and humanity's existence. And I hold in my hand the life of all things, including you and your friends."

Zann never took his eyes off of me, but the hand holding the gun swept to the side and there was the *pop pop* of a pistol blast. The first shot caught Guillaume in the arm; the second his chest. A scream rent the air and drowned out the fading thunder of the gunshots—the sound of a heart breaking.

Rachel and Margot both reacted at nearly the same time. Both tried to run to Guillaume's side. Henry, God bless him, grabbed Rachel, and despite her tears and her screams and her struggles he did not let her go. But there was no one for Margot. All she had was now laying on the ground, bleeding to death.

She stumbled to where Guillaume had fallen. If the Germans wished to shoot her, she did not care. At least she would die with the man she loved.

"You see, Carter. There truly is nothing you have that I cannot take. And that includes your very lives. I am in control now. Even Nyarlathotep himself would not dare to stand against me."

What happened next must have taken only a few moments, but as I watched, time seemed to stop altogether, as if we now stood in a place so far outside this good world that the laws of God and of man no longer applied.

Margot sobbed over Guillaume, and as the life fled from his body and the light from his eyes, he struggled to pass unto her his last words. They came in the form of a question.

"Would you do anything for me?"

The poor girl wept so fiercely she could barely answer. "Yes," she said finally. "I would do anything for you. I would give my life if it could bring back yours."

Then Guillaume smiled, but to my eyes it was more like a sneer, his teeth coated in his own blood, that dying light in his eyes suddenly roaring. The hand that Margot had been clasping was in an instant at her throat, and in the other, a blade.

"Of you," he said, "they will write songs the sound of which will drive men mad."

Before she could scream, he had slit her throat, the blood spewing forth and bathing him in its spray. No one moved, all of us, even Zann and his men, transfixed by what we saw.

A rushing, mighty wind fell upon us. One by one, the torches flared and then were extinguished, until all was but smoke and darkness. And yet, we were not blinded, the entirety of that great space bathed in a preternatural glow that hurt my eyes to even look upon. It was a light that was not of this world, one that was never meant to shine upon the paths of men.

The wind swirled about us, carrying the smoke of the dead torches into a column of whirling vapor that surrounded Guillaume. A cry echoed in the distance, and to a man we all clutched our ears in agony at that sound, the sound of slaughter, of pain, and of death.

The scream was cut off in an instant, sliced away like butter before a blade. Silence fell. The fog cleared.

He stood before us.

There are no words in this language or any of those of this earth to describe what we saw in those moments, none that do him justice at least. He was present before us, and yet not. He seemed to shift in and out of existence, as if he was both here and in some other place beyond. He towered over us, thin and gaunt and powerful, garbed in a yellow robe that flowed like smoke off of his shoulders and down his body.

Nyarlathotep had returned.

Chapter 34

Journal of Henry Armitage
July 28, 1933

At the last moment, I grabbed Rachel. I didn't even think about it. I just did it. I heard the shots, I saw her move, and I grabbed her and held on, deaf to her pleas and her tears. Thank God my nerve held.

I had not trusted Guillaume, not in the beginning. But I had come to think of him as one of us, and I knew that Carter saw in him a potential protégé, one to take up the torch that he would one day lay down. Oh, the bitter irony. Oh, the cruel fate. Yet there was no time for such sympathies or considerations. The wonder of what we were seeing overwhelmed all that.

I suppose I had witnessed many things in my years with Carter Weston, things that would have tested the nerves of less experienced men. But I had never seen anything like this, nor had I expected to. A god, rapped in dark majesty, clothed in the body of a man—for I had no illusions that this was his true form. He stood, and we stared. None moved. None breathed. Then the silence was pierced by a gun shot.

It was one of the Germans, one whose fear I suppose had finally ebbed enough for action. But only a small one. He had fired but one shot at the great colossus of a man who stood before him. Nyarlathotep—for I had no doubt that it was he—actually grinned. Then he stretched out his hand. What happened next bordered on disappointing. There was no flash of light. No explosion of fire. No demons swooping down from the swirling purple darkness above us. The German simply fell down in a crumpling heap, dead.

"We shall have no more of that," said Nyarlathotep. He turned where he stood, surveying the scene, his eyes passing over us all, and my soul turned to brittle ice when they fell upon me.

"So you have all come. How wonderful to have you all here. Those who would rule me," he said, bowing ever so slightly in the direction of Zann before turning to Carter, "and those who would banish me. Ah, Carter Weston, how I have longed for this day. To see the crusader face-to-face again. There are few who have stood against us, fewer still who survived with their lives and minds intact. And yet here you are. I underestimated you before, in the cold waste. I will not be so foolish again."

His eyes passed from Carter to me, but it was not me that he saw. Rachel struggled against me again, and I released her.

"I can smell your anger, your hate," he said. "In the midst of so much fear, it burns like the heart of a star. Such a strange thing, this Guillaume. His love for poor Margot was intense, and hers for him. And yet so easily he turned to you. Oh, you can rest assured in this, little one—I remained below the surface, only acting when need be. Perhaps I nudged him a bit, but he very much betrayed this child for you. I wonder, in your simple mind, how that makes you feel. To be the thief of something so precious. But do not weep for her. She was destined, you see? Destined to a higher purpose. I have removed her from a world of pain and betrayal. Your kind flower but for a season; she will live forever in me."

He stepped forward, and the air seemed to shimmer around him, the ground quake at the touch of his feet. "Of course, your anger is far more personal, is it not? You do not rage for her, it is not for her death that you would seek revenge. It is for your own foolishness, your own petty shortcomings. How quickly this boy beguiled you. It was the eyes, was it not? Yes, I changed them for you. I wanted them to remind you of another. I was inside of him too, though I must say, taking him was nowhere near as pleasurable."

"You bastard!" Rachel spat, as if she were speaking to a common tramp and not one who walked the earth before man was even imagined. "This isn't over. Not yet. Not here."

The lord of darkness turned back to Weston. "Her father's daughter, I see. So quaint. So charming. So simple-minded. Do you think, because I take this form, and because I speak your tongue, that we are somehow equals? Child, when this world was a ball of fire and smoke, I was. I have walked half the galaxy in a stride. Before He, whose name I shall not utter here, called light into being, I clothed myself in the darkness of the ancients. I bathed in the primordial deep; I swam in the wine-dark abyss. Before all you know was created, I am. You curse me and you hate me. And yet, who else of my kind will stand before you? You call to your God. Does he answer back? Does he even know that you are here? For I can tell you this, the gods that stand in the outer chaos, that await the end of all things, they do not see you, and they do not hear you, and they do not care whether you live or you die. Only I, Nyarlathotep, move amongst you. Only I care for you. For I do care. I love you. I love you all."

"Enough," Carter said. "Enough of your lies. If you are going to kill us, at least do us the courtesy of not boring us to death with your absurdities."

Thunder rumbled through the clouds. I wondered if Carter had finally done it, if after all these years, he would lay us low. But Nyarlathotep had other plans, and the thunder turned to his own laughter.

"Would you give them to me then?" he said with a smile. "Would you make forfeit their lives, sacrifice them for your greater good? Ah, I see in your eyes that you are tempted. You didn't consider that, did you? That perhaps if the sacrifice is great indeed, it might be enough to consign me once again to the light, until another time when the stars come right and my servants tear down the wall that divides the here from the there? Would it be worth it to you, to kill them all to kill me?"

In that moment, I admit that I feared what I saw in my old friend's face as much as I feared the demon before me. We were truly pawns in a game I did not fully comprehend, and these two masters were determined to pin the other, no matter the cost of the gambit. Then Nyarlathotep's eyes fell upon me.

"Ah, yes, what a blow it would be to lose dear Henry." He stepped forward, and in an instant he had crossed the yards between us, as fast as lightning might travel a mile. He was inches from my face. His hand reached up and caressed my cheek. He was cold personified, and the air turned to ice around us, and even my thoughts seemed to freeze. "He who has stood with you through so many confrontations. Perhaps that would add power to the spell, his blood. Perhaps in spilling it you would undo me. Perhaps you should try."

"There are other ways," Carter cried. "Other ways to defeat you. You may revel in the blood of the innocent, but we do not. The holy have tools you cannot imagine. Our ways are not your ways."

Now there was no question that the thunder that followed bellowed from the mouth of Nyarlathotep, so deep was his cackling cry.

"Holy. Good. Evil. You cling to these like a child to its mother's breast. But they are only illusions. In this world as in all others, there is only will and power and sacrifice."

Nyarlathotep stretched forth his hands. Across the stone plain, Zann stood. His eyes went wide, and then they went to the rod that he clasped in his hands, the one he had taken from the soldier beside him, I suppose in an effort to defend himself. The Staff of Dyzan began to quake. Cracks formed along its surface, from which blood red light poured. The air around us rippled. There was a sound of splitting rock and crashing waves. In one instant of dark fire and unaccountable sound the staff exploded. Down we all went, and even Nyarlathotep stumbled. In that instant, he seemed diminished, as if all the life had gone from him. I wondered then what ungodly power it must have taken to destroy the staff, a power of the purest hate drawn from a sacrifice of the purest love.

I know Nyarlathotep intended to kill us all then, but as he stood, bent over, his face a mask of rage and pain, I saw a tinge of fear in his eyes, too. Great was his triumph, but mighty was the cost, and if ever he was vulnerable to some hitherto unknown attack, it was now. He stumbled to the parapet overlooking the salt flat. He glanced back at us as we struggled to our feet, and there was a promise in his gaze that we would see him soon.

"You think that before your beginning there was nothing?" he almost whispered. "You are wrong. There was the deep, and the dark, and the void. And there shall be again."

He dropped over the side of the wall, there was a sound like a clapping of hands, and he was gone.

The German soldiers—the ones who remained alive—ran. Carter pulled himself up from his knees and stumbled to where Zann lay. A shard of the staff had driven through his throat, and blood poured out around it. Zann reached up and grasped Carter by the shoulder. Carter leaned over, and Zann whispered into his ear. When he released his grip, he took two more gasps, and he was gone.

We stood on the summit of that ancient cathedral, bathed in blood and death. And all hope, it seemed, was lost.

Chapter 35

Excerpt from *Enûma Anu Enlil*, Tablet 71, as translated by Dr. John Dee, 1567

When upon the unseen plains of Leng,
The night black stars of Yorn align,
The ancients of days will unite to sing
The coming of the Yellow Sign.

Journal of Henry Armitage
July 28, 1933

The night was passed fitfully by all. The brothers generously provided us lodging, and we did not need to leave the island. Their kindness was surprising, perhaps, given that we had only a few hours hence broken into their cloister with the intentions of stealing their most prized possession. But now, whatever we had been before, whatever crimes we might have committed against them, all was forgotten and forgiven. They, the Tzadikim Nistarim, had sworn a solemn oath to guard the world against Nyarlathotep's return. With the staff destroyed and the dark one walking free, new alliances were necessary.

When I went to Carter's room this morning, it was evident to me that he had slept little, if at all. The *Incendium Maleficarum* lay open before him; with Zann's death, its old master had become the new.

"Anything?" I said as I walked over to where he sat. Carter turned a page and sighed.

"Nothing. I stare at pages I have studied more times than I wished, looking for a secret, a code. But I don't even know where to start." He closed it with a thud. "The monastery's library is vast and deep, but it would take a lifetime to understand it. And I don't think we have that much time."

He picked up an open volume and flipped it around to where I could see it.

"It's an English translation of the 71st tablet of the *Enûma Anu Enlil*. Done by John Dee, of all people. I'd know that handwriting anywhere."

I was astonished. "The *71st* tablet, you say? But it was lost, if it ever even existed…and even that's unlikely."

Carter smiled, albeit wearily. The exhaustion hung heavily on him. "In a collision between your learning and your eyes, Henry, believe your eyes."

And Carter was right. The handwriting was distinctly Dee's, the phrasing and syntax, a classic Elizabethan take on a Babylonian text. The document was short, the central thrust some sort of riddle I did not understand.

"I take it you have a theory."

"I do."

"And what do you make of it then? The 'night black stars of Yorn'? 'The plains of Leng'? It's a riddle if I've ever seen one, with no key to break it."

Carter leaned back in his chair and fixed me with that gaze I knew too well. Even now, the excitement was still there, the daring. "I don't think so," he said. "I think it's pretty straight forward."

"But the Plains of Leng…"

"A limitless plateau in a world beyond our own, where darkness and light collide, and the Great Old Ones await the time of their return. The ancient texts tell us that the gods will rise when the stars are right. Now we know what that means. It's an astronomical alignment all right, just not one in the sky we know. And when it happens..." He held up a hand, and in doing so waved away all of human existence and all we've ever known.

"And how exactly does that help us?" I asked as I sat in a chair on the other side of the room. "If we can't see it, how can we know it's happening?"

"Well, I have a theory about that, too."

"I suspected you might."

"Take what we know. The darkness and the light, the eternal dichotomy, the mirror of this world and the next. What if it really is that simple? What if, when the black stars of Yorn align above the plains of Leng, we experience our own astronomical phenomenon?"

"All right, given that we have absolutely nothing to go on, I'll accept that as a possibility. But I still don't see how it helps us."

"It was 1919 when we last faced Nyarlathotep, when we stopped him the first time, albeit temporarily. He came back then for a reason, and had we not interrupted his plans, I have no doubt he would have accomplished the task set before him." Carter searched through the pile of books on the desk. It could not be denied—he'd done quite a bit of reading while I pretended to sleep. "Ah, here it is." His hands found an astronomical almanac. "Now look at this. Some six months later, in June 1920, Venus, Mercury, Earth, and Mars, all the inner planets, stood in perfect alignment to the sun. It's a rare occurrence. It happens only twice every few hundred years, exactly thirteen years apart."

"Thirteen years?" Like the switch of a light, illumination.

"Precisely. If you take a look at that French newspaper on the table next to you, a few pages in is a story from the Académie des Sciences. It confirms it. That same alignment is upon us again, in three days' time."

"Three days?"

Carter nodded gravely. "The stars are right, my friend. The veil is thin. And if we don't stop him, Nyarlathotep will open the gate, and this time there will be no closing it."

"But how can we? The Staff is destroyed. The Oculus, still missing. We have nothing."

There was a knock on the door, and Rachel entered without waiting for an answer.

"Hi, Henry," she said casually. "Figured I'd find you here."

"I'll leave you two to it," I said and began to rise. But she would have none of it.

"No, no. Stay. It's about time we stopped walking on egg shells around each other. We have much to discuss."

"And we were just discussing it," I said, as I fell back into my chair.

"You don't look like you've slept," she said, as she sat beside her father's desk. "In fact, if I'm being honest with you, you look terrible."

Carter coughed a little laugh, and Rachel rested her hand against his cheek. For a long while, she simply looked at him. Her eyes were soft, softer than I had seen them in some time. The events of the night before had shaken her, as they had shaken us all. Perhaps they had done more than that.

"I'm sorry," she said finally. "I know you both did what you thought you must, all those years ago. And after what I saw last night, maybe you were right to do it. In fact, I'd say you probably were."

I was surprised to see Carter shake his head. "No," he said. "No, I don't think so. Something Nyarlathotep said last night struck me. In the midst of his lies was a moment of truth. I've always thought, as a matter of faith, I suppose, that the lines between good and evil were bright and clear. I believed it was possible that one who would see the righteous triumph could keep himself pure. I guess I had to believe that. But it's not true. I can't say I put much stock in Nietzsche, but on this point he was right. In a conflict such as this, it is not only our blood that we sacrifice, not only the price of our lives that must be paid to keep men safe. It is our virtue and, if need be, our very souls."

The sun crept through the ancient panes of the great windows that made up the eastern wall of the chamber. Outside, a gull called. Life moved on, and I wished fervently that I could be amongst it, instead of there, the weight of all things bearing down on us.

"I guess what I'm trying to say," Carter continued, smiling wanly, "is that there is no need to apologize. We did what we had to do. That doesn't make it right."

For several minutes no one spoke. I watched as Rachel held her father's hands across the desk, him deep in thought, her studying him with an expression that almost seemed pitying.

"Well," she said finally. "No use sitting around feeling sorry for ourselves. What do we do now? And before you try to cut me out of this, you can forget it. Inspector Villard left this morning to conduct the body of Margot and..." She hesitated over the name. "And...the others back to Paris. He'll have a lot to work out between the German embassy and the French government, not to mention explaining what happened here. That leaves just us. Just the three of us. Whatever needs to be done, we will be the ones doing it."

"And time is short," I added, leaning forward. "Your father has worked out that we only have three days before Nyarlathotep will make his move."

"Even more reason to act quickly."

"But how?" I asked. "The last time we faced him we were fortunate, and even for that fortune we paid a horrible price."

"Rachel," Carter said finally, "do you still have the necklace I gave you the day after William's funeral? The golden sphere?"

Rachel's hand went to her neck. "Of course. I never take it off."

"Can you make an exception, just this once?"

Rachel's eyes were filled with confusion, but there was also trust there, trust that perhaps had been missing in recent days. She nodded almost imperceptibly and reached behind her back. A moment's fumbling, and the chain came loose. Rachel lifted the orb from within her blouse and dropped it into Carter's outstretched hand.

Carter held it between his thumb and his forefinger, and it shimmered in the morning light. He slid the chain out from the tiny circle of gold that ringed it, and took the sphere in his hands.

"I'm sorry I lied to you."

He continued to work the orb, and Rachel leaned forward to see exactly what he was doing.

"I had my reasons. Some of them were selfish. I knew that you would hate me. I knew that you would blame me. And why not? I blamed myself. It was my fault."

Carter's hands jerked once, and there was an audible "click" that seemed to fill the room.

"But I had other reasons to keep some things from you. And now it is time to tell you what really happened all those years ago. Hold out your hand."

Rachel did as she was asked. Carter separated the orb in half, and for an instant, something inside caught the light and burned like a fire. He turned the hemisphere over Rachel's hand. I stood, and Rachel gasped.

"Now you should know the truth."

Chapter 36

Tunguska Field Journal of Dr. Carter Weston
December 7, 1919

I raised my pistol. I pointed it at William's heart. I said the words.

"A ne a mai. Ma lei. Ma dooz."

I pulled the trigger, and time slowed down. The bullet struck William. The fire extinguished. The evil fled. And for one brief moment, what had been William was with us again. For one brief moment, before he died in my arms.

I held him there. I did not feel the cold. I did not feel the wind. I felt only this man, this boy, the only son I had ever had, the life gone from him. The things I have seen in this life. The evils. And yet it was then I finally lost the last shred of innocence I still held.

I had murdered him. Whatever else could be said for what we did, for what we had to do, it all came down to that. I had murdered him, and long before that moment. When I took him away from Rachel. I might as well have put a bullet in his brain.

"Carter..."

I looked at Henry and I could not bear the pity in his eyes.

"We have to go, Carter. We don't know what else is out there."

I clutched William's body close to mine. "Go get a sheet, from the horses. Go get it and bring it back."

"Carter, there's no time..."

"There's time! We aren't leaving him. Not like this. Not here."

Henry and Rostov exchanged worried glances. But they both knew that I would not be moved. They might leave me there, but I would not leave William.

"Come, doctor. We'll go together and get the sheet. Leave him for now."

I nodded to Rostov in thanks. Henry said nothing. Soon, I was alone.

I wept. Wept for all that had been lost, all that had been sacrificed. I let myself fall into despair, to question all that I had done, all the choices that I had made. Every turn I had taken now seemed to be the wrong one. And I wondered what future was now forever foreclosed, what doors were shut, what paths untraveled. For William. For Rachel. For their children that would have been. For their child that would be. All of it, lost. All of it, sacrificed. And I had done it on purpose. I had made that choice. It was the power that I needed, and I had taken it.

So deep in my own sorrow was I that I barely noticed that the shadow in which I sat had retreated. The sun was still absent, the gloom that covered the copse of trees total, but the darkness around me had lifted.

A glow moved amongst the bone-white cabers. I lowered William to the earth and stood, my grief replaced with rage.

"Come out!" I said, drawing my pistol. "Show yourself!"

The light seemed to move away. I ran to the nearest tree, throwing myself behind it. Even in the cold, the sweat broke across my brow. I led with my gun, glancing around the trunk. The light faded into the distance. I would not let it escape.

I ran after it, heedless of the danger, the skeletal remains of the forest whooshing past me in a blur. My feet did not stumble, my path was true. Hatred drove me, revenge prodded me on. I wanted to see Nyarlathotep again. I wanted to kill him one more time. Even if it was at the cost of my own life.

I ran after the light until I seemed to plunge into its midst, until it surrounded me, bathing me in its luminance. Yet no torch, no man-made fire cast it. It was the cloak of a power beyond anything I had experienced in that frozen tundra.

Before me stood William.

He was alive. Smiling, standing relaxed with his hands in his pockets, that cocky gleam in the eye that we all loved. My mouth fell open, and for a long moment in that dim glow we gazed across the middle distance at each other. I turned and looked back from where I had run. Through the trees, I could see the shadowed figure of William's body lying on the cold earth.

"Who are you?"

He shook his head and grinned, putting one finger to his mouth. "Shhhh!"

The sound filled my mind. The apparition turned away, a pirouette completed in half-time, and began to walk further into the forest. I watched him go, rooted to the spot. He turned back and looked over his shoulder. He beckoned to me, his hand moving as if through water, and I knew I must follow.

It wasn't William. Of course it wasn't. He was dead, and I had killed him, and no power on earth or in heaven could bring him back. In hindsight, it was foolish to follow, there, in a place of so much evil. But that voice in my head, the one that I had heeded so many times before, told me that whatever spirit moved through the trees that day was benevolent.

I kept pace. William never wavered. When he came to a clearing, he stopped. He did not turn, not until I arrived. We stood together, side by side, on the shore of a small brook, nothing more than a creek.

William gazed down into the depths of that shimmering water. A mad notion struck me that perhaps this was the only free-flowing water for a thousand miles, all else locked beneath a sheet of solid ice. And yet, other than its mere existence, there was nothing remarkable about that little stream.

A thought came to my mind, unbidden. A voice that was not mine, nor any I had ever heard before. It was not spoken. William continued to stare into the stream as if within its shallow depths resided the most beautiful image in the world.

The words were hazy at first, jumbled. It even struck me that perhaps they were in a language I did not know and, in fact, had never heard. Then the haze began to clear, and though the words did not change, I could understand them as if they were my native tongue.

Fire and flame. That's what the old legends foretold. That is the how, but not the why. The stone will come to him who is worthy of it. To him who is willing to sacrifice, to give all to save all.

A roar filled the air. The light that surrounded us was outshone by a fire from above. A column of flame fell from the sky. It thundered down and crashed into the stream where William still stared. The water hissed and steam boiled up from the earth. My gaze matched William's, and I saw it. He turned to me and smiled.

The light faded, the darkness returned, and I found myself still kneeling next to William's dead body. And yet, in my clinched fist, I held…

* * *

Journal of Henry Armitage, July 28, 1933

"And that is how I found it."

Rachel held the small jewel in the palm of her hand, and she looked as stunned as I felt. The ruby-colored diamond burned with an inner flame, and I thought that if one so desired, one could illuminate the night with its light. For more than a decade she had worn it around her neck, concealed in that golden globe with the Arabic script that Carter had purchased at a bazaar in Marrakesh. And he had never mentioned it.

I stumbled towards the desk where they sat. "You never said anything," I said. "Even when it became clear we would need it. Why?"

Carter looked up at me and smiled. "I would have told you, old friend. But I knew that if the Eye had returned, so would Nyarlathotep. I had to keep the stone hidden. And that meant keeping the knowledge of its existence to myself and keeping the Oculus in a place of utmost safety. I could think of none better than with my daughter."

"It's so small," Rachel said. She laughed. "I thought it would be bigger."

"I have a feeling," said Carter, "that in this case size may be deceiving and that perhaps it will grow to meet whatever challenges we face."

"And yet, with the staff destroyed…" I could not finish the sentence. Even the thought filled me with despair.

"Our mission is more difficult," said Carter. "But I must believe that the solution will present itself. That our situation is not hopeless. That faith is all we have left."

"To those who wait beyond the veil," I quoted, "the men who teem across the surface of the earth are little more than insects, ants to be swept away by the cleansing fire."

"The *Necronomicon*," Carter said with a wry smile. "Doesn't leave much for hoping, does it?"

"Well," said Rachel as she held the crystal out to her father, "then at least we will make them feel our sting."

"Yes," Carter said. "That we will."

"And where do you propose we look for Nyarlathotep?" I asked. "Have your books told you that?"

Carter leaned forward on the desk and clasped his hands. "No, they have not. They didn't need to. Herr Zann proved that as long as there is breath, there is the possibility of redemption. And he used the last of that breath to give us the last piece of the puzzle."

Carter stood and walked to one of the bookcases that adorned the walls. He pulled down a narrow folio and turned to us.

"'Beyond sky,'" he said, "'where the gods came down and set their foot on the earth.' That is all he told me."

"And what does that mean? Where is beyond the sky?"

"Not *the sky*."

He opened the book and dropped it on the table to where Rachel and I could see it. It was an atlas of the British Isles, turned to a page that showed us the north of Scotland.

"Beyond Skye," he said, pointing to the isle of myth and legend. His finger traced west to a group of tiny outcroppings in the midst of the North Sea. "To the place the Norse Sagas named *Alfheim*, and the Romans *Basilia*, and the ancient Britons *Avalon*, and the Celts *Caledonia*. It is where they say the gods came down to earth, and it is where they will return. One of these islands. We just have to identify which one."

"Then *that* is where we will find him." We both turned to Rachel, and when she looked up from the map, her countenance was not one I had seen before on her, and not one I particularly liked. It was determined, yes, but anger and hate rippled just below the surface. "And we've not got a moment to lose."

Chapter 37

The Diary of Rachel Jones
July 29, 1933

So it goes.

Today we make our way to England and then to Scotland beyond. Henry, ever the organizer, booked passage for us on a trans-channel ferry immediately after leaving my father's room. He didn't need help, and I stayed behind.

We talked of everything and nothing, and it was as if we weren't watching the clock tick down on the end of the world. I suppose this must be how soldiers feel, on the eve of battle, when the next day might be their last. And yet whatever might come seemed so far away in those moments. I had my father back, and that was something.

He had done what he thought was necessary. There was a time when I wouldn't have understood that. He knew that about me, and he kept the truth from me for no other reason than that I couldn't have handled it. There are those who would never forgive such a seeming betrayal. I understand that sentiment, too. If someone had asked me about it before, I'd probably have been squarely in their camp.

But the old saying that you cannot judge a man until you walk a mile in his shoes has proven true. After what I have seen, after all that I know, I have come to fully understand.

Guillaume...

I would say that I was a fool, but that would be a convenient lie. To be a fool is easy. To be fooled, forgivable, particularly in this case, given the one doing the fooling. But it was not so simple, not for me, not for him. Thinking on it too much is enough to drive a woman to madness, but I believe that there was truth in those moments we shared, however dark and damnable they ended up being. And yet...

Losing him is not like losing William. Of course it's not—I knew Guillaume for a matter of days. But to see him die. To know what took him. And to know that it was the same as that which took William.

I hate him. I hate him with as much fervor as I have ever loved anything. And I will see this through to the bitterest of ends.

* * *

Journal of Carter Weston

Passage from Mont Saint-Michel to England proved more difficult than expected. First, a train to Granville, a small fishing village some twenty miles north of the Mont. Then, a boat, if one can call it that. It was little more than a fishing trawler, really, and I wondered by what hook or crook Henry had procured it. From Granville we "sailed" to the isle of Jersey, where we caught a trawler to Guernsey, ending our cattle tour with our arrival in the port of Southampton.

It was a somewhat ignominious beginning to our grand quest.

Yet our spirits were high. Unfortunately, by the time our epic Channel journey came to a close, the sun had long since set and the last train north long since departed the station. So there we were, a day lost, the constant drizzle of a late spring rain soaking us to the bone. We retired to the Dolphin, an ancient inn in the heart of the city and one of the finest such establishments in Southampton. With tomorrow not assured, it seemed wise to eat, drink, and be merry.

As we stepped into the lobby of the Dolphin, the rain ceased, the clouds broke, and the moon shone through. It was near to fullness, and the rain-slicked cobblestones glistened in its light. From the docks the harbor bells rang, and the people of Southampton went about their business, oblivious to the danger that surrounded them. I wondered how often it was so, how many near misses with disaster the human race has endured but blindly, how many nights of peace and quiet for the many tipped towards disaster, a fate only avoided by the sacrifices of the few.

Tomorrow we go north, to Skye and beyond.

* * *

It is late. Or perhaps it is early. There is no clock in this room, and the empty night tells nothing. I have had a dream, and I cannot wait till morning to relate it. I must record it now, while it is fresh in my mind, in the event that the details thereof might be of help to us all.

Sleep came quickly to me, an unusual if not altogether unwelcome development. Now, in the glow of a pale electric light, I wonder if a dark power brought the spirit of Hypnos down upon me.

I remember only that as I began to drift into slumber, I heard a soft tinkling somewhere in the night, as if a mirror had shattered, casting broken glass upon the floor. When my eyes opened, I was no longer in Southampton or England or on this earth. I was somewhere else entirely.

I stood upon a high mountain. My familiar clothing was gone, and I wore the black robe of a Benedictine. A mighty wind whipped up from below, driving the pitch black clouds that boiled and raced above me. I was glad that they obscured the sky, for somehow I knew that whatever floated above them was not meant for the eyes of man, and that to see it was to invite insanity.

I looked out over a vast, stone plain, a flat sea of granite that continued on to the far horizon, endless and infinite and empty. From the dark clouds above, the whip-crack of thunder sounded as a great lightning bolt, larger than any I had seen before, slashed down to the stone in the outer distance. The smell of distant rain filled me.

"Leng," I whispered to myself.

"Beautiful, isn't it?"

The very sound of the words chilled my blood. I turned to find him waiting, and never before in my life have I felt so small, so naked, so alone. He was seated in a chair made of stone. Another sat across from him, empty, a small tor forming a table between them.

"This is only a dream," I said, but I found no strength in the assertion. Nyarlathotep smiled, and the perfect, pearly white of his razor-blade-straight teeth only made him all the more uncanny.

"Isn't everything?"

He gestured at the seat across from him. I stood, unmoving.

"Come, Carter Weston. There will be a time for unpleasantness in the future, of that I am sure. Not now. Sit a while. Think of all we have to discuss."

He pointed again at the stone chair. I stepped forward and he rose, as if he were the courteous host and I a guest in his home. I suppose in a way, I was. The two of us sat down together, he and I, and so the game began, far more literally than I expected.

He sat across from me, his fingers steepled. He wore the sallow robe that was his trademark, and his eyes shone from a face that was long and lined with the burden of command. He had no hair, either on his head or his face, and I wondered if that contrivance was simply too much for him to create. That perhaps of all the things he had mastered, hair was not one. Or maybe he simply did not care to fabricate it. But of one thing I was sure—the legends were right; he really did look like an ancient pharaoh.

He waved his hand across the stone. It rumbled and cracked, dust and smoke erupting from the crevices that formed beneath his hands. Shapes rose from the rock, its surface darkening in spots as if burned by a fire. When the figure on my right resolved into the image of a castle's turret, the shocking realization of what I was witnessing broke across me like a wave.

"You play, I presume?"

I nodded.

"Then you can play with me. It is, I have found, a singular invention of your race, perhaps the only one for which you merit attention. A diversion unlike any other. A mirror of life, where power is gained only through loss."

I picked up the king. It pulsed in my hand, hot to the touch.

"And what do I get if I win?"

That almost reptilian smile returned.

"Why nothing, my dear Carter. I am not here to make deals or wagers. This is but a friendly game. Something to occupy our time, while we have our little chat."

"Well," I said, for no other reason than defiance, "I guess we know who will take black."

The grin broadened beyond what might be possible for a human being. "Quite."

I picked up the white pawn that sat before my king and moved it two spaces forward, e4.

"So it begins." His long narrow fingers clasped the pawn across from mine by its head, which, in the pale orange light of whatever fire burned in the sky above us, looked like a skeletal face caught forever in a scream. e5. It was then I made the decision—I would throw everything I had against him. If I were to lose, I would lose with style. f4, attacking his middle pawn.

"King's gambit?"

I nodded.

"Accepted."

I watched him, seated in a cold stone throne, yellow cloak tangled in the dying breeze, as he moved a pawn to capture my own, exf4, and I wondered.

"So why this?" I asked. "Of all the ways that you could have appeared, why this one?" Bishop to c4.

His mouth twisted into a smirk.

"What we are and what we seem, these things are all illusion," he said. He casually dropped his queen across the board, putting my king in check. Qh4+. "When Dr. Henry Armitage asks you to his house for a drink or for dinner, you dress for the occasion, do you not? And not just in any attire, but in that which is appropriate. I learned long ago that of all the forms and fancies I might take, this is the one that pleases men the most. And of course, your mind is such a fragile thing. So easily damaged by the truth. If you were to see me as I am, well, it wouldn't be pleasant. For you, at least."

I moved my king to f1 and temporary safety, and he responded by harassing my bishop with a pawn to b5. Perhaps I was feeling fragile, because I took it. Bxb5.

"I remember," he said, "I watched a boy once, a child no older than three." Nf6. "He had a treasure that he seemed to value above all other things. A common hen's egg, nothing special or important." While he talked of eggs, I challenged his queen, Nf3. "I'm not sure how he got it. Whether his mother gave it to him or whether he found it. But he clung to that little white ovoid as if it were the most precious thing in the world." Qh6. "Of course, you see where this is going. He was clumsy, as your kind often are, even when childhood has fled from you. And he dropped the egg. And it did what eggs do. He wept for it." d3. My center was secure.

"That is what your mind is like, that egg. I hold it in my hands. And it takes so little to crack it." Nh5. "So if I were to reveal my true form, if you were to see me as my father made me, then I think you might break, right before my eyes. And I would hate to see Rachel mourn for you, as that boy mourned for his egg." Nh4.

At this point, I felt rather secure in my position. The center held by my forces; our material, even.

"You can leave Rachel out of it." I said. Qg5. Now he was harassing my knight. Nf5 to save him.

"Oh, but it was not I who brought her into it." c6. Now my bishop was under attack. So I threatened his knight, g4. He didn't seem all that concerned. "That was your friend Henry. And you, of course. From the moment she was born." Nf6.

"This is between us," I said, as another crackle of lightning scarred the plain below. Rg1. Nyarlathotep's laughter drowned out the thunder.

"No, my dear Carter. No, it is not. It never was. And it never could be. You are but the player on the stage in the moment, whose career passes in the blink of a season, never to rise again. Before you were, I was. When you are gone, I will be. This that I give to you now is the greatest gift one of your kind could ever hope to receive. How many times have men fallen upon their knees and called in vain to gods who do not hear, who do not see? I see you, Carter Weston. I hear you. And you would do well to hear me."

cxb5.

He had taken my bishop right from underneath me. And there was nothing I could do to strike back. A shadow of a grin passed his face, and I did not know if it was a reflection of what he had said or what he had done, that haughty face of triumph. Or maybe I had misread it altogether. Either way, I would not go so easily into the night. h4. The grin faded. For my sacrifice, I had gained a tempo on his queen. She was trapped in a box, both literal and figurative. She was in retreat, Qg6.

"I don't understand," I said. "What could you possibly want from me?" I advanced a pawn forward, closing the noose around his queen's throat. h5.

Here, if I had not known it to be impossible, I would have thought that he faltered, as if he were uncertain. The mask of composure, of supreme confidence, had slipped. His move was a simple forward jump one square by the queen. Qg5.

"You don't have to die, Carter. And neither does your daughter. This world will be changed, yes, and many will perish. But some will remain."

"As slaves." I slammed down my queen, Qf3.

He tilted his head to one side. "Alive." Ng8. He was in retreat.

"And what did I do to deserve this honor?" I pushed my bishop forward in a slashing stroke, taking a pawn and threatening his queen again. Bxf4.

The smirk returned. "Because I know you, Carter. You will do anything to stop us, anything to stave off the inevitable, to buy your species a few more years of dominion." Qf6. His queen was free, and she was threatening to attack.

"But the staff was destroyed."

"And will that keep you from trying?" I moved my knight to c3 in answer, blocking his queen's advance. "As I thought." Bc5.

"Then why not kill me? Why all this?" Nd5.

"You assume too much. Your life is not your own to give, and neither is it mine to take. You were fated, before you were born, by ancestors buried in the sands of time, who chose to stand where you stand. I can no more kill you than I can alter the paths of the stars in the sky. But if you stay this course, succeed or fail, you will die, and your daughter, as well. And while you rot, we will wait, as we have waited for tens of thousands of years. We are patient, and we are ageless. It is inevitable. Just as you will die, so too will your race. Why give your life, why give your daughter's life, for nothing more than a temporary reprieve? Is her safety not worth more than that?"

Qxb2. His queen had swung down and struck my pawn. Now not only was my rook under assault, but my king as well. But his words did not match his play. In fact, he almost seemed to be pleading with me.

"You lie. All of it is lies." Bd6.

"No lies, Carter. No lies. A chance. And if you let this pass, if your eye is fixed only on my destruction, you might miss something. And who knows what it might cost you." He thrust his bishop forward like a dagger, and its point found my rook across the board. Bxg1. A crushing blow, and one that I had not seen coming. There was no point in finesse now. I pushed my pawn, e5. If he had had an eyebrow, he would have arched it.

"An interesting strategy," he said. "Hopeless, but that is your way." His queen took my other rook, Qxa1+. I was in check, pinned between a queen and a bishop. I moved up to hide my king behind a protecting pawn. It was a temporary reprieve, but maybe it would buy me time. Ke2.

"I wish you could understand. This would be so much easier if you could. That we are adversaries does not mean that we must despise one another." Na6. "We can glory in the fight, like Hector and Achilles of old. But like Hector, you cannot see the truth beyond your own anger. We did not steal your Helen. We did not take what was not ours to possess. You did that, in the long ago. And in exile we have waited, for what is rightfully ours, for that which you have defiled."

I advanced my knight, putting his king in check. Nxg7+.

"All I know is the here and the now. The millions who live that you wish to kill."

He leaned forward in his chair. "But I know so much more. I have seen so much more. I saw the fall. I watched as the first light split the darkness, as all that we were was destroyed, as our cities sank beneath the surface of the deep. Imagine it, Carter. The truth you claim to serve, the purpose you live to uphold? We fight for the same thing—the salvation of our races. The difference between us is that I am willing to give all to have it. Are you?" Kd8.

"Whatever it takes." Qf6+

"Whatever it takes?" he said. "Whatever you must sacrifice for victory?" A silence filled the space between us, and in that space our thoughts seemed to shimmer. But his eyes, his amber eyes, they shone. And in the light of them, if I hadn't known it were impossible, I might have thought I saw pity, or longing, or even a touch of sadness.

"I wonder, Carter," he said finally. "What are you truly willing to give up, just to defeat me." He reached out and, without taking his eyes off of me, picked up his knight. Down and over it slid, until he dropped it where my queen sat. Nxf6. She was gone, but that was the cost, the price I had to pay, and I had known it when I left her there to draw him. I moved my bishop up and over one spot. Be7#.

"Checkmate."

The scene split and shifted. The rocks shattered, and the earth plummeted away. I started to fall, until with a jerk and a shudder I awoke in my bed in England, the scent of distant rain still with me.

Chapter 38

Journal of Carter Weston
July 30, 1933

I did not return to sleep. Instead I lay in bed, gazing out the window while the black night faded to purple and then pale blue as the sun finally rose. I knew that it had not been a dream, at least, not as most people would so term them. My enemy had taken me beyond the wall of sleep, into some other place and time. Another world, or perhaps something even more distant and alien than that.

I thought of Rachel. I thought of the message Nyarlathotep meant to send, the clear intention of the game, of what it had taken to beat him. Of what I had been forced to give up in exchange for victory. He and his kind are old, and they are patient. Unlike us, they will never die. And thus, death was the one power we have over them, our lives the one thing that we can give that they cannot comprehend. An end to existence. And while to some that might seem a weakness, it was in fact a source of unimaginable power. For to make that choice, to give our lives willingly for something else? That was old magic.

So Nyarlathotep's message was clear.

Diary of Rachel Jones

We left the town of Southampton early, on the first train north to Glasgow. From there we would take the rail line to the shores of the

North Sea and on to Skye, then a boat to beyond the Outer Hebrides. There, with luck and more than a few pounds, we'll convince a local captain to make the passage to the small, barren shards of rock that jut from the waters. What happens after, no one can say.

My father is distant today. I suppose the immensity of what we face weighs upon him. Still, I have never seen him so pale, so distracted, so sad, even. And Lord knows we have witnessed our share of difficulty before.

* * *

We have arrived in Uig, a small hamlet on the shores of the Isle of Skye where, for the right price, boats may be hired. It is the high season, and there is a merriness about the village that belies what must surely have passed here before us. But if any cloud follows the dark one, it has gone on with him across the waters.

In fact, all of today has been positively delightful. The train traversed English countryside as green and fresh as any I have seen in my Massachusetts. The sun shone down upon us for the entirety of our journey as we cut between rolling hills and over endless plains, past golden farmland and the smoke stacks of busy foundries, whisking by tiny hamlets and through mighty cities. I fancied I saw Stonehenge in the distance as we went just west of Salisbury, but my father assured me it was unlikely. It was the only thing he has said to me all day.

I asked him, should we make it through this, if perhaps we could stop at the ancient monument and picnic beneath the stones in celebration. It was a jest, of course, as I know the odds of return are slim, a fool's chance at best. But even still, my words seemed to pain him. He smiled, and his eyes fell away from mine. He was suddenly distant from me, in another place, in another time. I took his hand in mine, and it was trembling. He covered it with his other, and clasped them so tightly I thought he might hurt me. Then he returned to his book.

He has sat with that evil thing in his lap for hours, staring at the words, following them with his finger, flipping back and forth. That accursed tome, that albatross about the neck of our family. I wonder, sometimes, how he can stand it, the incessant song, the whisperings. I tell myself that he keeps it to prevent others from taking it, from doing evil with it. And yet, there is more to it than that.

The *Incendium Maleficarum* does not choose its master lightly. It seeks only its own purpose—to find its way to those who would return the Old Ones to dominance, who would use it to bring about the end of mankind. Thus, it might seem ironic that my father, a man long dedicated to keeping the gate between the worlds shut, would be its master for all of these decades. And yet, do we not take it now where it seeks to go? Is it even possible that by pursuing Nyarlathotep, we are in fact helping him to achieve his ends? That perhaps if we simply stayed behind he would fail? But the knot of uncertainty is twisted tight, and how can we do anything other than slice through it and pursue? It is a terrible choice, between the Scylla of inaction and the Charybdis of unintended consequences.

I know now why my father has been gray all the years that I have known him.

* * *

I dreamt last night of Leng. I dreamt of *him*.

I knew the place; I am my father's daughter, after all. And I knew him, of course, for one does not forget the thing that one hates.

We stood upon that endless plateau, he and I. He waited for me, the arid wind whipping his yellow cloak about his incorporeal body. Did any of it exist? The cloak, the man, the wind? Would that I could believe it was a dream.

This was real, and I had come here by some force that I could not comprehend.

"Hello, Rachel," he said, though I am not sure even now whether he uttered those words or if the sound was entirely within my mind.

"Don't speak to me," I said.

"But we are here, aren't we? Why waste this opportunity?" He stepped towards me, palms up, questioning, as if we were old friends. "Perhaps you would prefer a more idyllic setting."

I felt faint, and the scene swirled. I was falling. There was a flash of light, and we were no longer on that accursed plain. Instead, we stood within a forest, but one unlike anything I had seen before. The trees were dead, the earth with them. It was cold, very cold, but a little stream flowed freely before me. Although the stars were obscured, a strange incandescence lit the night. I recognized the place, even if I had never been there before.

"This is a cruel trick," I said, as he moved within the trees. "Even for you." He stepped into the circle of the light.

"You don't approve? I thought that perhaps you would want to see it, where he drew his last breath."

"You mean where you took it from him?"

He shook that regal head of his, an almost sympathetic frown upon the face he had worn for five thousand years. "No, my child. I was not the one who killed your William."

If this was a fantasy, if it were a dream, then I thought that I might be able to control it, if even to the smallest extent. One second my hand was empty. The next, I held a knife. I kept it close to my body, lest he see.

"Why did you bring me here? Not to kill me. You could have done that by now."

"Maybe I have other purposes for you. Maybe you have a different role to play in all of this. You know, I spoke to your father last night. Did he tell you that?"

"Can't say that he mentioned it."

"No, I didn't expect that he would. He keeps things from you, doesn't he?"

"You didn't bring me here to talk about my father. Why don't you get to the point?"

"The point?" he said, as he lowered himself onto a fallen tree. "The point is that what started here in this place all those years ago is coming to an end. And when it does, all that you know will end with it. Your father understands. He also understands what he must do to stop it. He knows that there is power in blood, power in loss, power in sacrifice. And the greater the loss, the greater the sacrifice, the greater the power."

"I don't understand," I said. A shadow passed across him. If such a creature could display remorse, I would have believed I saw it in him then.

"You must die, Rachel. You must die to save the world. Your father knows that, and he knows that it must be by his hand."

"I don't believe you," I said, but my voice trembled, and I was ashamed of my weakness.

"Yes, you do. You are Isaac to his Abraham, and only your blood can save mankind."

I stood there before him, angry, helpless, naked. He cocked his head to the side and regarded me.

"I do not hate you, you know? Despite what you have been taught. What they have written about me. I always found your kind to be curious. That is why I have walked among you for so long, even as my brethren slept, as they waited to return, to cleanse this planet as you might burn off a field for planting. They would destroy you without even knowing you are here, so insignificant are you in their eyes. But not mine."

"So you're a benevolent god, then? Do you grant wishes too?"

He smiled again.

"It is a rare thing," he said, "such reckless bravery. And yet a mark of your kind. I know you fear me, and yet you stand there, defiant, sarcastic. But believe me when I say this—you do not have to die. Neither does your father. You can have your life. You will be changed, yes, as the world must be changed. But that, I suppose, has always been the fate of mortals. I simply offer you eternal life of a different sort than you might have imagined in your Sunday school."

"You've already taken the only thing I care to have."

"Yes," he said. "But I can give it back."

I felt faint again, and I believe my heart may even have stopped. There was a boom, like the sound of falling lightning. I opened my eyes, my vision cleared, and William stood before me.

He was exactly as I remembered him, even though more than a decade had passed since my eyes last beheld him. He hadn't aged a day. He looked bewildered, confused, as if he had no idea where he was or how he came to be there. He spun around, eyes scanning the forest. Then he turned back and saw me.

"Rachel?" he murmured, taking a stumbling step forward. "How did you get here?"

It took all I had to stand there, seeing him. My voice caught in my throat, tears came to my eyes, and it seemed as though all I ever dreamed had finally come true. I don't even remember how it happened, whether he came to me or I to him, but before I knew it my arms were around him and I was holding him close.

"William," I said, "William." There were no other words. No words of love or loss or words to explain how I had felt, what I had suffered those many years. For a few blessed moments, I lost myself in that feeling, the feeling of him, the chance to say goodbye to the man I had cherished.

And I cursed Nyarlathotep for it, cursed the feeling of a debt owed, even as I knew it was all a lie. Even as I knew that this could not be real, that it was only an illusion.

I still held the knife in my hand.

"William," I said. "I'm so sorry."

I plunged the blade into his back.

It felt like I had grabbed a live wire.

A surge of energy pulsed through my body. I was flying, and then the world went black. I saw things as they are, as they were, and as they would be if we fail. I saw the sun extinguished and the earth cast into a shadow blacker than any comprehensible by the human mind. Within that infinite veil walked beings unimagined and unimaginable, and the force of their intellect alone thrust me into the void.

I was carried along, across galaxies and past dying stars as the darkness spread like a black fire, consuming all in its path. Nyarlathotep carried me on the wings of his hate, and he spoke to me as we touched the edge of the universe, past the swirling abyss where rests the ultimate chaos.

"You worship the light," he said, "but the light is destruction. Darkness is the natural order of things. Light consumes. It lives only as it kills. It gives only what it takes. It devours all before it until there is nothing left and then, only then, is it extinguished. You think you fight for the truth, you think you fight for the right, but *you* are the evil one. You are the enemy. But you cannot hold the darkness at bay forever."

I awoke with a start in my bed. The bells of the nearby port rang as the sun crested the horizon. Nothing could have made me question the reality of what I had seen, nothing could have shaken my confidence that it was no simple dream, even if I did not still hold the dagger in my hand.

Chapter 39

Journal of Henry Armitage
August 1, 1933

This morning we left Uig for the Isle of Berneray, which lies in the sound of Harris, the narrow stretch of water that splits the Outer Hebrides and opens into the Atlantic. Carter is convinced that there we can discern the place of power from which Nyarlathotep will do his work. I hope that he is correct. When the day burns away and the night comes, the time of the alignment will be upon us. Unless we move quickly, there will not be a dawn.

As it stands, we are on a small ferry that regularly plies its trade between the two islands. A miserable little vessel. I have always hated the sea, and I do not care for crossings. I prefer my own two feet upon the land, though I have no aversion to rail travel or even aeroplanes. There is something about the water, however, the bottomless abyss below, the endless back and forth. It does not agree with my stomach or my soul.

The passage took several hours, much longer than we could have predicted. The wind was against us and so were the waves, and I wondered if some foul magic had bewitched us, if perhaps the very forces of the earth herself had turned against us, if maybe they preferred their old masters to the new. That was fancy, of course. Or at least, I told myself so.

Carter was stoic, indefatigable perhaps, if one can be so bold. Rachel was the same. Rarely in this life have I felt myself the superfluous man, particularly in my relation to Carter. But whatever joined the two of them was not for me. It seemed that they had forged some silent understanding, as if both knew what was required of them and had accepted it. But whatever it was, I was not a party nor was I informed. In truth, I was rather envious, though something told me that what passed between them was not a matter I should want any part of.

Berneray is an idyllic place, the sort of village that neither time nor technology will ever reach. Children here dream of either escape or of nothing more than following in the footsteps of their fathers. So it has been since the beginning of time. So it will always be.

There is a single inn. It serves more as a tavern than a true hostelry. But it has rooms to rent, and here we shall make our base of operations and perhaps even take our rest, should we succeed on this night, the night the stars come right.

The people of the isle are quiet, and they look upon us with suspicious eyes. I would not call them insular, but it is certainly the case that they do not see many travelers. Of course, Carter and I know such people well; we have found them in towns and villages from the Kamchatka peninsula to the Straits of Magellan. They are kind in their own way, and in them is something old and strong that we do not have in the great cities of the West. A goodness and a willingness to stand before the forces of evil, forces that they, on the borders between civilization and the wild, know all too well.

We are to meet a man named Diarmad who is apparently the most skilled boatman these waters have seen, a man whose trade stretches back down into the distant memory of his forefathers. He is also said to be something of a local historian, and it is Carter's belief that he can provide some clue as to what barren stack Nyarlathotep has chosen to make his final stand.

* * *

The sun hung low in the sky by the time Diarmad made his way to the dark corner of the inn where we waited. He was a solid man, gray hairs streaking his full beard and framing his iron-blue eyes. He said nothing, dragging the ancient stool on the other side of the table back with a dull scraping of wood on wood. He collapsed on top of it, and I wondered if it would hold the weight of him and the extra pounds of his great coat. He removed his cap and dropped it onto the table.

"Mr. Brodie, I presume," said Carter. The man nodded.

"Diarmad will do," he said. He glanced toward Rachel. "A pleasure to make your acquaintance."

"Do you know why we asked you here?"

"I've heard speculation from some of the men at the wharf. I take it you and your friends are in quite the rush to make whatever the destination it is that you seek, calling me here like this and offering to pay what you are."

"We *are* in quite the rush, in fact. It is a matter of life or death."

He pulled a pipe from inside his coat and lit it with a long wooden match. Soon the thick smoke of Scottish tobacco filled the air.

"Your business is your own," he said between draws. "And if you pay the rate, I dunna care whether it is life or death, by the law or against it. My boat is good and true, and so is her captain. Where are you headed, and when do you need to get there?"

I exchanged a glance with Carter, and the old sailor not only saw it but deciphered its meaning. He threw his head back and howled with laughter. This continued for some time. Carter, for his part, showed no emotion.

"You don't know, do you?"

"We were hoping," I said, "that you could help us to figure that out."

"Were you now? And how, precisely, might I do that?"

"You know the area," Carter said, "and you know its history. I have a feeling you know much more than that. I have a feeling you know many things."

Diarmad grinned. "Go on."

"We are looking for a place of power," Carter said. "A place likely of legends, and dark ones at that. Perhaps a place where something strange happened recently."

Diarmad leaned back and crossed his arms. His brow furrowed, and while he might have been mistaken as deep in thought, I believed something else was going on, something else entirely. He was studying us, weighing us, deciding whether the knowledge that he held was best kept to himself or shared with those who sought it.

"There are many places in this world where strange things can be found. Many places, indeed. Tell me, what do you know of this island?"

"Very little," Carter answered. "I know only that it lies at the edge of things, and that beyond that edge is the fall. That, if this village is the last outpost of civilization, it would be the beginning of the frontier. That past its breakers they would have written 'here there be dragons' on the old maps."

"Yes," he said, "yes, perhaps they would. But there is one thing you have wrong, my friend. This place, this island where you find yourself this blessed evening, it is *not* the last outpost of civilization before the wilding sea."

Carter seemed to deflate. Had we misjudged?

"Or, at least," and a sparkle came into the man's eyes, "it wasn't always."

Carter leaned forward, the old energy back. "Something happened here."

Diarmad nodded. "Yes, a few years back now. There is an island, some fifty nautical miles to the west. It is a place that we do not speak of, particularly with strangers. A dark place, marred by ancient stone monuments to an unknown god. But there have always been those who are drawn to it. Strange folk. They would come here from places near and far, and to the island of Hirta they would travel. Often times, they'd never return from that place.

"Three years ago, a naval expedition from England stopped here to refuel and resupply. The steamed off in the direction of Hirta. Four days later, they returned, but with far fewer men than before. We were curious, of course, to know what had happened. But no one had the courage to go."

"Except you."

A half-grin. "Some men are more foolish than others."

"And what did you find?"

"I left in the morning, for I did not want to chance the place at night. The sea was calm, but the sun was obscured by thick and unyielding clouds. It wasn't long before I thought that my eyes were deceiving me, that one of those clouds had descended from the heavens to rest upon the sea. As I drew near I realized it was the island, shrouded in mist.

"I circled it once at a distance, past the cliffs of Conachair and between the stacks of Sgeir Domhnuill, for I was hesitant to come within that bank of fog. And yet nothing revealed itself. Nothing of the island, and certainly nothing of the disaster that had befallen it. There is only one inlet suitable for a landing, the harbor of Village Bay. I made for it, and I entered the fog.

"It was eerily peaceful, silent, with nothing but the lapping of the waves and my own engine to break the calm. I approached deliberately, slowly, lest I ground myself on some jagged rock that hid beneath the waves and the mist. Perhaps I delayed for other reasons, too. Perhaps, in the part of my heart that feared, I did not wish to see what had become of the Isle of Hirta. But as with all things, one cannot delay forever.

"My boat clanked against the wooden dock, and I made sure the mooring lines were tied double secure before my feet left the deck. I had no intention of staying for long. With my rifle in hand, I made my way into Village Bay."

"And what did you find there?" I asked. It seemed that the light had dimmed in that place, that the darkness from Diarmad's story had infected us all. For his part, he only shook his head.

"I'm not sure what I expected to find there," he said. "Blood. Bodies of the dead. Signs of violence and struggle. Instead, there was nothing. It was as if the few hundred souls that had inhabited that island had simply disappeared. Nothing was out of place. Nothing was broken. If the navy had found a fight when they made landfall, they covered their tracks, that much is for sure.

"I thought about leaving. The air about the place was foul. The feeling of menace, immense. Evil had come to that little village. I knew that then, and I know it now, as surely as you sit across from me tonight. But I didn't leave. I needed to see more. I needed to know more.

"I made my way to the little dirt road where most of the people of Hirta lived. I suppose I thought that if I saw where they had dwelt I would know where they had gone. But there was nothing to be found, nothing except a Bible in each of the little hovels."

"A Bible?"

He nodded.

"Some upon the tables, some upon the hearth, some in chairs or even on the floor. And all of them, every one of them, open to the same page. Revelation, chapter 8."

A chill rippled through me, and Carter spoke. "'And I beheld, and heard an angel flying through the midst of heaven, saying with a loud voice, Woe, woe, woe, to the inhabitants of the earth.'"

"Yes," he said. "Yes. So I returned to my boat, and I left that accursed place. I am not eager to go back."

Carter leaned forward, the fire flashing in his smiling eyes. "Well then," he said. "How soon can we leave?"

Chapter 40

The Diary of Rachel Jones
August 1, 1933

We approach the island from the east. The sun is sinking in the distance, and the wind howls and the rain falls with unceasing fury. Diarmad was exceedingly wary of embarking tonight, and he warned us that these conditions were in no way ideal or even safe. But we were insistent, and I must believe that some preternatural sense of the captain told him that we were more than fools seeking folly.

I watch the sun as it descends. Even through the lashing rain, the sunset is beautiful here on the sea. The clouds seem to have parted around it, and the brilliant crimson sky promises that a new and better day is coming. I've never been one for sunsets. Not until this moment.

I have decided to maintain this diary for as long as I can, come what may. Someone should keep a record of what we face tonight. I have seen Henry hunched over his own journal, scribbling away between bouts of sea sickness. I am glad. If we survive, people should know. They should know what we had to do here, what we had to sacrifice here.

My father does not write. He simply stares ahead, into the coming dark, the wakening gloom. His thoughts are his own. He does not share them with me.

He has not spoken to me of his dream, of his walk with Nyarlathotep. Nor has he spoken of what we both know we must do, of our only chance to keep the gate closed. I do not expect this cup to pass from me. I do not expect to see the dawn.

Later

The island is close now, and I hear his voice. It echoes in my mind.

I can feel you, Rachel. It is not too late to turn back. It is not too late to choose life. It is not too late not to die.

I wonder if my father feels him, too. I wonder if my father hears him, too. I wonder what he says to him. What he offers. What price he is willing to give in exchange for our souls.

Journal of Henry Armitage, August 1, 1933

I hate boats. If I am to die tonight, at least I will never have to set foot on one again. This is a strange comfort, albeit a small one.

Everyone is silent. Sitting in quiet reflection, as I imagine soldiers before they face the enemy. Only Diarmad moves about the boat, tending to it, fighting a losing battle against the wind and the rain. So it goes.

I know, of course, that this journal must end soon. There is, for me, great sadness in that. It has been my companion for so long, throughout this and countless other adventures before. And when I close its cover and bind it again, it may well be for the last time. So I make a promise here, on this sacred parchment. If I survive tonight, if I see the dawn, I shall record truly and faithfully all that I witness this eve. For good or ill. For fair or foul. So help me God.

Journal of Carter Weston, August 1, 1933

We stand now on the silent docks, listening to the lapping of the waves. What began a decade ago in Siberia will end tonight. Of that I am sure.

Diarmad is a good captain, honest, brave, and true. He grasped my hands after the others had left the boat, and drew me close.

"I don't know what you are seeking out there," he said, nodding into the dark. "And there is no need in you telling. But I give you my word, I won't leave this place without you and yours."

And I believe him, too. In fact, I know what he said is true.

"Listen carefully," I said. "Whatever happens out there, whatever you see or hear, do not come after us. There's nothing you could do to help anyway. Stay with the boat. Keep her safe. Hopefully we will be back to you soon. But if we don't arrive by noon tomorrow, leave this place, forget about us, and never return."

I could tell by the glint in his eyes that he didn't like that last bit. Didn't like it at all. But after some hesitation, he nodded once and released my hand.

"You take care of yourself, professor. And you take care of that girl of yours, too."

The simplest request of a father, and yet, can I keep it? Can I even begin to?

Now we depart. A great hill towers above the inlet where the people of Village Bay once made their home. Diarmad spoke of its strangeness, how it looks a bit like a pyramid, its top sheered clean off, leaving nothing but a flat plain at its summit.

But I know this is not strange at all. In fact, it is precisely what I would expect. It is just as the legends predicted.

Chapter 41

Statement of Henry A. Armitage of Arkham, Massachusetts, United States, before D.I. John Jacobs, Scotland Yard, 11 August 1933, regarding unexplained events of 1 August 1933

You have asked me to swear an oath to speak the truth of what happened on that accursed hill, ten days ago. No oath is needed. When one witnesses that which I have seen, it is a duty to share with those who come after. That much I know for sure.

As to my recollection, I can tell you only what I believe I witnessed, for no man who claims sanity would be so bold as to assert that the things I saw on Hirta, beyond the Kildean straits, were anything more than illusion. And yet I am certain of them, as certain as I am that you are sitting here before me, as certain as I am that you will not believe me. It is for you to judge my sanity. I can only tell you what I know.

We did not tarry long in Village Bay. Time was short, and the sun had long since fallen behind the accursed pyramidal hill that was our destination, bathing it in an unearthly glow, and casting its shadow upon us all. The clouds above us swirled and danced, and though no breeze blew upon the land to cool our faces, it was as if a hurricane raged above.

It was beginning.

Up we climbed, Carter burdened by the great crimson tome he carried, the *Incendium Maleficarum*, and I hoped that within its pages he had found a spell or an incantation that would save us. The ascent was not difficult; paths had been cut through the trees by countless men and beasts before us. But we labored under unearthly burdens, and every step was heavy. We did not speak, not for long minutes, not until we reached the final berm, the traversing of which would take us to the unnatural plateau that was our destination.

Carter turned and looked at his daughter. Carter, a man of limitless intelligence, a man who could speak ten languages like they were his own, and yet the question of what to say then was one he simply could not answer.

I thought it was simply that he feared we would not survive our quest, that he wanted to tell his daughter one last time that he loved her before we made what might be a futile charge against the creatures of the night. It was only later that I understood the storm that was raging within his mind, that I knew what he planned, what he felt he must do.

I cannot know how it weighed upon him, the burden, the guilt. I pray that I never do. He had stared into the abyss and seen its depths. He had fought monsters for so long that he had now become one himself.

The words did not come. Rachel reached out and took his hand. She cocked her head to the side and smiled.

"It's all right, father," she said. "We'll do what we came to do. We'll do what we must." Then she kissed him on the cheek. "I love you." When she let go his hand, his arm fell to his side, as if he didn't have the strength to hold it up.

I watched him, watched them both, like a fool. I suppose I could not have known what passed between them. It was impossible, really. How could I? The language between fathers and daughters is always a mystery. How much more so then?

Still I blame myself. I should have known. I should have been part of it. I should have helped them to carry a weight that was so much more than any two people should be asked to bear.

Instead we stood on the precipice of the ultimate darkness, standing, waiting, loving, planning, wondering. We stood there until whatever needed to pass between them had made its way, until Rachel said, "Let's go." So we followed her over the berm and into shadow.

We stepped into another world when we set foot upon that plateau, the flat plain that stretched from one edge of the ancient pyramid to the other. I could no longer fool myself into believing the structure I stood upon was natural, even as I was certain it was not man-made.

It was not night there, at least, no night that I had ever seen. But it wasn't day either. A purple radiance lit the very air, and as we moved across the plateau it was as if we were walking through the ocean. The air was thick and unyielding, and it was foul to the taste and burned my lungs. The wind blew with a ferocity I had rarely seen, one that belied the calm we had just left. We had passed beyond something, some narrow membrane that separated our world from theirs, that divided the light from the dark. And in that instant, I was certain that this was the place destiny and whatever dark eminence moved within had chosen where the fate of the world was to be decided.

I was wrong.

We moved forward, pushing through the night made manifest. We had not walked for long before we saw him.

He stood in the midst of it all, his great yellow cloak caught up in the wind, its edges gleaming with unnatural luminescence. His arms were raised, and the sound of discordant piping floated down from the heavens, where clouds swirled in a vortex of purple fire. Whatever fate had brought him to that place to summon, it was coming.

Carter reached into his pocket and drew forth the Oculus. He held it in the palm of his hand, as if its very presence in that place would activate it, would enflame the fire legend held burned within it. But it simply sat there, cold and small, a flawless gem that was as worthless to us as a lump of coal.

He opened the *Incendium Maleficarum*, finding almost immediately the page he sought. He scanned it with his index finger, mumbling as he did. Then he held the Oculus in the air and recited three lines, an incantation in a language I did not recognize. We waited...and still nothing happened.

Carter glanced at Rachel. Something passed between them. It was then that Nyarlathotep noticed us, or at least acknowledged our presence.

"You came, dear Carter. Of course, you did not disappoint." He lowered his arms as green flames seemed to dance about them. "I knew you would come. I knew that I would see you again. We are drawn to each other, don't you know? Two adversaries, down through the ages. How many times have we met in a place such as this? If only you could remember, as I do."

Carter shouted above the howling wind. "And yet every time, it seems, I come out on top."

The old adversary grinned. "Yes. I suppose I am Prometheus, and you are the eagle sent daily to peck at my hubris. One is left to wonder who the hero of this tale might be, but the ending is not in doubt. Not anymore."

"I have the Oculus," Carter said, holding it up between his thumb and his forefinger. "You cannot escape its power."

Nyarlathotep laughed, and it carried on the wind and off into whatever lay beyond that place.

"Yes, my dear Carter. You do. But you do not know how to use it. And even if you did, you have not the heart to do what must be done."

Carter faltered, and so did my strength. I had assumed he had discovered the way, at the last moment, as it always had been before. That he knew what was necessary to save the day, to win the battle, to emerge victorious. Another story to tell, another legend to weave. Maybe not this time.

Then Carter spoke, and I knew that I had misjudged. The truth was far more terrible than I could have imagined.

"Oh, I know," he said. "I know all too well."

He drew aside the coat he wore and unsheathed a dagger, long and curved, the kind that had but one purpose—the drawing of blood for sacrifice.

Nyarlathotep's smile grew wider than should be possible, his face a mass of sharpened teeth, shark's teeth. "Oh, do you now? But do you have the strength to do it? Can you live with yourself if you do? We cannot die, Carter. We sleep, and we dream, and a time will come when even death shall fade away, and we will rise. But you must live with what you do today. Sleep will not come so easily for you, and when it does, you will wake screaming, the taste of blood in your mouth, an image of *her* burned into your eyes. Can you do it? I wonder. But there's not time for delay. Enough words. Time to choose."

The world hung in the balance. I was rooted to the spot on which I stood. If I had been compelled to move to save my life, then death would have taken me as sure as the sun rises in the east. I was paralyzed by that place, by the one who stood before us, but so much more by the choice I now realized that Carter had to make.

The knife shook in his hands. He looked up at Rachel, tears in his eyes. All the while Nyarlathotep stood perfectly still, watching. He made no move to stop him, no effort to interfere.

He was enjoying this bit of sick theater.

"Rachel..." Carter murmured.

"It's all right," she said, and her face shone, her countenance that of an angel. "I understand. I understand everything now. Do what you have to do. For me. For everyone."

Carter stepped forward and grabbed Rachel by the neck. He pushed back her head, the vein throbbing with every beat of her heart. He raised the knife to the sky, and lightning cracked through the glowing haze.

For an instant the blade hung there, suspended, gods and men enraptured, unable to turn away. For an instant only, and then it fell. If I had had more of my faculties about me, I might have looked away. But if I had done that, I wouldn't have seen what happened.

The blade swung down and cut only air. Carter held it by his side, a look of almost unimaginable failure in his eyes, matched only by the desperation in Rachel's.

"Father! You must."

But it was over. Carter couldn't do it. He couldn't have raised that blade again any more than if his muscles had been shredded, his tendons gone.

Nyarlathotep laughed.

"I knew it," he said with triumphant hate. "I knew you could not do it. You are weaker than the other ones. Far weaker. And now it's too late."

He brought his hands together in a mighty crash. The churning chaos above us flashed with an evil radiance and then fell to the earth, stopping directly behind where the demon stood. The swirling darkness was more than it seemed. It was a door, a portal to the place beyond. And through that door those who had ruled the earth in the long ago would return.

"I go to prepare the way." He reached out his hand. "And I'll take that."

The book flew from Carter's grasp as if it were pulled by a rope. It rocketed across the distance and slammed into the demon's waiting claws.

Nyarlathotep turned and stepped into the portal. A howling echoed across the plain.

"Oh, God," Rachel moaned.

Carter looked from her to me, and the pain that had been etched into every wrinkle suddenly melted away. Resolve replaced it.

"We follow," he said. "This is not over."

With that, he broke into a run toward the spiral of night in our midst. Rachel hesitated for only a moment before she followed. I was right behind her. I didn't break stride, even as I watched them both vanish before my eyes.

Chapter 42

Statement of Henry A. Armitage, cont'd.

The passage was extraordinary, and beautiful. I would say that it was *as if* we had left this world and become beings that could traverse time and space and dimensions, but I believe that was, in fact, what occurred.

Stars, burning masses of celestial fire, streaked by us. Nebulae, constellations, entire galaxies, were nothing to us. What beauty. What wonder. And I considered myself blessed to see something no one, save my friends, had ever witnessed before.

Yet the price to stand witness to such glory was high indeed, for then we looked upon horrors the likes of which have never been imagined.

Everyone, if honest, is afraid of the dark. And yet, few if any have ever experienced its depth. In those moments, we were bathed in it.

We passed into a region of time and space beyond the world of light. And as the stars faded behind us, it seemed to me as though we were coming to a great wall, an ink-black curtain, a Stygian veil that separated the lesser darkness from the greater. I did not want to pass beyond it, but I had no choice. I tried to scream, but I believe the sound echoed only in my own mind.

It has been my habit, in the years I have known him, to criticize Carter's inability to describe properly the things he has seen. I have mocked the many times he claimed that there were "no words in the English language" to encapsulate the wonders of the invisible world he has witnessed with his own eyes. But in that moment, I repented my judgment. Still, in the interest of completeness and for the scientific record, I will attempt to describe what I saw.

Beyond the veil was chaos. There were stars, yes, but unlike any I had ever seen before. They shone down darkness, not light, on worlds that were as black as if formed from coal and pitch. *Things* moved there, winged and tentacled things, mad amalgamations of form undreamt of even in the wildest fancies of the Pharaohs.

You disbelieve, don't you? I see it in your eyes. No, don't bother to protest. I understand. If I hadn't witnessed it, I wouldn't believe it myself. I'm not even sure how to explain what I saw, what I experienced. And I did see, but not with my eyes. Through something else, another sensory organ altogether, one vestigial and primordial.

But I know this now, as surely as I know anything—there are worlds of light and worlds of darkness, and beings that move within both.

I can't say how long our travel lasted, whether an instant or an age. One moment we were speeding through that eternal void. The next, we had come to rest on an endless plain, a flat sea of granite. The air glowed red, and the sky was clear and empty, save for four dark stars that, even as we watched, slid across the black dome above. Three in the center, so close that they seemed as though they were fused, and one at the bottom. It was the sign of the crawling chaos, the mark of Nyarlathotep, the alignment we had been waiting for.

"Come on," Rachel said. "We don't have much time."

We didn't have to think about where to go. The plain was vast, but it was not empty. A great tower stood in the distance. Around its crown swirled oily tendrils that seemed to reach down from the dark stars.

Toward it we raced.

"That wasn't here before," Carter said. "Not in my vision."

"Mine either," Rachel answered. "Maybe it's always been here. Maybe he hid it from us. Or maybe it only appears when the time is right."

I didn't know what they were talking about, of course. They had shared something that I was not a part of. Only then was I coming to understand my role in all this. I was a watcher, a scribe. I would record for posterity what was to happen in that place, but it would fall to Rachel and Carter to see it done.

We ran across the plain, as fast as age and senescence would allow us. And I couldn't help but wonder—when would we be struck down? When would the creatures that ruled this place decide to rip us apart? We could not survive, surely. We had come to stop them, to stand against unimaginable power and limitless hate. To prevent their conquest. Or perhaps, their liberation. That interference, they would not allow.

And yet, as the tower loomed larger ahead of us, nothing happened. Nothing reached up from the ground to pull us below. Nothing swooped down from the heavens to carry us away. I couldn't understand it then. I don't understand it now.

The tower was unlike anything I had encountered before. Sheer walls of obsidian. There were no doors, only a yawning maw of an entrance. No windows. I wondered if it were actually a tower, or if that was just the only way our minds could conceive of it. I wondered if perhaps anything we were seeing was truly real, or if to see the truth would lead only to madness. There was no time to ponder such philosophical musings then. We dashed up the mighty steps and into the void.

The maw opened into more stairs that curled around the wall and spiraled toward our destination. There were no images, no words, no sigils or glyphs. Just blank, black stone.

How long did we climb? An eternity perhaps. I am in no great shape, so I would have thought that after only a few stories I should have been exhausted. Whether because of the adrenaline pumping through my veins or something extraordinary—perhaps, for instance, we were traveling through a metaphysical space outside of the normal order—I never even broke a sweat.

Still, no matter what hallucination or flight of fancy might have beguiled us, there was one thing that seemed certain to me. As we rose, the sounds from above that drifted to us grew louder and louder. That music, if music it could be called, was unlike anything one would ever wish to hear, a discordant piping and manic drumming that made a mockery of melody. If sound could drive men mad, then that horrid noise would be a weapon unlike any before conceived.

Still we pressed on, until my thoughts were driven from my mind by that dizzying sound. A landing appeared before us, lit by a spill of pallid red light.

For an instant, we paused on the next to last step. None of us knew what we would see, what visions the next turn would present. And none of us knew what would be required of us. But I was certain that if the fool's chance proved true and we succeeded, only two of us would leave that place alive. And, of course, I was right.

Rachel led the way. She was, I suppose, the bravest of us all. Even with all Carter and I had faced, I'm not so sure we could have made those last few steps without her. But when she led, we could not help but follow.

What did we see when we crossed that threshold, you ask? Only the beginning and end of all things.

The battlement of the tower was open to the mad sky. I chanced a glance upward and wished I had not. Titanic beings floated in the living blackness of space that swirled above, bleeding coils of multi-colored, tentacle-like things that groped and probed around the edge of the tower. In the midst of it all stood Nyarlathotep, his back to us, bending over something that we could not see, his great yellow cloak billowing in the wind. The unseen pipers and drummers continued their devilish work, and we stood silent, waiting for the last tumbler in the lock to fall into place.

Nyarlathotep, of course, sensed our presence. He looked up from whatever he hovered over and turned. He smiled, and for an instant the mask slipped, and I saw beyond it, to his true form. But only for an instant, thank God, for then I could dismiss it as a trick of the eye and save my own sanity. He held the *Incendium Maleficarum* in his hand, and I knew that it had finally returned home. There, in the place from whence it came, we all heard its song, dancing in the air with the pipes and the drums.

"You came," he said, as he slammed the book shut with the sound of waking thunder, "to bear witness to the rebirth. To the wakening of our lord, Azathoth."

"No," Carter whispered, "even you couldn't be so mad. You have heard the prophecy, the promise. If he wakes, so they say, 'there will be worlds nor gods no more.' You must know this."

Nyarlathotep bowed. "Of course, dear Carter. Did you think you were the only one willing to sacrifice all to save your world? Or, in this case, to know it reborn? What is this life, but pain and loss? What is this cruel existence that any would see it saved?

"The truth? All of this, all that you see or know, is but a dream of the sleeper. His dream."

He stepped to the side, and the three of us gasped in shock at what we saw.

I cannot say for sure what actually lay there, squirming in the tiny bed. Without a doubt, our perceptions were not to be trusted, and our eyes had been deceiving us since we entered that realm. And yet, somehow I knew that the thing that lay before us naked and small and defenseless was the only truth I'd ever really known.

It was an ordinary child, a babe, an infant. It slept, though its body was wracked with tremors, with shudders brought on by some unseen horror.

"What witchcraft is this?" Carter said.

"Does it surprise you so much? Think about all you know, the horror of this world. The hate, the pain, the suffering. What else could it be, but the nightmare of a child? Surely you don't still believe that a just god made you and put you into this manifest sickness to wallow until you die? This is the truth, Carter," he said, gesturing toward the child, "the one you claim to seek, the one you have dedicated your life to pursuing. This is your god, the god that sleeps, the god that dreams. And when he wakes, the dream will cease, and a new world will be born. A better world where the light is finally banished and darkness rules, as was intended."

The three of us stood there, a gulf of seemingly endless distance between us and the child. The pipes played. The drums beat. The stars moved. Nyarlathotep looked up and grinned.

"The stars are almost aligned," he said. "The time has come for all of us to make our choices."

He opened the book and held a hand high. He began to shout words that I did not understand or recognize into the howling wind. There was a flash of dark light from above; the alignment was complete. The child began to stir.

Rachel grabbed Carter by the arm and pulled him toward her. I feared the grimace on his face. It was one of confusion, of loss. He seemed as though he had no idea what to do.

"Father!" she screamed above the wailing wind. The piping had begun to thin and fade, the drums to slow. "You have to do it," she said, and tears followed. "You have to do it now!"

Carter glanced at her with a look I had seen before. Wheels were turning. He reached into his pocket and removed the jewel, the Oculus. Nyarlathotep continued to chant, the child to stir towards wakening.

Rachel held the dagger up and pressed it into Carter's hand. He glanced from the blade to the jewel, and then to Nyarlathotep and the babe.

"I wonder…" he whispered to himself.

"Father, now!"

Carter's trance broke. He turned toward Rachel, took her chin in his hand. "I love you, child," he said, before turning to me. Something deep inside the gem began to sparkle faintly. "You too, old friend." Then he dropped the knife, the blade clattering upon the ground. He stepped towards Nyarlathotep.

"Father!"

"It's all right," he said with a smile, looking over his shoulder. "There's more than one kind of sacrifice."

He turned and continued toward the dark one.

"Father, no!" Rachel tried to go to him, I suppose to stop him, but I grabbed her and held her back. What Carter had to do, he had to do on his own.

"Nyarlathotep!"

The old wizard looked up from his book and locked eyes with Carter.

"You once said that you'd waited for thousands of years for this chance. I hope you're prepared to wait a thousand more."

Carter held the stone up to the sky, and from within burst a light so brilliant that it blinded us. The flash cleared, and by some power beyond our ken, the jewel had grown many times its original size. Even more, it now burned with a holy fire. And in that singular moment, I saw fear in Nyarlathotep's eyes.

"No!" He took a step toward Carter, but it was too late. Carter took the jewel with both hands and drove it into his chest. That which had been broken was now remade. He had become the staff.

There was a roar like a mighty, rushing wind. It whirled about us, and great lightning bolts streaked down the solid stone walls that surrounded us. The piping grew to a shrieking, the drums beat feverishly. The earth trembled and quaked.

And then—it all stopped.

The drums, the pipes, the shaking, the thunder. One moment it roared, and then it ceased. Just as quickly as it had begun. The world froze. And in that silence, a still, small voice. There was a brilliant flash, and I knew it was Carter. He had become a column of light. It filled the room. The walls of the tower began to break. Stone tumbled from above. The last thing I remember seeing was the light striking Nyarlathotep full on, ripping him apart.

Chapter 43

The Hebrides Post, 13 August, 1933, Front Page

An unusual event in the St. Kildan Archipelago continues to mystify both local authorities and investigators dispatched from London's Scotland Yard. What we do know, we report here.

A fortnight ago, three Americans were transported to the deserted island of Hirta by way of Berneray, carried in a fishing boat owned by a local seaman, Diarmad Brodie. We can report here, for the first time, that the visitors were two professors from the famed Miskatonic University in America—Henry Armitage and Carter Weston—along with the latter's daughter, Rachel Jones (née Weston). Remarkably, Professor Weston was reported missing and presumed dead in Arkham, Massachusetts, nearly a year ago. How he came to be in Scotland and why his colleague and daughter were traveling with him is, as of this writing, unknown.

Moreover, inquiries made of Mr. Brodie have failed to reveal the purpose of the voyage to Hirta, and we can only assume that some strange curiosity drove them. Whatever the case may be, the events of 1 August are truly extraordinary.

Upon arriving at the island, Mr. Brodie reports that the three visitors struck off on their own while he tended the boat. Brodie claims that, after surveying the abandoned village, the Americans headed to what he describes as "a mountain, a kind of flat-top pyramid on the other end of the island." Brodie is embellishing, of course. There is no such mountain on Hirta, the most prominent rise being a small hill just beyond Village Bay. In any event, Brodie reported to the police that he waited for several hours for the visitors and had in fact begun to prepare to find them when there was, and we quote now from his testimony, "a crash unlike any I have heard upon God's earth. There was a flash of light that turned the night to day, and then an explosion upon the hill. I ran to the rise, climbing as quick as I could. When I reached the top, there was one of the professors and the Miss, passed out on the plain. But the other gentleman, her father, he was nowhere to be found, and by God, I do not think you'll ever see him again."

Investigators are said to have questioned both Dr. Armitage and Mrs. Jones extensively as to the whereabouts of Professor Weston, but no satisfactory answer was forthcoming. In fact, there are reports that the two remaining visitors both offered a strange and fantastic story to explain the Professor's disappearance, one that investigators have dismissed as a joint-hallucination, brought on by extreme stress.

In any event, with Professor Weston's complicated status and the lack of any evidence of foul play, investigators were forced to release both Dr. Armitage and Mrs. Jones to the American authorities. What truly happened on the Isle of Hirta, we may never know.

Diary of Rachel Jones
August 22, 1933

It's been a week since we came home from Scotland, and three since my father gave his life for the cause he had lived to uphold. Carter Weston spoke often of turning back the night, of the light that shines in the darkness. On the plains of Leng, at Kadath in the cold waste, he became that light.

Henry may never be the same. Before, when my father disappeared, he was so certain that he was still alive. And he was right, of course. My father did live. But now, his death seems without question. Of course, it's hard to say exactly what his fate might have been. Did he die? Or was he transformed? Perhaps it wasn't just that he became the light. Perhaps he is now also the guardian of that light. Someone to watch over us all.

I hope that one day Henry can see it that way.

He came to visit me two days ago. He wanted me to know about something he discovered in his research. There is a legend, it seems, that holds that the Old Ones cannot return without a sacrifice. A human sacrifice. One given freely, and with very specific requirements. It must be a woman, and she must be killed by her own father. Henry believes that this explains much, that Nyarlathotep had allowed us to follow him for a special reason. And that had my father killed me instead of himself, all would have been lost.

Perhaps, but I think it goes beyond even that. I think, in that place of fear and shadow, Carter Weston proved a truth older than time—that love is stronger than hate, kindness more powerful than cruelty, light far greater than darkness. That it was my father's love, more than his sacrifice, that saved us all.

As for my future, I'm not sure where I go from here. My father taught me, from a very young age, about the things that move beyond the civilized world. But the old saw is true—seeing is believing. And once you see, there is no unseeing.

He taught me something else, too. Knowledge is a burden, and ignorance is bliss. If most people knew the truths we know, they could never go on. They could never go to work, raise families, live their lives or do a million other ordinary, everyday things if they knew that in the deep woods and empty plains and wild places of the earth there waited beings ready to devour them. And since they cannot, it falls to those of us who do know to stand against those forces. That was the burden my father took up. Now it falls to his daughter.

Of course, Henry does not agree. He thinks the world should know. And that's fine, too. But the fact of the matter is simple in my view—it's not just that people cannot handle the reality of this world; it is that they *will not* accept it. Nyarlathotep, Cthulhu, Shub-Niggurath, and all the other unpronounceables, to most, will remain nothing more than dark tales and legends, scary stories to tell in the dark around the campfire.

So it is, and so it shall be. I'd have it no other way.

And whatever I face in the days and years to come, I do not walk this path alone. Yes, there is Henry, my friend, my mentor, and an ally till the end. But there is another now, too. I hear it even as I write this, calling to me, singing its song, urging me to open it, to read it, to learn its secrets. For it was not just Henry and me that the good Captain Diarmad found on that desolate plain, a fortnight and a half ago. The book was there, too.

And it has chosen a new master.

Epilogue

Arkham Advertiser, May 1, 1934, Page D-1

We at the *Arkham Advertiser* rarely make editorial comments on personal announcements, but in this instance, we have deemed an exception appropriate. It is our great pleasure to announce that last night, former *Arkham Advertiser* investigative reporter Rachel Jones safely delivered a healthy baby boy, Carter Weston Jones. We understand that mother and baby have been discharged from the hospital and are recovering at home.

The father of the new arrival is unknown and we understand, of course, that certain members of the community may look askance at celebrating an unwed mother. Nevertheless, we believe that, given the tragedies that have befallen Mrs. Jones over the past few years—including the loss of her husband fourteen years ago and her father in recent days—we can both uphold the moral standard that has long marked the *Arkham Advertiser* while still acknowledging this happy event.

So to Mrs. Jones and the baby, we at the *Arkham Advertiser* offer hearty congratulations.

Truly, the blessings of the Lord are without limit.

THE END

Brett J. Talley is the Bram Stoker Award nominated author of *That Which Should Not Be* and *The Void*. His work has been featured in the shared-world anthology, *Limbus, Inc.*, and he is the editor of the forthcoming sequel, *Limbus 2*. He is also a lawyer, speechwriter, and an avid fan of the Alabama Crimson Tide. He makes his internet home on his website, www.brettjtalley.com.

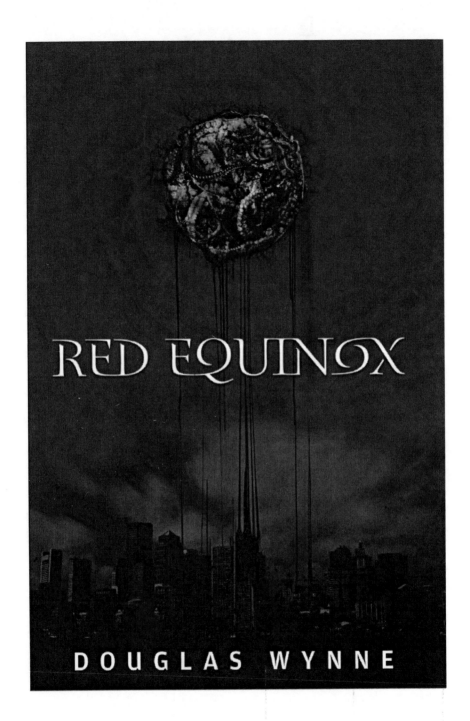

RED EQUINOX

DOUGLAS WYNNE

DIVINE SCREAM

A NOVEL

BENJAMIN KANE ETHRIDGE

BRAM STOKER AWARD® WINNING AUTHOR

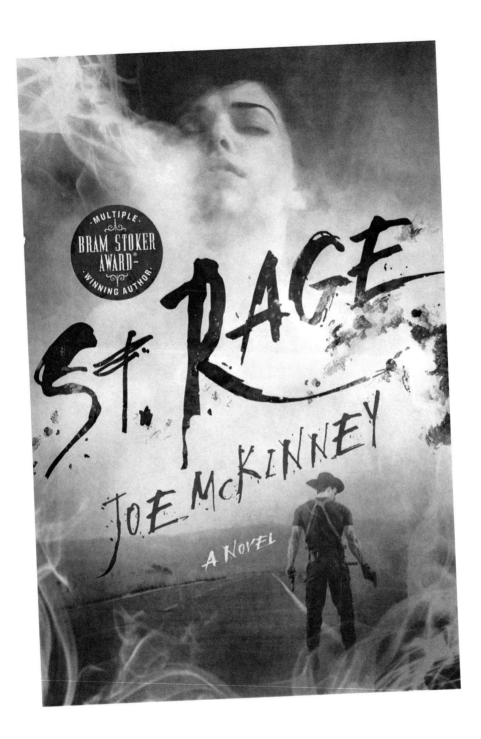

CPSIA information can be obtained at www.ICGtesting.com
Printed in the USA
LVOW08s1208250516

489870LV00001B/98/P